COMMUNITY LIBRARY
3 2301 00246209 5
P9-DWH-552

# HOW COULD SHE

# HOW COULD SHE

· Lauren Mechling ·

VIKING

VIKING
An imprint of Penguin Random House LLC
penguinrandomhouse.com



LIBRARY OF CONGRESS CATALOGING-IN-PUBLICATION DATA
Names: Mechling, Lauren, author.
Title: How could she : a novel / Lauren Mechling.
Description: New York, New York : Viking, 2019. |
Identifiers: LCCN 2018052453 (print) | LCCN 2018052914 (ebook) |
ISBN 9780525559399 (ebook) | ISBN 9780525559382 (hardback)
Subjects: | BISAC: FICTION / Contemporary Women. | FICTION / Satire. |
FICTION / Literary.
Classification: LCC PS3613.E29 (ebook) | LCC PS3613.E29 H69 2019 (print) |
DDC 813/.6—dc23
LC record available at https://lccn.loc.gov/2018052453

Printed in the United States of America
1 3 5 7 9 10 8 6 4 2

Set in Janson MT Pro
BOOK DESIGN BY LUCIA BERNARD

*For Ben*

*December 23, 2016*
*New York City*

Dear friends near and far,

After a beautiful eight-year streak, my annual holiday card shame-walks its way back onto the scene as a New Year's card. Things have been crazier than usual these past few months, and the election certainly didn't help matters. I'm writing this a few days before Christmas, you'll have to take my word. I like imagining all of you in the not-too-distant future, holding my message in your hands. The winter-flower watercolors are the individual part. I focused on each of you as I painted yours, so that love had better come through. Goodness knows we all need it more than ever.

On to the annual report, the one you won't find in the newspaper. . . . The year got off to a rough start, with my mother's skiing accident. Once we knew she was going to be able to walk again, it was nice to have an excuse to hang out at my parents' home, but we were all shaken up for a little while there, and I couldn't be more grateful to all of you who helped us through it. The phone calls, the overnighted cookies, the amazing Sylvia Plath poem screen-printed onto a pillowcase by a particularly superheroish one of you. Mum loved it all. She's been diligent about her physical therapy and is determined to get back on the slopes soon. My parents are talking about a trip to Chile next summer.

After two years of nomadic life, Nick and I finally moved into the town house that Nick's owned forever but never really dealt with. We left our Chelsea sublet in June, and the renovations went all the way through the fall, so after several months of living on the run (out on the North Fork and a few weeks at Nick's friend Fernando's house in Majorca, so don't think I'm complaining), we're only starting to settle into our home. It's funny seeing our furniture mixed up together and trying to get along in the space that has always been starkly, midcenturyishly "his." My studio is on the top floor, with a ceiling that slopes so low I have to duck my head when I reach over to change the radio station. The window overlooks a courtyard where an old greyhound naps all day long. I have a dog bed for Stanley, so he hangs out up there with me. It's my new favorite place on earth.

Nick has been working on a hostel project and a few other things, mostly in Berlin, so when we see each other, it can feel as if we're on a date (sometimes it's more like we have dementia—it's impossible to keep track of anything when somebody is a ghost most of the time!). He's finally given in to my prodding and gotten back into tennis. After what I will admit was a promiscuous spring, with work in magazines and galleries, I've just agreed to the sweetest invitation to participate in a group show about "the cold" at the Brooklyn Public Library. Being Canadian and all, I suspect they want me to contribute a couple of paintings of infinite tundras, but I'm not in a chilly state of mind. I've been busy making watercolors of snowflakes and snow cones in all sorts of psychedelic colors. Sort of like the paintings I'm sending you.

Those of you who live in town, come to the opening on Feb. 14 (yes, I know) and I'll feed you banana bread and cream or possibly a gingerbread snow castle like the ones I made in grammar school. If you're in the faraway club, please know I love and miss you dearly, and I'd be honored to save a piece of castle just for you.

Here's to a safe and not-too-surreal 2017!

Love, Sunny

*Geraldine: If you're planning on visiting nyc anytime soon, come to the opening? I'm sure Gus will be there. xxxxx*

# 1

Geraldine considered her grapefruit. To an observer it might have appeared that she was snacking, but anyone who knew her could attest that Geraldine Despont was a considerer. Perched on the window seat in her living room, her back upright against the washed-out January sky, she peeled the skin into careful ribbons and arranged them in a pile beside her. Rotating the heavy pink sphere in her palm, she was suddenly overcome by the grapefruit's erotic aspect. It was the fruit kingdom's breast or, she determined with a little squeeze, more likely a buttock. Geraldine contemplated her own backside, which was rosy and muscular, with slight puckering by the thighs. The citrus connection certainly held up.

Geraldine let loose a snort and flushed, remembering she wasn't alone this evening. Her roommate, Barrett, was in the den with his girlfriend, Katrina, who took epic showers in Geraldine's bathroom most mornings and availed herself of other people's bath products.

Ever since Geraldine had taken to keeping her shampoo and cleansing gel in a hunter-green canvas kit that traveled with her to and from the bathroom each day, Barrett felt free to accuse her of not liking Katrina. Liking had nothing to do with it. It was just that she didn't *get* Katrina. Her unintended roommate was a twenty-something woman who dressed in rave pants and baby-size T-shirts, as if airing out her navel ring were more important than avoiding looking like she'd wandered in from the mid-nineties. Barrett, too, was bepierced and no stranger to the Toronto rave scene—God, could there be three uglier words in the English language?—but at least he was serious about his work and in the process of losing his hair. His head now resembled a half-blown-off dandelion, which Geraldine found touching.

And they had history. Back when Geraldine was assisting the managing editor at *Province*, Canada's weekly newsmagazine, Barrett, then in his second year at York University, was an editorial intern. He showed up for work in shiny button-down shirts and, because no one else talked to him, eagerly fetched Geraldine cups of tea and typed up detailed pitches for long-form features—mostly to do with food politics or the changing Canadian city (Jane Jacobs was a big influence). Geraldine had no clue whether his ideas were special, but she was always good for a dose of encouragement. She even invited him to join her for tea a couple of times. Barrett had been terribly respectful of his colleague, never realizing that she was merely a twenty-five-year-old who was planning on going to law school once she dug her way out of student debt. Geraldine did nothing to disabuse her intern of his perception that she was some all-powerful entity, never explicitly telling him that she simply passed his memos on to her boss, Barb McLaughlin. Barrett felt safe in Geraldine's hands, and who was she to take that away from him?

There'd been a chance encounter at Kensington Market nearly a decade later, and now here they were, living together in the second-floor apartment of a peeling Victorian. Geraldine was no longer his superior, barely in his industry at this point, but he still viewed her with enough respect not to constantly make her feel like a loser for being on the verge of thirty-seven and renting out the second bedroom of an apartment that wasn't even her own. She was indefinitely subletting from her old friend Sunny MacLeod, who'd ages ago left town and moved to New York, where she was by all standards, measurable and not, winning the game of life.

"I'm not eating God-knows-how-old leftovers. They're stinking up the fridge." Katrina's husky voice entered the room before she did. Geraldine wiped her hands on her sweatpants and considered running into her bedroom and shutting the door, but it was too late. Now Katrina was on the couch, one hand fiddling with her limp ponytail, the remote control dangling from the other.

"Is it okay if Bear and I watch TV before we go out?" Katrina stared through Geraldine, her eyes blue orbs of indifference. She stalled at a promo for a *Kids in the Hall* marathon, then moved on to HGTV. A man with frost-tipped hair and his Eastern European wife were touring a three-bedroom condo on Vancouver Island. Garth, Geraldine's boss, had urged her to spend time watching these shows that might inspire new ideas. Garth was editorial director of Blankenship Media, the company that had acquired *Province* seven years ago, after its longtime owner, the Ricker Family Trust, in a fit of consultant-inflicted financial prudence, had decided to sell rather than fix it. She was a senior editor at Blankenship's Special Titles, a division responsible for creating cheerful one-off publications tied to holidays or popular movies or Canadian personalities. Geraldine didn't know anybody who ever purchased these heavy-stock magazines posing as coffee-table books, yet they were a surprisingly profitable business. The Drake special issue kept reprinting, and copies with a limited-edition fold-out poster now fetched nearly eighty dollars on eBay.

"You in for the night?" Katrina asked.

"There's a film screening I'm supposed to go to at eight," Geraldine said, and when Katrina didn't follow up with any questions, Geraldine made no mention of its being a science-fiction movie, some of which had been filmed in Toronto.

"Oh, I thought since you were . . . ," Katrina said.

"In my happy pants?" Geraldine was wearing her beloved Kermit-green sweats with interlocking tennis rackets and orange stripes along the seams. When she'd found them in the bottom of a thrift-store bin, they'd reminded her of childhood. Not *her* childhood specifically, which she'd gone through mostly dressed in cheap princess costumes from Winners, but an alternative version in which she'd cavorted in primary colors with an unbroken family.

"Hey." Barrett arrived from the kitchen, cradling a bowl of microwaved popcorn that smelled vaguely vinegary. "Hungry?" he asked Geraldine. "It's vegan."

"Sure, but I'm not vegan," she said with a slight laugh, and stood up to take a handful.

"I thought you'd converted for January?" Barrett cocked his head.

"I did a dairy cleanse," Geraldine reminded him. "For five days."

Barrett settled onto the couch next to his girlfriend. "Want to watch with us?"

"Sure, for a little bit," Geraldine said. One of her New Year's resolutions had been to work at improving her home life. She was over thinking she had a shot at doing anything about her career. There was more room for growth on the home front. Living with harmless weirdos was so much better than cohabiting with a fiancé who thought it was his right to insert himself into any available orifice. Those days were over, thank goodness. Arranging herself on a low-slung armchair by the couch—with limbs as long as Geraldine's, she was never so much seated as she was arranged—she reached out for a second handful of popcorn and met Katrina's curious gaze with a warm smile. Such was Geraldine's determination to make nice.

Last month Barrett had spent a grand total of zero weekend nights at home, and he'd gone to his parents' house in Winnipeg for Christmas week. Yet December had been stressful for Geraldine, an endless procession of holiday parties, with their identical oozing baked-brie wheels and inevitable token single man in velvet. Why did they always wear velvet? When Geraldine was among the coupled, she could ignore these predatory bachelors. Her ex-fiancé, Peter Ricker, had brought ruin on her life, yet sometimes she missed having him at her side, if only to carry the conversation at gatherings. Now on her own, Geraldine was expected to show up wearing something sharp and not grumble about the often exorbitant carfare home.

Even tonight, on this bleak, frostbitten evening, she was expected to be out and about. Geraldine really did not want to go all the way to Richmond Street to watch a movie that undoubtedly would contain not a single joke or snatch of genuine conversation. But Garth had more or less ordered her to go as some sort of an ambassador to the production company, to say hello to whichever bright-eyed assistant would be clutching a tablet at the theater entrance and waiting to cross Geraldine's name off an electronic list. Devoting the past month of her life to cobbling together a collectors' issue pegged to the latest release in the franchise had not been enough, Geraldine gathered. She would much rather stay in and read the book she'd bought at the Upper Yonge Street library sale, a paperback of *You'll Never Eat Lunch in This Town Again.* Or, more realistically, she'd look up her online horoscope and settle in to near infinite refreshes of her social media feeds. Gus Di Paolo, whom she had slept with on her last trip to New York and who was her very occasional correspondent and possibly the next true love of her life, had been tweeting some weird shit. Perhaps his latest, "Life can only be understood backwards, but it must be lived forwards," was meant to telegraph that he spent his free time mulling Danish philosophers, but the only conclusion Geraldine could draw was that something sudden and important was up with Gus and his ex, Sarah.

Geraldine had never met Sarah, but Sunny had filled her in. Sarah and Gus had been together for nearly a decade, and they hadn't had any problems save for Sarah's desire to make babies and Gus's unwillingness to propose. Last summer Sarah had startled everybody in her and Gus's circle by leaving him for a guy she'd met surfing on Rockaway Beach. Gus, who had crinkly blue eyes and meaty hands that made things that sold for ridiculous sums of money, was crushed. Geraldine had met him a couple of months after that and Sunny had coached her to give him his space in their courtship. "I know how he comes across, but he's far more sensitive than he appears," Sunny said.

On the television the house hunters were wearing hard hats and inspecting a basement. The man was knocking on the beams while his wife expressed her burning desire to build an at-home spinning studio. Geraldine realized she was the only one watching. Barrett and Katrina were exchanging strange glances, and then Katrina was looking at a message on Barrett's phone. "What's up?" Geraldine asked. "Everything okay?"

"Nothing's up." Katrina sounded jumpy. "We're fine."

Cupping his hand over his girlfriend's knee, Barrett slowly turned to Geraldine. "Maybe we should talk," he said. Geraldine willed her features into a serene expression, as if she could fend off the dread closing in on her. She knew exactly where this was going.

"Kat and I are thinking about . . . looking at apartments."

"Apartments!" Geraldine exclaimed.

"We've seen one," Katrina said. "But it was way above our price range."

"You've worked out a budget?" Geraldine said. The room was becoming slightly blurry.

"Nothing's definite," Barrett replied.

"But you're moving in together." Geraldine tried to maintain her composure but couldn't help gulping. "That's huge. Wow." She stopped short of congratulating them; she and Barrett were past insincerities. "I'm going to miss you, buddy."

"I know, it's bittersweet," Barrett said. "But I don't want to be keeping a secret from you until the last minute. Last Sunday morning when you asked where we were going, I felt lousy lying."

Geraldine recalled talking to the two about the restaurant they were running out to—Ondine East, a Vancouver-based chef's hot new spot in the Beaches. At the time she'd felt envious, not of their plan but of their enthusiasm for waiting in line to eat brunch, a made-up meal that was entirely unnecessary in a city whose streets went dead at midnight. "You didn't go to brunch?"

"We got bagels." Barrett cleared his throat. "Of course we'll help you find a replacement when it's time. I'm not going to leave you with some psycho."

"My friend Mabel met her boyfriend through a roommate-search app," Katrina said.

"Oh! I just remembered something." Geraldine refused to meet

Barrett's eye as she sprang off the chair and headed for her bedroom door.

Once she was safely alone in her room, the sensation of despair only became more piercing. Barrett was Geraldine's third roommate in four years to move on in order to cohabit with a significant other. Geraldine had attended two weddings that resulted from these departures. Gracelessly she dropped to her knees and pulled a blue plastic crate out from under her bed. She flipped through a couple of photo albums and spiral notebooks filled with diary entries before she even fastened on what she was doing. Some animal instinct had pushed her to find the composition journal with the marble-patterned cover that she'd started writing in some years ago. It was a greatest-hits of sorts: Only the very lowest of Geraldine's lows occasioned an entry in the Book of Indignities. And now she was faced with what might be the greatest indignity of all: She didn't even have her book. In one of the more poorly thought-out gestures of her life, she'd lent the journal to Sunny, who'd vowed to return it once she'd illustrated the scenes in it. The closest Sunny had come to keeping her promise was emailing Geraldine a picture of her Cray-Pas rendering of one of the original indignities: *Dad Moves to Alberta, Age 3.* That had been two years ago. Surely she wasn't still working on it.

Geraldine collapsed on top of her bed, her coral tendrils fanning out on the duvet's cloud print, and felt stupid for letting Barrett's news take her unawares. That's what men did, even the sweet ones. They left. She tried to figure out which was worse, Barrett's forthcoming abandonment or the added disgrace of needing to remind Sunny to return the journal. Sunny forgot things only when it suited her, when she didn't stand to gain anything. The book was probably stashed away with a jumble of treasures Sunny had picked up on one of her international jaunts and some dried-up art supplies.

The only way Geraldine could imagine reclaiming it was to finagle her way into Sunny's house. An invitation to stay at Sunny's for any longer than the length of an afternoon had not come in years and years. Geraldine pictured herself looking like some deranged assassin as she marched through a throng of Sunny's bubble-dress-clad admirers at one of her painfully curated all-women get-togethers to demand she hand over the composition book. She could picture Sunny's disorientation, her nervous chuckle as the reed of her body tilted five degrees away from her friend as she realized the magnitude of Geraldine's sense of injury. Sunny had been kinder to Geraldine during her darkest hour than anybody else, and certainly kinder than she needed to be to somebody who had no way of repaying favors. She'd been there for Geraldine during her crack-up and had bequeathed her Toronto apartment, with its crooked floorboards and plastered-off fireplace, to her friend. But on some level Sunny had to know the truth. Holding on to the journal was a means of keeping Geraldine in her place, serving as insurance against Geraldine's ever thinking, God forbid, that she was equal to Sunny.

Geraldine flexed her toes and pried off her woolen reindeer socks. Even her feet were in a state—her nails overgrown and patched with the aquamarine remains of a pedicure. How had she ended up here? If only the question were rhetorical. She knew her mistake. When Barb had asked her to come down and work for her at the CBC's New York bureau, Geraldine should have jumped, not said that she wasn't looking to leave Toronto. There was a time following her decision when Geraldine had nearly forgotten about Barb's offer. Now she thought about it constantly, occasionally while crying in a bathroom stall, her one refuge from Blankenship Media's open-plan office.

Geraldine could feel her mouth quivering as she took in her surroundings. The painting that Sunny had included in her holiday card, a jubilant mess of seed shapes in pinks and blues, leaned against a scented candle on top of her bureau. Geraldine rolled onto her side, facing away from the dresser. If only she had said yes to Barb. Geraldine would have made a stellar deputy. Few possessed her talent for executing the vision of those ranking above her while buoying the morale of all those underfoot. To think of where she'd be at this very instant in her parallel life, of whose voices she would be overhearing in the next room. No—it would be a single voice, and he'd be talking to her. Geraldine looked up at the ceiling and crossed her arms over her torso, more straitjacket than hug, and rocked herself as tenderly as she could manage. New York was her solution, but it was also six years in her past.

# 2

The sidewalk was paved with half an inch of slush, but Rachel walked down Lafayette Street with an uncontainable bounce. She couldn't help feeling encouraged. It wasn't just that she was having lunch with her agent, Josie. The greater victory lay in, for once, not having been the one to initiate the face-to-face. Rachel had nearly deleted the email from Sabrina, Josie's assistant who sent the agency's biannual author-sales reports—or, in Rachel's case, returns. This time there was no spreadsheet attached. Sabrina was simply asking if Rachel might be free to have lunch with her boss and suggested a date four weeks away.

After Rachel confirmed, all her lingering fears were squashed when Sabrina replied, "Great. Give that little guy Leo a squeeze from me!" That Rachel's baby was a girl and her name was Cleo did not matter. Rachel had to believe that Sabrina would not bother to break her ice-queen façade if she were setting up a client termination. And Rachel was fairly positive that getting fired never happened over a nice lunch.

Rachel and Josie hadn't broken bread since they went out to celebrate the publication of *The Girl from Bird Street*, Rachel's fourth book, which was no longer in print. The publisher hadn't even bothered to press whatever button made it available as an ebook. This stung, but Rachel was done Googling the competition. Now she Googled the competition from the Clinton Hill writers' space, where she spent three days a week working on a new novel, one that was totally different from any of the semiautobiographical ones she had written in the past.

Rachel felt a fluttering in her stomach and pulled out her phone to double-check the restaurant's address. A text had come in from her old friend Geraldine. The message couldn't possibly rate an immediate read; Geraldine lived in Toronto. Then again, Geraldine was careful about international texting rates and ordinarily emailed.

> Rach, I have a meeting with Barb McLaughlin on Feb. 15, a Wednesday. Do you think I could stay over a couple nights? xx

As if you need to ask! Rachel typed. If you can get away from work, stay through the weekend! As she wove her way through a knot of SoHo tourists outside the Supreme shop, Rachel's mind cast back to Barb, who'd been her first editor at *Province* and only tolerated Rachel's contributions because the men who ran the magazine told her to. Barb had covered the war in Afghanistan, whereas Rachel's beat was Rachel, which meant she wrote about her adventures in pet-sitting or embedding as a dance-floor motivator at a Forest Hill bar mitzvah.

Rachel had run into Barb a couple of years ago at a holiday party thrown by the Canadian consulate. It had been an elaborate affair in a Sutton Place town house, with a raw bar and a trio of fiddlers flown in from New Brunswick. Rachel hadn't received an invitation from the consulate since then, she now realized. The office must have removed her from the guest list when they learned she wasn't actually Canadian.

Barb had been quite drunk and uncharacteristically nice to Rachel at the consulate reception, cupping Rachel's cheek in her warm palm. "Still got that cookie face! Does everybody tell you that you could be Debbie Harry's daughter?" Barb frowned. "You never took yourself seriously is what killed me."

Rachel bristled at the memory and turned right on Bond Street. There was truth to what Barb had said. And now here she was at thirty-six, killing herself to make up for lost time and get the world to take her seriously. Which might never happen. At least Rachel had Cleo and a husband she loved. Not everyone could say as much. Even Sunny had married somebody who always looked stiff in party pictures, with his groomed hair and rictus smile. Could Sunny possibly love Nick, much less want to be alone with him?

Rachel glanced at her phone and saw another text from Geraldine.

> That's so nice of you. If you and Matt want to go out for Valentine's Day, I'm happy to babysit!

Rachel's heart moved a little at Geraldine's selflessness. Whenever Geraldine came into town, Rachel put her up on an air mattress wedged between the changing table and the diaper pail in Cleo's room. Geraldine never showed up empty-handed, never brought up that camping out in Cleo's room was a far cry from the Gramercy lodgings she'd enjoyed when she'd come to New York with Peter.

V Day is nearly a month away, Rachel replied. I wish you'd come sooner! The city is sad without you. xxxxxxx

Rachel swerved around a woman handing out samples outside a pop-up cheese shop and kept walking. How crazy that Peter had been free to seduce Geraldine more or less out in the open and nobody seemed to fault him for his borderline-pervy management practices. It was just the way things were.

The restaurant's façade was free of an address, the only signifier a snail-like glyph on its awning. Rachel watched a pair of men with fashionable laptop cases descend the restaurant steps while she unfastened the hood of her winter jacket and pushed it over her shoulders. She glanced at her phone and made sure it was not yet one o'clock. She had time to go to the bathroom and tidy her frizzing bun.

But the second that Rachel set foot in the restaurant, she saw Josie waving at her from the back of the room. Her hair, which used to be in a side-parted lob, was now shorter and blonder. She sat at a corner table already crowded with vegetable-laden plates, a few of which were so delicately arranged that the produce appeared to sway.

"I'm obsessed with this place," Josie said when Rachel took her seat.

"I've been wanting to come here." Rachel unfolded her napkin and draped it across her lap. She should have worn a cool top; nobody could see her floral skirt. "With Cleo on the scene, my feasts consist mostly of avocado puree and chicken nuggets."

Josie narrowed her eyes. "Hilarious."

Rachel felt a slightly sad stirring within. It had been so long since she'd seen Josie that she'd forgotten about her agent's tic. You could announce a cancer diagnosis and Josie would pronounce it hilarious.

Perhaps it was her way to compensate for her obvious inability to laugh.

"You're probably wondering why I asked you here," Josie said, and Rachel felt her stomach twist. "I'll be honest. An author of mine found new representation and said it was because I wasn't sufficiently present." Her gray eyes widened to convey her feelings about her former client's expectations. Rachel was sure it was Cassie Burkheim who'd dumped Josie. Cassie was a twenty-something prodigy who wrote bestsellers about fairies and was perpetually on the road. She and Rachel had met through Josie and kept up a rich Twitter friendship. Cassie was always threatening to bring Rachel to one of her YA conferences. "So," Josie said, "I'm doing check-ins with all my people. And you, missy, are one of my people."

"I never think of you as absent," Rachel forced herself to say. "You're always there when I need you. And I know I'm not exactly bankrolling your lunch tour."

"Well, neither was he," Josie said. Huh. So Cassie was off the list of potential dumpers. "I have faith in you," Josie declared. "You're going to figure it out."

"I actually might have already. I'm nearly done with something different." Josie stopped spreading white-bean puree on her toast. Rachel drew in a bracing breath. She had one chance to hook Josie on the project. "It's about a young mother in a Gypsy community in Queens," Rachel went on. "You know how when you're riding the subway and a young woman comes onto the car begging for money while she's holding a toddler's hand or has a baby strapped to her chest? I always wondered how they can do that to their children, and this is a tragic saga of immigration and the ties that . . ." Josie's head had begun to bob up and down, and she wasn't looking at Rachel anymore. "You hate it," Rachel said.

"No, no, I love tragedy. I'm just surprised to hear you're ready to move out of the teen market."

Rachel felt heat rise in her cheeks. She'd messed up her pitch. This was supposed to be a YA book—just not another supposedly funny one that was doomed to fail.

"I'm not moving to adult," Rachel replied. "The main character is sixteen."

"Oh," Josie said. "I find that what's working in the market is stuff like Cassie Burkheim's books. Things that are supernatural and sexy. This sounds different, but we can try." Light came to Josie's face. "Check him out," she whispered. "Jake!" Josie clasped her hands excitedly and rose to hug a sinewy boy-man. He had on a clean white jacket, his straw-blond hair twisted into dreadlocks.

"Jacob Marsden, meet another client of mine, Rachel Ziff. Rachel, Jake is going to write the most incredible cookbook for Clarkson Potter."

Rachel took another look at him. "This is your restaurant? It's delicious."

"Josie better be making a killing for you," Jacob said with a grin.

"We're working on it," Josie said.

Rachel forced her shoulders to remain straight. Josie's and Jacob's heads tilted closer together, and Rachel was suddenly left on her own. Her boss, Ceri, would take her back full-time, wouldn't she? Ceri ran *Cassette*, the magazine where for two days a week Rachel "edited" but actually rewrote other women. Basically she was a word janitor. Rachel didn't hate the work. She didn't really care about it one way or the other, which was probably why she was good at it. Egos didn't ship magazines. Rachel could go to social-work school, the way everyone else who'd lost their way, suddenly on the wrong side of thirty, seemed to. Or she could lean harder into what she knew best and try to write a book about sex-crazed adolescent fairies.

"You should come see the kitchen," Jacob insisted. "We installed a woodstove that my brother and I salvaged up in the Maine backwoods."

Josie's eyes filled with lust. "Do you mind, Rachel?" Before Rachel could determine whether Josie was asking her to join them, her agent stood up and assured her that the bill was covered. "We'll do this again soon," Josie said as she departed the table.

Left to her own devices—literally, she realized—Rachel speared her fork into a cumin-dusted carrot coin and consulted her phone. Nothing from Tanya, the babysitter; just another message from Geraldine, who must have switched phone plans. First meeting about a new job in . . . too embarrassing to admit. I'd better not die before it happens.

Eat lots of greens and don't jaywalk! Rachel fired back. Seriously, this is so exciting. xx

Rachel meant it. She had grown to believe that Geraldine was never going to move on from the weird job for which she was exquisitely overqualified. She was going to die recycling second-rate content for memorabilia magazines that moldered on airport newsstands and in hospital waiting rooms. Rachel secretly thought that only somebody with Geraldine's brittle upbringing would accept her present circumstances. Geraldine's mother, a night nurse with a soft spot for hockey players, was never that emotive, and her father was alive but not present.

Rachel was happy to give Geraldine whatever support she needed. Besides, she liked having her old friend around. In the presence of Geraldine, Rachel instantly returned to a twenty-five-year-old girl-about-town. Rachel had been somewhat miserable in Toronto, yes, stressed out about work and dating as if it were a high-intensity aerobic activity. But her beauty was in full flower then, and even the people who didn't want to kiss her used to find her intriguing. It was nice to be reminded of that.

And there was always news about Sunny, whom Geraldine invariably saw during her visits, at some preposterously glamorous event. Rachel would listen to Geraldine's recaps and chew over the details like a dog sucking marrow out of a bone. Information about Sunny was bitter poison to Rachel's sense of self and sanity, yet she couldn't get enough.

Rachel looked up to see a busboy bearing down on her table. "Are you still working on that?" he asked. Rachel swallowed the bread she'd been absentmindedly chewing and fumbled to her feet. She took the long way out so she could pass the kitchen and wave goodbye to Josie through the kitchen door's porthole window. As Rachel made her approach, it swung open, barely missing her face.

# 3

She doesn't even drop hints anymore," Sunny said. Her elbows were on the tiny marble table, her chin propped on her fists as she mulled the rather startling email she'd received earlier that morning. Geraldine understood how busy Sunny was, but perhaps they could get a tea. "It's like she enjoys throwing my inhospitality in my face."

"When she used to ask if she could crash at our place, you always came up with excuses for why it was a bad time for a visit," Nick reminded her.

"That's not true," Sunny said, knowing full well that she hadn't put Geraldine up in two years, not since Rachel, her regular host, was thirty-seven weeks pregnant and bedridden. "I'm going to tell her she should stay with us. It just might be hard with my show, but I can make it work."

When Geraldine had last been in New York, in early November,

Sunny had blown off their afternoon snack date at the last minute, citing a migraine. The truth was she had just a regular headache and too much work to do.

"Don't tell her to stay if you don't mean it. You'll regret it." Nick emptied the remnants of a sugar packet into his cup.

"By which you mean I'll drive you crazy with my groaning." Sunny gave him a playful kick.

Sunny and Nick were at a window booth in Nero's, the table strewn with the *New York Post*, the *New York Times*, and the *FT.* The couple's breakfast consisted of double cappuccinos that they were nearly done with and croissants that they habitually ordered and tore apart without finishing, as if they might find a wonderful toy inside.

Sunny reached both arms across the table and took hold of Nick. He had good, big hands. Nick's shirt, which he'd had made for him by his Singaporean tailor, was nearly as rumpled as his face. Sunny wore oversize black glasses that she'd chosen because they reminded her of one of her most beloved fellow Canadians, Rick Moranis. That they also made her nose look dainty didn't hurt. Her thick black hair was in a high bun that had taken her a solid five minutes to arrange into an adequate mess.

"You think I'm a lousy friend," Sunny told Nick.

"You want to know what I really think?" Nick chuckled. "That your friend is batshit to be trying to move down here."

"Why?" Sunny said, though she completely agreed. "You did it. I did it."

Nick, who'd come over from Johannesburg so long ago that he bore only the barest trace of an accent, shook his head. "Not now we didn't. Must I remind you she's a foreigner, she's a woman, and she's broke? Does she know anything about health insurance? Why would anyone want to become an illegal immigrant?"

"Stop," Sunny tutted. "This is New York, not—"

"It's still America," Nick said. "And right now it feels like garbage. I half wish I'd stayed put."

"Thanks a lot, honey."

"That's why I said 'half,'" Nick told her.

Sunny bit her lip and surveyed her surroundings. "America" was not the first word to spring to mind. Nero's was best known as the place where *Vanity Fair* threw book parties for its staff writers. It was mobbed at night but quiet in the mornings, with tone-deaf prices and a no-laptop policy that drove away most people who needed to spend typical working hours doing work. Nick had taken Sunny there the morning after their fourth date. During the six years they'd been together, Nero's had always been their place. Now that they were in the habit of having coffee at home, often separately, they came when they needed some sense of grounding. The only other time they spent together before dark was when they walked Stanley, their aging Scottish terrier, to the dog run in Washington Square Park. Stanley had originally been Sunny's, rescued from a shelter in Long Island City, but Nick had come to love him like his own.

Sunny looked over at Nick, who was peering into his phone. She reached for hers and then stopped. She didn't want to be like every other couple, silent at the table, connected only by a shared Wi-Fi signal. Nick was leaving for a work trip in four hours, and even though he had only a couple days of site visits and meetings in Germany, by the time he made it there and back, they would have been apart for a week.

Low-grade anxiety pulsed through Sunny. She had meant to spend the day working on her watercolors for her show at the Brooklyn Public Library. It was nearly a month away, but she needed to make the pictures great. Her determination to throw herself into a group show that included who-knew-who-else in a back room of a public library rather than take the simpler route of having a solo exhibition at the Drawing Center was what made her quirky and impossible to predict. She knew that, though she never let herself get engaged with thinking that way, so at the same time she did not know that. She sighed. What was the difference between coming off as calculating and doing exactly what you wanted to, all the time? She'd long ago lost access to that answer. Now, though, everything felt loose, which made her so nervous she'd put on two pounds in the past week. She'd heard someone talking about the Trump Fifteen. Perhaps that's what was going on. Maybe she'd come up with a project based on bathroom scales. Projects, that's what Sunny did. Her dreams of becoming a proper artist had given way to the satisfaction of earning affection as a simulacrum of one. Besides, fewer and fewer people seemed able to tell the difference.

Her cookbook memoir project, due at the end of the summer, was still in heavy research phase, which was just a fancy way of saying she was endlessly shopping for vintage Canadian volumes on Biblio.com. She was also contracted to design the labels for a range of candles to be sold at the boutiques of a fashiony hotel group designed by a Brooklyn restaurateur and backed by a dashing Colombian. The pitch had been to base the artwork on the animal wallpaper so prevalent in bathrooms when she was growing up in Hamilton, Ontario. And her *Cassette* column was due by the end of the week. She hadn't gotten started, let alone come up with a topic. Each month she was supposed to share her "latest inspiration" and supply a short essay along with images of her favorite real-life examples and a couple of original watercolors. The one time Sunny had asked for help planning future columns, her editor, Miriam, had laughed. "But that's what we've brought you in for—our readers want to know what

Sunny MacLeod is thinking about. It's not *my* taste they're after!" When Sunny had muttered something about baked beans and toast, Miriam had told her it was brilliant and scheduled it for a fall issue. Sunny had found a French-Canadian recipe, a Brighton-based artist who painted Heinz cans, and a trio of Mexican beaded necklaces that looked as if they were constructed from silver beans. By the time she was done with the column, she couldn't help agreeing with Miriam. It was sharp. Sunny lived in fear of Miriam's leaving the magazine and being told her new editor would be Rachel Ziff. Rachel was one of the most judgmental people Sunny had ever met, and she made no secret of her dislike of Sunny, who saw no point in trying to win her over. When the two found themselves at work events, Sunny simply stared through Rachel as if she weren't there.

"That's it." Sunny drew out her phone. "I'm going to tell Geraldine she's more than welcome to stay with us," she said.

Nick looked up and took a long sip of what had to be cold cappuccino. "You've earned yourself an Amnesty International tote bag."

"Oh, come off it," Sunny said. She started typing and paused in mid-message. She loved Geraldine like a little sister. But when it came down to the prospect of actually opening her home to her, seeing Geraldine in the morning before she'd had adequate quiet time, having to chitchat about Geraldine's dreams while setting up the toaster oven and an array of condiments, Sunny's bigness of spirit calcified into a brick of obligation. Who was Sunny kidding, offering use of the guest room? Toast with homemade preserves wasn't going to solve Geraldine's problems. She needed real talk that Sunny couldn't possibly provide.

"I have a bad feeling," Sunny said.

"What do you mean?"

"Peter Ricker's been sending me strange emails. His mother just died, and he's a wreck, going on and on about the past." Peter was losing his bearings. He'd bought a plot of land off Algonquin Park and built a yurt, he'd told Sunny. He'd started seeing a Transcendental Meditation coach. In his last email, he'd dropped the rakish tone. No more calling her "Sunshine," no more signing off with a row of lowercase *x*'s. Peter now used words like "humble" and "reckoning."

"He's talking about Geraldine, asking me whether I think she's completely moved on."

Nick looked up at Sunny. "Has she?"

"Yes, four years later. To her great credit."

"She's still single, right? Maybe there's hope."

"*Hope*—are you kidding me? She should stay far away from Peter. Not just as punishment for what he did to her but because he's the worst. Trust me, you don't know him like I do."

"Mum's passing has opened up a sense of clarity," Peter had written. "Not marrying Geraldine was the greatest mistake of my life." Sunny knew that this was nonsense. The greatest error of Peter's life was his complete inability to see how much damage he brought upon others. Even Sunny, who'd made the mistake of getting a little too close to Peter when she was in his employ, had suffered as a result of his cashmere-clad existence. Most of the unspeakably rich people she and Nick were friends with were self-aware enough to understand that they did not count as good souls. Even if they voted and donated in the right direction, there was no shaking off the shame inextricably bound up in their privilege. Peter, on the other hand, indulged his tendency for self-torment and melancholy. He had the gall to wear his fucked-upped-ness as a badge of purity. Poor little Ricker boy.

Sunny had half a mind to tell him to stay in his yurt and leave Geraldine alone. But she worried it would only provoke Peter to stop pontificating on email and go after Geraldine. If he wore her down, Geraldine would never find the happiness that had eluded her. Sunny knew Peter's kind. He was only going to get more selfish and crazy with age. He would disrespect sweet Geraldine again and again.

"You should not get tangled up in this mess," Nick said. "Let them work it out."

Sunny scowled. She wished she could tell Nick the whole story, but that was out of the question. Honesty had never been Sunny's priority. As far as she could see, it just slowed things down. She had come to believe in a supertruth, a version of reality that cut through the fog of other people's hang-ups and never hurt them. What was she going to do? Geraldine's one other actual friend who'd been around for the Peter fallout was Rachel, and they had worked so hard to build a wall of non-engagement that it would be a shame to knock it down.

She'd known Rachel back when Sunny shopped at department stores and had encountered so few Jewish people that she didn't know better than to wish Rachel a "happy holiday" on Yom Kippur. Sunny went clammy every time she remembered how Rachel had chuckled and explained to her that there was nothing festive about the Day of Atonement—in front of their Jewish editor in chief, Edward Simonov, no less. Rachel still bugged Sunny to no end. It was obvious that Rachel took great pleasure in their class differences, as if there were something wrong with Sunny for liking nice things while Rachel's decision to live in the borough where she'd grown up and churn out pulp fiction made her some kind of Rosie the Riveter.

And maybe Geraldine couldn't be helped. Sunny used to trade long emails with Geraldine, trudging through her friend's sentences of self-pity and despair, parrying them with whatever comfort and film recommendations she could locate within herself. Geraldine's boss, Garth, had called Sunny when Geraldine hadn't shown up to work for three days in the wake of Peter's leaving her. Garth was considering filing a missing-persons report, and it fell to Sunny to contact her old landlord, Mrs. Wang, and ask her to confirm that her sublessee was spending her days curled up in her bed watching *Sherlock* on her laptop. Now, though, even if Geraldine wasn't thriving, she was surviving, talking about making a change. Sunny had no choice but to play along and be supportive, while keeping a healthy distance. Geraldine was a lot of work; even thinking about her was exhausting. Sunny squeezed her eyes shut.

"I need an April theme," Sunny said to her husband. "Sailing?"

"Plums," he said without looking up from the sports page.

Sunny considered this. "Aren't they a fall fruit?" The moment she said it, she knew she needn't have bothered. There was never any reason to second-guess Nick's suggestions. Though he had no firsthand experience in media and did not make art, he had a near-perfect understanding of what people wanted next.

"Plums will be good," he said. "A homemade tart, mail-order sugarplums, and you can throw in a plummy lipstick." He raised his eyebrows at Sunny. "The advertising side will love that."

Sunny granted her husband a sheepish smile. She knew that he was partly making fun of her, but she didn't mind. If anything, she wished more people would challenge her, call her out on the ridiculously covetable business of Being Sunny MacLeod. Yes, she was hardworking. But so were a lot of people, and they weren't here, enjoying the luxury of being expensively yet comfortably dressed and nowhere close to doing anything productive at past ten o'clock on a Thursday morning.

"That could work. . . ." Sunny's voice trailed off when she detected the telltale vibration. It was for Nick. While most men had fewer friends the older they got, her fifty-something husband spoke on the phone with a frequency and variety of conversational partners that put Sunny to shame.

During the great split of 2014, when Sunny was breaking Nick down into a list of flaws in an attempt to get over him, she'd created a small counterlist of his positive attributes. That his phone rang more than hers had made the number-two slot. (His ability to make her laugh and his beautiful hair were numbers one and three, respectively.) And when he came crawling back with a marriage proposal, she was willing to overlook his distracted affect and his ambivalence about having a child—not that Sunny was lobbying for one.

"Of course I'm on for lunch," he was saying into the phone. Sunny studied his forehead, which was collapsing deeper into its folds. She could tell that he'd forgotten about the plan until this minute.

"You have to pack," she whispered. Nick brought his finger to his lips.

"Okay, she can come by at twelve thirty," he said.

"Who's coming?" Sunny asked when Nick had hung up.

"Agnes. That was her mother." Sunny nodded in understanding. "Aggie's staying till four, and then Fatimah will come get her. It will be fine. You can make everybody tuna-and-caper sammies and stick around after I split, right?" Nick had a way of wording things that reminded Sunny of Paddington Bear.

"Doesn't she have school? Or does Zoya not believe in school this week?"

Zoya, Nick's ex-wife, was an architect who worked primarily on Nick's projects, though she and Nick barely spoke. Zoya seemed to spend an awful lot of her time pulling Agnes out of school and taking her on vacation.

"It's some holiday," Nick said, rolling his eyes. "You know how her school is."

"I have work I need to do, remember?" Sunny said weakly. She wasn't going to foul up Nick's visitation rights. In addition to the odd lunch, Agnes spent the night on alternating Wednesdays, and though it had gotten off to an awkward start, Sunny had come to no longer mind the sleepovers. Agnes was nine, obsessed with the library books she hoarded, and wonderfully oblivious to her monobrow, which snaked from temple to temple.

When Sunny and Nick had first gotten together, she'd viewed his three-year-old daughter as a liability in leopard leggings and an ill-fitting tutu. Because of this moppet, Nick was able to go away only on certain weekends. Because of her—or rather his guilt over leaving her—he was opposed to fathering another child. Some women in Sunny's shoes might have handled this by embracing their stepmother role and consoling themselves with the knowledge that they *could* have it all—a child, in a part-time way, as well as a career and tight pelvic-floor muscles. What Sunny hadn't accounted for was how much she would come to love the girl. More and more, when Aggie was munching on pretzel nubs in front of Netflix, Sunny had to fight the urge to bust into the den and smother her with cuddles.

Nick cocked his head. "You want me to call Zoya back and say that nobody will be around to supervise Aggie on my day? Because she'd love that."

"Of course not." Sunny felt her shoulders slump. She'd take care of Agnes, and when she was done with that, she would get back to Geraldine. Her day had tumbled out of her hands. At least she had her plums.

# 4

The Tuesday-afternoon flight from Toronto Pearson International Airport to New York's La Guardia was one hour and twenty-five minutes, less time than Geraldine's Wednesday-night Afro-pop dance workshop at the Y. And yet when all the anticipatory shopping excursions, salon blowouts, and *New York* magazine reading sessions were totted up, the journey began to feel like the international expedition that it was.

Geraldine arrived at Rachel's door feeling exhausted and preemptively irritated with her host before even placing her index finger on the scuffed buzzer. Snow fell from the sky in desultory drifts. It was a little past four in the afternoon, which barely gave Geraldine the time she'd need to wash off the airplane's barf-bag smell before showing her face at Sunny's opening. Rachel was going to want to "catch up," even though they'd been in constant email touch and they had the whole five days ahead of them for that. A car drove past, Frank Ocean blasting out of its open windows. Geraldine turned around and smiled as the vehicle sailed toward the corner. People lacked the audacity to do that sort of thing where she lived, and not for the first time since her plane had touched down, she was reminded that her being here, and not in Toronto, made every kind of sense.

When she'd talked to Barb last month, her former boss had been able to offer encouragement only of the noncommittal variety. Barb had rattled off words like "hamstrung" and "head count" on their call, explaining that she had been promoted to senior vice president and, ironically, no longer had much clout in hiring. Barb offered to introduce Geraldine to the new bureau chief, Tom Newlin, the next time she was passing through New York. "There's a way to return you to the world of real news. I just have no idea what that way, that *path*, looks like."

But of course Geraldine was able to envision it with a bit more clarity and orchestrated this pass-through just a few weeks later. She emailed Barb about coming in for Sunny's show, making it sound as if she were a guest of honor rather than just a name on a list. Wonderfully, Barb had stayed true to her word and arranged to bring Geraldine in. "I can't do any more than put you in the same room as Tom, but I'll tell him to be nice to you." Geraldine had a good feeling about Barb. She was too charmless to be a liar. She was more of a jerk, which Geraldine could handle.

A disconcerting fuzz blared from the intercom. This was Geraldine's cue to announce herself, slam her weight against the door, and trudge up to the fourth floor. Rachel and her husband, Matt, lived on the eastern edge of Clinton Hill, in one of the last run-down multi-unit buildings on a block of recently renovated frame houses.

"I'd come help you with your suitcase, but I don't want us to get locked out," Rachel said. She was standing in the doorway, a slippered foot holding the heavy metal door ajar. She was as pretty as ever, with her heart-shaped face and smudgy blue eyes that always looked as if she'd rubbed a little sunscreen into them by mistake.

Geraldine set down her suitcase and shook the snow off her insulated duck boots.

"Your hair looks good. Did you cut it?" Rachel asked.

Geraldine felt her eyes crinkle. "Not in months."

"I'm glad you're back," Rachel said, taking Geraldine in for a hug. "We can actually hang out this time."

"New dress?" Geraldine said once they were inside.

"You mean my potato sack? I can barely squeeze into any of my pants. I should just bring them all to the swap. You're coming, right?"

Geraldine made a confused face. "Swap?"

"Sorry, I thought I forwarded you the invite. It's on Saturday. I have a ton of crap you can donate."

Rachel's apartment felt cluttered, but maybe that was just a side effect of having a child in New York. All of Geraldine's parent friends in Toronto lived in houses with hockey-rink-size basements and pantries stocked with enough fruit squeezie packs to last through several years. Geraldine saw that the door to Cleo's room was shut, so she set down her bags in the living room.

"Can I get you something?" Rachel stood over the dining table, which doubled as her office, and attended to her laptop. It was open to a Word document, a couple of Gchat windows blinking in the background. Geraldine knew Rachel down to her number of sexual partners and struggles with getting off Nicorette yet had no idea about the people she talked to during the day. "Seltzer? Wine?"

"I'm fine, really." Geraldine shook her head and took in the chaos. Sunny had told her she was welcome to use her guest room but had quickly slipped out of touch. Sunny had been preparing for her show tonight and was clearly too busy to keep up with email or remember her promises. It was still nice of her to offer in the first place. Sunny hadn't done anything that magnanimous in a long time. Geraldine sighed and said, "Why don't you finish whatever you were doing and I'll shower?"

"No, no, please talk to me. I've been writing all day. Yolanda was here looking after Cleo." It took Geraldine a second to remember that Yolanda was Rachel's hard-to-handle mother-in-law. She wasn't even Matt's birth mother, but Geraldine had witnessed her spend the entirety of his and Rachel's wedding in operatic tears.

Geraldine struggled for an anecdote that would entertain Rachel. This chapter of their friendship, with Geraldine a frequent overnight guest and Rachel a bed-and-breakfast matron, was relatively fresh. There had been a time in her not-too-distant past when Geraldine's visits to the city meant staying at the Gramercy Park Hotel, with Peter. She hadn't seen much of Rachel in those days. Rachel and Matt had lived in Hell's Kitchen then, but Rachel did not get along with Peter. The one time the two couples had met for a drink, Rachel had brought up Peter's unwillingness to move to New York, which Geraldine had always said she wanted to do. "If you're going to hold her hostage in Toronto, you should at least make an honest woman out of her," Rachel had said. It was almost funny, Geraldine thought, that it wasn't until Peter had asked her to marry him that her life had imploded. When Peter pulled out of the deal, Geraldine moved out of the apartment she shared with him and lived like a student again, using other people's secondhand furniture and eating frozen cod sticks. It had changed her in other ways she didn't like to admit, even to herself. She was more prone to emotional injury now, tuned in to a radio frequency she'd once had the luxury of skipping over.

"So are you excited for your big interview tomorrow?" Rachel said.

"It's not an interview," Geraldine said. "It's a meeting."

"And that attention to detail is going to get you the gig." Rachel raised her eyebrows. "I have a good feeling. The bureau chief must not ask a lot of people to come in from other countries."

"Well, it's not like he paid for my ticket," Geraldine said in a bashful tone. "Barb is arranging the visit. I told her I was coming in anyway, for tonight's thing."

"Ah, the thing. What is it again?" Rachel asked, innocently enough, before turning away to gather the parts of Geraldine's bed.

Geraldine stiffened and calculated her response. She'd already told Rachel that Sunny was having an opening, and she knew this wasn't the sort of information Rachel would forget. Geraldine knew that Rachel couldn't remember the plot of the show she'd streamed the previous night, but about Sunny she'd recall the name of the town in Vermont where she and Nick had rented out a farm for a couple dozen of their closest friends three Christmases ago. Sometimes the enmity between Rachel and Sunny felt so electric that Geraldine found herself jealous. Their mutual dislike for each other seemed to have grown in the years since they'd both moved to New York, which made little sense to Geraldine. They barely ever saw each other, even though their regular paychecks came from the same source. In her meaner moments, Geraldine thought of her two friends' relationship as akin to that of a chambermaid and a VIP guest at a grand hotel.

Though Rachel occasionally implied as much, Geraldine did not actively keep Sunny and Rachel away from each other. No, they had done that to themselves, by simply sliding too far apart on the ladder of life to ever be friends. Sunny never acknowledged Rachel's existence to Geraldine, but Rachel was always full of questions and loaded pauses. Geraldine kept her Sunny references to a minimum, omitting far more than she reported.

"Sunny has an opening this evening, and since I'm in town, I thought I should go and say hi," Geraldine said.

"Where is it?" Rachel pulled at the hair band on her wrist.

"I forget, some space," Geraldine lied. She felt a flash of guilt. Clearly Rachel wanted to come. How bad would it be to show up with her host, rather than by herself? But Sunny wouldn't like that, Geraldine thought uncharitably. And neither would Geraldine. "I'd totally bring you, but I'm not sure if it's some of us just meeting there and going to dinner, and that might be—"

"Oh, no, I can't go anywhere tonight. Or ever." Rachel smiled and motioned toward the room that used to be her office. "It's not that bad. Tanya stayed late last week so Matt and I could have a 'date night.'" She made air quotes with her fingers. "Six to nine. Your assignations don't *start* till mine are over, right?"

"Oh, whatever," Geraldine said, trying not to feel hurt by Rachel's implication that Geraldine never met up with men at a proper time and was some sort of night prowler. "You and Matt have this perfect marriage. He rented a fricking castle for your birthday. And here I am pining for a guy who can barely respond to my text messages."

"It was a *cabin*," Rachel said. "What's going on with Gus anyway?" Rachel looked at Geraldine with heightened interest. Ever since she'd stopped having romantic dramas of her own, she lived for hearing about other people's love lives. Rachel had been twenty-nine when she met Matt—or technically when Rachel's family went out to Di Fara Pizza and her father started talking baseball with a couple of fellow Chowhounds at the next table.

Geraldine rarely had anything to offer up during these interrogations. Though she did sometimes experiment with dating apps, if only just to have a story to share with Rachel and her other married friends, she couldn't imagine completely going through with it and having sex with a stranger—let alone an overeager one she'd met on the Internet. Men liked the look of her, so that was never her problem. She needed to meet people organically, the way she'd gotten to know Peter. This was the only way her crushes could build up, over dozens of nights of lying in bed by herself and obsessing over the outline of somebody she'd met in passing. Rachel was no use in helping Geraldine meet people. "I wish I could think of anybody," she'd say, even though Matt commuted to a neurology lab at Columbia University filled with men, and her brother, Jesse, worked out of a Red Hook studio shared by carpenters, set builders, and comic-book artists.

"You didn't see Gus last time, right?" Rachel pressed.

Geraldine shook her head. "He was in L.A. for a wedding," she said. "He might be there tonight. He told me he'd try."

"Try?" Rachel rolled her eyes. "You're the one who came all the way from Canada. He can be there." Her gaze drifted to the nursery door. Fussing noises were coming from the other side. "You'll get to see Cleo before you go," Rachel said brightly as she stood up and walked toward the source of the cries. It took Geraldine a second to remember she was expected to dig the present she'd brought for Cleo out of her bag and follow behind.

Geraldine arrived at the Brooklyn Public Library an hour after the sun had dropped out of sight. The air was cool but not cold, and the snow was softening to slush. She watched middle-aged people carefully make their way up the steps and kids hunched under the weight of their backpacks stream out of the library's revolving door. An aroma of ham sandwiches and pencil erasers filled the main hall.

She rode up on the escalator and stared over the balcony, down at the people waiting in line to return books, realizing suddenly that she felt self-conscious in her new designer outfit. Sunny's openings only very occasionally took place in proper art galleries. More often they were in back rooms in private clubs and restaurants that didn't exist unless you knew to ask for them. But of course that made the choice of this venue even more frustratingly brilliant.

Everything fell into place when Geraldine opened the door to the Hijuelos Room. It had already started to fill up with people making chitchat that bounced musically off the drawings and paintings of various styles lining the walls. The works bearing Sunny's artistic fingerprint, all thick brushstrokes and bruisy shadows, put the other pieces to shame. Sunny was across the room, holding a glass of white wine beside her complicated updo and aiming her smile at a man whose mouth was moving at nervous speed. There was nothing quite so sweet as having Sunny's full attention.

Geraldine threaded her way through the crowd, discerning notes of apricot and black pepper in the mingled perfumes. She spotted Christian, the rakish Icelandic yogurt impresario she'd been introduced to and had spent some time flirting with at a previous art opening—not Sunny's but a member of her circle's. Several of Sunny's ex-boyfriends from her first few years in the city stood in a cluster around Servane Klein, Sunny's first roommate in New York. The daughter of a famous gallerist, Servane was gorgeous as well as tall and big-hipped, which gave her an ageless quality that worked in her favor. Whatever Sunny had paid to live in Servane's loft on Lafayette Street had been worth it. All the young as well as not-so-young somebodies in the New York art world used to filter through their apartment. Sunny had been in the city for barely a year when Servane and a few friends set up a gallery on the Lower East Side. She included a quartet of Sunny's paintings in their opening show.

Geraldine realized she was staring and steered herself to the left. She saw Jeremy Cleeve and changed course yet again. She wasn't in the mood. Jeremy had originally been a friend of Rachel's husband, Matt. He owed his presence at the party to Geraldine, but he was such a comer that she was sure he no longer remembered that, or cared. Jeremy had created a company that helped baby boomers digitize their photo archives, which had made him ridiculously rich. Now he did something with microfinance and socks. He had snaggly teeth and was always offering to give Geraldine rides home. At the bar she took a single almond and fixed herself a glass of white wine. When she looked at the room again, Jeremy was gone.

Something jutted into Geraldine's hip. "Congratulations," came a deep voice. She looked up and saw the yogurt maker, his teeth and lips purple with drink. "Last time I saw you, you told me you were going to move here," he said.

"It's still in progress," Geraldine said, and saw his face fall. "I'm here for an interview, with the CBC." The yogurt maker looked at Geraldine with a blank expression. "The BBC of Canada," she clarified, and he gave a high laugh. "Though you're welcome to streamline the process and hire me yourself and give me a visa."

"I would just marry him." A new voice entered the conversation. It belonged to Benny Tait, one of Sunny's exes. He was a self-appointed intellectual, with wire-rim glasses and curly brown hair that was starting to recede. "You could be the dairy queen."

Geraldine forced a smile and scanned the room. As far as she could tell, Gus hadn't bothered to come. Probably for the best. She needed to focus on tomorrow. And for the time being, she was sandwiched by two cute guys from Sunny's world who seemed to be alternately vying for her attention and working together to ignore her. She felt her status as entourage member acutely. Geraldine thought back to the early days, when she and Sunny were more or less on a par with each other. There was even a period, however fleeting, when Sunny reported to *Province*'s tempestuous creative director, Françoise, and the scales tipped in Geraldine's favor. The Sunday after Geraldine's official promotion, Sunny sneaked into Geraldine's new office and installed a towering rubber tree and a congratulatory carton of Vernors diet ginger ale. Geraldine now glanced across the room at Sunny, who was talking to the same man as before, her smile barely tolerant as she plotted her next move.

Geraldine directed her attention back to the men, who were comparing tasting notes on the mince pies Sunny had baked and arranged around a ziggurat of colorful vintage wooden blocks. There was a competitive edge to their banter. The guys Geraldine knew in Toronto also did this. When exactly had men decided they would rather joust over food than sports?

She was preparing to express her opinion when something at the other end of the room made her breath go shallow. Gus peeled off a black overcoat and slowly hung it on the coatrack without bothering to survey the scene. There was a steadiness to Gus that extended to all actions he performed. Even when he'd pushed Geraldine's body onto his bed and ministered to her, his excitement had manifested only as an air of intense concentration. Flat against his duvet, Geraldine had joked about her Silly Putty–colored bra, which she'd nicknamed her "Pilly Slutty," but he'd ignored her and run his hand beneath the undergarment. Geraldine's insides fluttered as she remembered the ticklish feeling of his breath against her thigh. At the time she was officially happy, yet she'd been too nervous to enjoy it. Afterward, when she was still on her back, Gus reached for his phone and ordered an Uber. It wasn't until the car was on Rachel's block that Geraldine realized he hadn't even asked how long she'd be in town.

Geraldine slunk away from Benny and Christian and spent the next hour circling the room, making sure that Gus would witness her having more people to talk to than she could possibly accommodate. Luckily, she'd been to enough Sunny gatherings to know nearly everybody, and Sunny's friends were always happy to ask questions about life in Canada. Sunny was from Canada, so that made it interesting. Geraldine obliged, saying what they wanted to hear, which D-list movie stars had been rotating through the temporary apartment she could see into from her bathroom window, and how everyone in her odd little city was obsessed with a new gourmet store where you could point at ingredients through a window and design your own "hand-ground" chip dip.

At last she found her way to the woman of the hour. Sunny raised her arms in the air like a sorceress before taking Geraldine in for a hug. "Sweetie! Why aren't you staying with me?"

Geraldine was speechless.

"We got a new guest bureau and everything," Sunny went on. "Promise me you will next time."

"It's a date," Geraldine said in confusion. She had barely congratulated Sunny on the show when Gus joined them. Geraldine couldn't help noticing he'd waited to come say hello until she was talking to Sunny. Standing this close to Gus, Geraldine was reminded that he was just a human being. Chocolate-colored dog hair clung to his shirtsleeves, and he was a full two or three inches shorter than Geraldine—even tonight, when she'd worn fur-lined snow boots that had barely any lift at all.

"Can everyone come closer together?" A mousy woman with an oversize black camera crouched in front of the three of them. Sunny barely moved, and the other two drifted in to bookend her.

"I'll catch you both later," Sunny said after the library photographer had wandered off. "I should probably go save Nick." Geraldine knew this wasn't true—Nick never stayed in place at cocktail parties long enough to necessitate any rescuing.

Gus shuffled his feet as he and Geraldine exchanged glances. "I wasn't sure if I'd see you here," he said.

Her laugh came out sounding a little deranged. "But I told you I was coming," she said.

He squinted, looked sheepish. "Are you staying with Sunny?"

"I was . . . I was supposed to," she sputtered. "I have a job interview tomorrow."

"That's exciting," he said, without looking remotely excited or asking who it was with. "I mean, is it?"

"I hope so. As long as I don't mess it up. I haven't had one in a while."

"Let me know how it goes." Gus's eyes lingered on Geraldine's face, and she understood a beat too late that he was gearing up to say good-bye. The party was winding down; a line was forming by the coatrack.

"Hey," she said, a desperate edge to her voice. "Are you going to the drinks thing?"

"Where is it?"

Something lifted within her. "I don't know—I can ask Sunny?"

"Nah." Gus shook his head and looked down. "I'm supposed to meet someone in the city, actually." He didn't need to say any more. Another woman was written all over his face. Geraldine's heart snapped. "I'm probably not going to stay for long," she said, managing her tone into neutral. "It's just that I promised Sunny."

He nodded, seemed relieved. "Good luck tomorrow," he said. "Maybe next time you're in town, we can have lunch."

"For sure," Geraldine said, and concentrated on holding her poise as Gus kissed her lightly on the cheek and walked away. She was humiliated, but also slightly relieved that he was leaving so she wouldn't have to spend the drinks portion of the evening being rejected.

Sunny's contingent moved on to a loud restaurant on Franklin Avenue, where Geraldine chatted with a circle of cool, mostly single women, including a sloe-eyed handbag designer who had just spent her fiftieth birthday surfing in Uruguay. At one point Sunny appeared and leaned her head on Geraldine's shoulder, a gesture that filled Geraldine with a sweet contentment that lingered long after Sunny sailed off to conspire in a corner with Servane.

Geraldine must have gone twenty minutes without thinking about Gus, and when she did, she relegated the memory to the back of her mind, then scanned her surroundings and gave a little swoon. There wasn't a dull person in sight. She didn't need Gus. New York was where she was meant to be, to the degree where she sometimes felt that she was already there, leading a parallel life in some alternate dimension, waiting for the Geraldine who was stuck in Toronto to figure out how to latch on to her fate. She was happy here, *and only here.* This understanding bloomed within her each time she visited New York, especially when she was basking in the margins of Sunny's life. Even if it was impossible to get close to Sunny, she still possessed a magical ability to make others feel like a slightly more satisfying version of themselves, or electrically close to it. The feeling that Geraldine began to experience at Sunny's afterparty took root overnight. It only began to dissipate the following afternoon, when Tom Newlin made it clear that he had no intention of hiring her.

Most of her twenty-five-minute meeting with Tom was given over to Canadian media gossip—he dropped that he knew a lot of the old *Province* crew. Geraldine changed the subject to Sunny's latest accomplishments before he could bring up Peter's name. Sometimes she could remain level when she heard people talk about Peter. Other times it sent her right back, to the hurt of being told by the man she loved with a blinding fierceness that she was, essentially, too decent to love. "I don't trust myself to do right by somebody as pure and good as you," he'd said. "Maybe it would be different if you were damaged, too, but you're ridiculously perfect, from every angle." The hardest part of hearing this was that she considered Peter to be the perfect one, perfectly flawed. She knew that she would never find somebody equal to him.

Tom was considerably younger than Geraldine, who suspected he'd cultivated his thick belly and Brillo-pad beard as strategic distractions from his lack of experience. "Barb speaks the world of you," Tom said when he finally picked Geraldine's résumé off his lap and moved it to a pile on his desk. "Too bad our business is on its last legs."

"Don't say that," Geraldine countered gamely. "People are still hungry for news. The models are just transitioning."

"Maybe." Tom pursed his lips and made a tiny sucking sound. "Web is more disappointing than you'd think. I mean, unless you crack Facebook, but otherwise you're looking at a whole lot of content with not a lot of page views. Video is working, but clearly that's not your thing."

Geraldine opened her mouth, but Tom kept talking. "The only

area where I can possibly imagine somebody with your background entering the picture is podcasts. They're cheap to make, and you wouldn't believe how people eat them up. Last year we saw double-digit growth. This year will be even higher."

"I listen to podcasts all the time."

"When?" He sounded skeptical.

"When I'm grocery shopping. Or cooking." She knew better than to mention that she often continued listening through dinner.

"Which ones?"

"Mostly news," Geraldine lied. "And there's one I just got hooked on, *Great White Gay*, where the host brings in a Broadway star and they unpack a famous show tune. It's really smart. I would love to produce one—or some . . ." Her voice trailed off.

Tom cracked his knuckles and tossed a longing glance at his computer screen. "We're not very deep in the podcast world, but we are certainly talking about expanding. So I'll keep your interest in mind, and maybe we'll talk again."

"Definitely, I'll send you some ideas." As Geraldine rose to her feet, she felt a pleasant sensation born less of standing up too quickly than of true excitement. The world had said no to her countless times. She'd heard the word so often that it had almost no impact at all. What mattered was that Tom had led her to an idea. Pointed her in the right direction at least. Not that he deserved much credit. She was the one who'd fought her way to him.

Geraldine beelined it for the subway station. She couldn't wait to get back to Rachel's and tell her about the meeting. She was going to move into podcasts. Not that podcasts themselves were necessarily so thrilling, but she was going to use them to pave the path to the life she deserved. It would be like Sunny's life, but without a skulking husband and multiple addresses. Which was fine. Money didn't excite Geraldine. She imagined her future self, waking up in a clean studio apartment and walking to the bodega, spending her days listening to interesting conversations. She was ready to stop thinking about running into Peter and worrying about Sunny's discarded Toronto apartment—which lonely soul she was going to share it with next and whether she was going to die in it too young or too old. Sunny was good at choosing interesting spaces, though, and maybe Geraldine should convince her to vet her new apartment when she moved to New York.

When Geraldine got off the subway, she headed down Greene Avenue to Sancerrely Yours. She was going to buy something special for Rachel and Matt, a wine that was better than the usual offering grabbed off the twelve-dollar-and-under table. She couldn't wait to see Rachel's face when she Googled the vintage, as Geraldine knew her friend would, and discovered it was a twenty-six-dollar bottle!

# 5

I got you." Rachel took Geraldine's elbow and helped her long-leg it over a treacherous puddle. The rain was shooting down in streaks, and Rachel was glad she'd changed out of the silk dress she'd been wearing and into the pleated canvas skirt she'd scored at the clothing swap earlier in the day. Geraldine had found it for her, balled up at the bottom of the pile. "It's perfectly Rachel," she'd said, a nicer way of saying it was Rachel's slightly larger size.

It was Saturday evening, and the three of them—Matt up ahead, sans umbrella—were heading west on Canal Street, to a dinner party at Jeremy's place. Geraldine had made the appropriate noises about not wanting to be a third wheel, and Rachel had done her duty and told Geraldine that Jeremy was borderline obsessed with her pretty friend from Canada. Even though Geraldine was not remotely interested in Jeremy, she could stand to soak up some male attention. Rachel did not mention that Jeremy had met somebody and was using the word "girlfriend" for the first time since Rachel had known him.

Geraldine kept up beside Rachel, her steps light and jaunty. Geraldine's emotional rainbow contained more hues than possibly any of the other people in Rachel's life, and she was in a particularly upbeat mood. She had been bound up in optimism since her total non-event and yet also sort of transcendent CBC interview three days ago. This gave Rachel some apprehension, but maybe things would work out, if not with the CBC then with something else, and it filled her with joy to glimpse the Geraldine who'd been her de facto life partner back when Rachel's romantic relationships lasted on average three weeks. There was light in Geraldine yet.

It was also in Rachel's interest to have a close friend on hand. Jeremy's get-togethers could be hard to live through. He was more of a collector of people than a friend to them. The one exception was Matt. They'd known each other since kindergarten in Great Neck, Long Island, when Jeremy had spent most of high school getting stoned and doing PhD-level math in Matt's basement.

Jeremy had met Geraldine at a picnic for Cleo's debut in Fort Greene Park. Even though he'd come on too strong, telling her she looked like an actress in an old Michael Caine movie he'd just seen at Metrograph and inviting her to go on a ride in the country the following day, he'd gotten something arguably better out of the connection: Somehow he'd talked her into introducing him to Sunny and Nick. Jeremy and Nick had clicked, and now Jeremy was often seen at their parties. Geraldine had confirmed that he'd been at Sunny's gathering the other night. Rachel's lungs went heavy as it occurred to her that Manhattan's golden couple might be at tonight's dinner. If they were, she might plead a migraine and relieve her brother of his babysitting duties.

She had no tolerance for Sunny. When Rachel had returned to Brooklyn after her stint at *Province*, she had been slightly surprised that Sunny never reached out, if not to welcome her home then to milk her for native tips. Rachel had finally moved out of her parents' house and into a three-bedroom in Windsor Terrace when she finally ran into Sunny. It was at a party for *Re-Vision*, a literary magazine whose tiny subscription base was offset by its renowned reputation. Sunny stood by a white brick wall, her arms draped by her sides, looking like a tulip. Buzzed on two and a half Coronas and a flickering sense of self-respect, Rachel went over to say hello. Sunny was friendly, but in a brazenly insincere way. "I'm on the magazine's advisory board," Sunny said. "You should really think about contributing an essay." Rachel chuckled nervously and said she'd love to make it work, but there was never a follow-up solicitation, and Rachel couldn't stand the idea of emailing an essay and saying that she was doing so at Sunny's suggestion, never to hear back from anyone on the matter.

The city glimmered in the drizzle. "Did Jeremy say who else is going to be there?" Rachel called out to her husband.

"Sorry, we didn't go over the seating plans." Matt stopped and dutifully waited for Rachel and Geraldine to catch up.

"Men don't tell each other anything," Rachel muttered to Geraldine.

"Maybe we have other things going on," Matt shot back. "Jeremy's busy taking meetings at Google."

Rachel laughed. "He's not Steve Jobs."

"He's always been nice to you," Matt said.

"Did Sunny mention if she's coming?" Rachel asked Geraldine in the lightest tone she could manage.

"I don't think so," Geraldine said.

They came upon the building, an aggressively sleek development on the westernmost stretch of Canal Street, and Rachel brushed her hand against Matt's as they rode the elevator up to Jeremy's. She kept her eyes trained on Geraldine as they entered the loft. Peter's place in Toronto had been nice, Rachel remembered, but Jeremy's was on another level. The ceilings were high enough to accommodate three other apartments, and Peter's view of the CN Tower had nothing on the sweep of the Hudson River beyond Jeremy's window.

"Where is everybody?" Rachel asked, looking around. There were no people, just a two-sided dish of olives and pits on the counter.

"More important, where are those cheese sticks he put out last time?" said Matt. "I'm starving."

Rachel noted that the table had been set for seven, a riotous floral arrangement at the center. It all seemed a bit girlie against Jeremy's masculine design scheme—he favored leather ottomans and art that spread its legs across entire walls.

Matt walked into the living room and crouched down to pull out a steel bin of records. He inspected the contents without envy or judgment, even though Matt was the one who'd been president of the radio station at MIT.

"Find anything good?" Geraldine asked.

Matt didn't reply. He just carefully removed a black disc from a paper sleeve and set it on the turntable. He made a gun with his fingers and pointed it at the ceiling, holding still as he waited for the funky instrumental to give way to the vocals.

"Betty?" Rachel said once the singing started, and Matt nodded. "Betty Davis was on one of the first mixes Matt made for me," she told Geraldine.

"I remember those mixes." Geraldine sounded wistful. "I still have the one you copied for me, with that psychedelic Brazil—"

"Matty! Ladies, you made it," said Jeremy. He and a few others came in a rush from the back. He must have acquired a new toy he needed to show everybody. Rachel saw, with a modicum of relief, that Jeremy had invited Don and Henry, a couple she'd met and utterly failed to make conversation with a few times before.

Rachel introduced herself to the girl at Jeremy's side. She had ruler-straight hair and full, pursed lips. Her youth was blinding. So were her teeth. "I'm Renata," she said. "I've heard so much about you." Her arm undulated at Rachel like a tentacle.

"And my favorite Torontonian. That's what you call yourselves, right?" Jeremy kept a courteous distance as he hugged Geraldine, his feet unmoving in spite of his tilting torso. "It's good to see you. We didn't get enough time together at Sunny's thing." Geraldine gave a graceful smile and tucked her chin. Something about the apartment's lighting made her hair look more golden than apricot-colored. Jeremy swiftly turned to Rachel. "No Cleo? I told Matt you could park her in one of the bedrooms."

"My brother's babysitting," Rachel told him. "Here, for you." She handed Jeremy two bottles—the one that Geraldine had brought home, the other that Rachel had swiped from a photo shoot at work. If anyone would appreciate this double-fisted gift, it was Jeremy.

"Cheers," he said, scanning the labels. "How's Jesse doing?"

"He's okay. Still smarting a little after his arrest." Rachel had meant it as a joke, but Jeremy's friends looked slightly freaked-out. "He got taken in for disorderly conduct at the rally in DC right after the inauguration," she explained. "He's not, like, a drug dealer."

"We're becoming a fascist state," Renata pronounced, fluttering her lips.

It wasn't long before they were all seated, spooning pureed parsnip soup into their mouths. Geraldine was earning her place at the table, laughing musically and recalling a book of Nordic fairy tales that she'd been obsessed with as a child. "There was one about a girl whose father sold her to a witch who trapped her in an attic. She ended up falling in love with a bat who covered her with kisses. It was possibly the most inappropriate thing ever," she said with a snort. Rachel felt a glow of appreciation for her friend. Geraldine was at her best when her self-consciousness fell to the floor like a dinner napkin. She'd light up from within and hopscotch through conversation, proffering oddly charming connections—"Romaine lettuce could not be a more buttoned-up vegetable" or "We should all be forced to spend a week of our lives as a puppeteer." Her artless delivery made her words all the more surprising and beguiling. This would have served her well in the life role everybody had believed she was meant to lead, Rachel thought, her remarks scattering magic dust around her and Peter's Toronto extravagant dinner parties.

Rachel hadn't known what to make of Peter at first. She'd never met anybody like him, not even at Amherst, which was rife with the entitled sons of scions. Peter had inherited the magazine from his family, erstwhile steel barons who'd once held control of the Canadian Pacific Railway company and who'd run the journalistic institution for the past century. The Rickers had a camp in British Columbia, and Peter seemed to spend an awful lot of time canoeing under the northern lights. When he showed up at work, Rachel spotted him flirting with the young women whom he employed. This was only a decade ago, but a wholly different era. Nobody seemed to fault Peter for his management practices. It was just the way things were. If Rachel were to be horribly honest, what made her bristle most was that he made it clear he didn't find her attractive. He preferred his women pale and enigmatic, a nicer way of saying Christian and quiet. Rachel wasn't the least bit surprised when Peter took up with Geraldine, who had a serene temperament and looked a little like Lauren Hutton minus the tooth gap.

By the second course, Rachel was able to deduce that Renata was a recent Columbia graduate and had been an intern at Jeremy's company. Now she worked for an interior decorator, primarily making inspiration boards.

"But Jeremy and I weren't together till I found another job," Renata said, as if anybody cared—or believed her.

"May I ask a random question?" Geraldine said during a conversational lull. "Does anyone here have a podcast they're obsessed with?"

Henry perked up. "Is this some personality test?"

"I'm supposed to be developing ideas for the CBC and could use some inspiration," she explained. This account didn't exactly square with Rachel's understanding of how Geraldine and her CBC interviewer had left things, but she respected Geraldine's optimism.

Rachel had glanced at Geraldine's email when she was taking a shower. How demoralizing it must be to keep flying into New York for meetings only to receive an email from Barb saying, "Sorry Tom didn't have better news for you. Chin up—we'll keep chatting." And the Barrett thing, *oof.* He'd written to tell Geraldine that Katrina knew somebody who might be interested in the room—was she comfortable living with a classical flutist who might want to practice when Geraldine was at work and only sometimes at night? Rachel wasn't proud of snooping in Geraldine's in-box, but she suspected that Geraldine did the same to her.

As Don gave Geraldine a hard sell on what sounded like a sleeping pill of a podcast that purported to make astrophysics understandable, Jeremy pulled his chair closer to Rachel's. "Is it terrible that I don't listen to podcasts?" he whispered. "Can you give me a list of them? Also books I should buy? I just got the new Colson Whitehead." This was what he always asked Rachel when he wanted to brag about whatever book he'd just picked up that day at McNally Jackson. He never seemed interested in discussing things he'd actually read—only what he planned to read soon.

"I haven't been reading much," Rachel admitted. "I'm in the throes of a project."

Rachel had recently dragged "Gypsy Girl" from her desktop to her "Dormant" folder and started a new document called "Monsters!" It was unlike anything she'd ever written. She'd banged out nearly sixty pages in less than a month. Assuming Cassie Burkheim was right and the market for "realistic mythical-creature" stories was hot, she just might get another lunch with her agent.

"Throes," Jeremy repeated. "I like the sound of that. Usually when somebody says 'throes,' they're talking about desperation. You're so good with words."

Rachel said nothing. Desperation had something to do with it, too. She was determined to finish before Cleo grew old enough to see her mother wrapped up in worry and defeat.

"Oh—there's something I wanted to show you." Jeremy rose from his seat and beckoned to Rachel.

Not wanting to be alone with Jeremy, Rachel motioned for Geraldine to get up and join her.

"Where are we?" Geraldine asked as Jeremy guided his visitors into a darkened room.

"The guest suite," he said. "It's got its own bathroom and everything. I store my toys in here."

He flicked on the light. The queen-size bed in the corner was dwarfed by all manner of expensive junk, some of which was inspired by the design pages of the very magazine where Rachel worked.

"What happened to the surfboard?" Rachel asked of the hand-painted piece he'd shown her last time she'd been here.

"Renata gave it to a friend of hers who actually surfs."

"I thought you said you wanted Matt to teach you," Rachel said with a laugh. Matt had all but given up trying to convert her into a surfer.

"You think Matt has time to hang out with me? You should know better, Rachel. I have nothing on his beloved zebra fish."

Rachel was touched that Jeremy remembered what type of fish Matt worked on. His love for her husband was genuine. Rachel could tell that Geraldine was reevaluating Jeremy, too. He'd been goofier at dinner than he usually was around Geraldine. Perhaps it was the girlfriend effect.

"You don't see the new thing I got? Turn around."

Rachel did as instructed and squinted at a painting that was hanging over a love seat. Though her face was obscured by a bush of red hair, the waifish girl was indisputably Boo Mierke, a fashion editor–turned–jewelry designer who was a fixture on the smug-people circuit.

"I know her!" Geraldine exclaimed. "We had a really nice conversation about Mexico. She's friends with Sunny. I thought she'd be there at the library show. . . ."

Now Rachel recognized more than the painting's subject. "You bought a Sunny MacLeod?"

"Indeed," Jeremy asked. "They had me over for dinner in December, and she showed me her studio. She was working on this at the time, and I was like, Want. Need."

"You should hang it out where everyone can see it," Geraldine said. Rachel looked at her friend and felt a jolt of protectiveness. Her unrelenting adulation of Sunny was ridiculous. Jeremy, too. Did he really think his studio tour had been spur-of-the-moment?

"Sunny might be our generation's greatest genius," Jeremy said.

"I wouldn't go that far," Rachel said with an effortful laugh. "Don't get me wrong, she's incredibly talented. . . ." Rachel trailed off, not wanting to sound churlish and definitely not wanting to provoke Geraldine.

"Anyhow, she's way cheaper than Elizabeth Peyton, and the girl in the picture is cuter-looking, too. Sorry—the woman," he said.

Geraldine wasn't listening. She'd moved over to the window and was gazing outside. The rain had let up, and the Hudson River ran dark and luminous, framed by a staggering of rooftops that overlapped like Matisse cutouts. "I can't believe nobody uses this room," she marveled.

# 6

Sunny hated the subway. She knew that this was an unpopular stance, and she did her best not to advertise it. Her unease at being trapped underground was too easy to mistake for snobbery. Usually she walked or biked, or she asked people to come to her corner of the world. Today she took a taxi. Traffic was worse than she'd accounted for; ten minutes after takeoff the vehicle was barely two blocks from where she'd hailed it. She was not going to be on time for her meeting at *Cassette*. This, too, would be mistaken for snobbery.

An outdated sign that somebody had forgotten to take down from the window of her local pizzeria advertised heart-shaped pies. Sunny used to love Valentine's Day. Now that she was thirty-seven, the holiday had lost its kitschy charm and become little more than a painful reminder of her predicament. For years she was unbothered by the prenup that Nick's lawyer insisted upon. It had even given her a feeling of hard-won independence. At the rate her career was going, *she* was the one who should be making *him* agree to terms, she'd told Nick over their post-signing lunch. The baby thing wasn't much of an issue. Sunny had never harbored fantasies of pushing a stroller or attending Mommy and Me music classes. She knew herself well enough to understand that caretaking was not her strength. When Nick was recovering from knee surgery last winter, Sunny had filled his hospital room with poppies and snuck in his favorite cabernet franc in a thermos. But she was secretly, awfully grateful when her editor, Miriam, had written to say there was a last-minute change in page count and they would have more space than they'd accounted for. Sunny had offered to run to her studio to bang out an additional item.

Nick was in no shape to become a father again, and at least he was self-aware enough not to be trying to spread his seed. His separation from Zoya had hardly done wonders for Agnes, who'd landed in therapy before she even learned to read. He felt terrible about the girl and had a funny way of dealing. Unless you counted picking stupid fights with Sunny over things like her disappointing grasp of current affairs, as he'd done last night. Sunny had resisted pointing out that Nick was too busy traipsing around the world to raise his daughter. He'd missed the bulk of Agnes's most recent visits, owing to work crises. The last time he and Agnes had been together, Nick had challenged her to a game of Scrabble. When he called her out for consulting her iPad on a word, she swept all the pieces off the board and said the game was boring and so was he. Nick handled the incident admirably, showing his daughter how to make a malted-peanut-butter milk shake. Soon after Agnes left, Sunny found him staring out at the garden and not just tearing up but fully crying. He had enough on his hands. But recently Sunny had found herself, if not wanting, then certainly wondering about having something tiny and warm and entirely her own.

The cab suddenly broke through traffic and sped up Sixth Avenue, and Sunny leaned her head back against the pleather seat. She needed to save her energy for the performance she would have to put on at the office. All the staffers had gone to Ivy League schools and had the social skills of staplers. They stared at her from their workstations and waited for her to talk, and she had to fill the air with references to her quirky travels and friends and obsessions. There was something profoundly sad about these once-brilliant people who clung to their perches in corporate media as if there were a chance in hell the industry would take care of them. *Get out while you still can,* Sunny wanted to tell them all, but she had to pretend to be operating under the same misapprehension as the rest of them. How else to justify the silly rate she charged for her column? The world certainly thought she was worth something. Sunny did, too. But, just lately, not with the same vehemence. She wondered if this new insecurity had come with age and if she should address it directly in her work—but no, she was still too young for that. She'd save it for once she turned forty.

Sunny walked out from the elevator bank to find Miriam waiting for her star columnist. Miriam had on a navy blazer that enhanced her gargantuan shoulders. She was really into rock climbing, Sunny remembered.

"They've just begun," Miriam whispered, ushering Sunny through a pair of ID-protected double doors. "Everyone's in there." Before Sunny could apologize for being late, Miriam said, "I'm so sorry for this nonsense. Thank you for coming."

All forty or so people assembled in the Luce Room looked up when Miriam entered with Sunny. The woman at the head of the table shot the latecomers a disapproving look, while Ceri, the editor in chief, appeared to melt in ecstasy at the sight of Sunny, who had cupped her hand over her mouth in a pantomime of embarrassment. Ceri had been a star fashion editor in the nineties and still wore wispy bangs and gold hoop earrings the size of bracelets.

Sporting slightly smaller hoops, Miriam pointed out a free chair at the table, near Ceri. Sunny instead chose to head to the back of the room and clambered up onto a spot on top of a massive filing cabinet that was serving as an overflow bench. As far as she could tell, the talk was about expenses and the need to clearly itemize them. Sunny felt herself zoning out; she just sent her receipts to an assistant at the magazine. The woman to Sunny's left pulled her phone out from under her notebook and looked down at a text from a sender named Mom: Cleo just made a beautiful poopie.

Sunny sat up straighter and glanced at her neighbor. If Rachel Ziff's hair hadn't been hanging over her face, Sunny would have instantly recognized her, especially considering all the thought she'd recently been giving to Peter. Rachel looked more or less the same, she now saw, with her moon face and milky blue eyes.

Sunny's thoughts wandered as the meeting droned on. She could recall the morning Rachel showed up for work at *Province*, brazenly flouting the custom of all-black office attire that every entry-level hire wore on her first day at the magazine. Rachel swooshed in wearing a cheeky nameplate necklace and a knee-length pleated skirt that took up a hell of a lot of space. Rachel was supposed to be an assistant, but Sunny never saw her ask senior staffers if she could help with anything. No, she strutted around the office as if she were its star correspondent and dropped the fact that she was from Brooklyn whenever she could. Rachel avoided putting together the sidebars that editors typically stuck on newbies. Her first piece was published two weeks after she began. It was about being the new girl at an office, written from her own point of view, with tips from career-management experts woven into her tale of feeling out of place. Sunny didn't buy it. The new girl seemed plenty comfortable.

A week or so after Rachel's start date, Sunny meandered over to the kitchen, where Rachel was preparing a cup of instant noodles. But before she could think of what to say, Rachel waved. "Hi. I'm Rachel."

"We've already met," Sunny said.

"Right—you do layouts! Stella, right?"

"Sunny. I'm an art director. And I do a lot of the illustrations."

"Sunny!" Rachel play-slapped her forehead. "Sorry, I knew it had to do with the sky. Can I ask you a favor?" She lowered her voice to a whisper and turned around. "I just got my period. Everything look okay back there?"

Sunny was so stunned that it took her a second to understand what Rachel was asking her to do. She squinted at the seat of Rachel's cream tuxedo pants. "You're fine," she managed. She'd given Françoise, her direct boss, an account of this incident, and from that point on, the art team referred to Rachel among themselves as Code Red.

Sunny wasn't sure what offended her more—that Rachel's lack of consideration was a violent affront to Sunny's Canadian sensibility or that she'd been too busy disrupting the magazine's ecosystem to learn that Sunny did not sit at the bottom of the pyramid, as her "layouts" gaffe had implied. Sunny was a proper artist. She had a studio in Chinatown that she shared with a ceramicist, and she'd had a show of her paintings at a used-book store on Queen Street East. Everyone else knew that.

Sunny glanced at Rachel's hands, which now rested on top of her phone, obstructing the screen. There was something else that bothered Sunny. Of all the people in the Greater Metropolitan Area of Toronto for Rachel to zero in on, she had chosen Geraldine.

Geraldine was Sunny's closest friend at work, and given all the hours they spent in the office, sometimes staying well after everybody had stopped working and departed for rounds of whiskey sours, Geraldine was Sunny's closest friend, period. Sunny did not appreciate Rachel's encroachment. The three of them had ended up having drinks one night when Rachel was still new in town, after they all ran into one another at a Thai restaurant. Rachel had been so aggressive, bragging about her screenwriter boyfriend and then interrogating Sunny about the cost of her shoes, tasseled Prada loafers that Rachel recognized from a magazine. "I don't know," Sunny murmured. Her mother had sent them as a gift.

A few months later, Geraldine obtained tickets to a secret Tragically Hip show at Lee's Palace and begged Sunny to give Rachel a second chance. The three met up at a wine bar, and Rachel was at it again, yammering about a poor guy she'd run out on before the dessert course—so much for the screenwriter. Then she pivoted to how she'd never heard the Tragically Hip until a week ago, practically flaunting her ignorance. "You make her nervous," Geraldine preemptively told Sunny when Rachel went to the washroom. "She's cool, trust me."

Rachel more or less ruined the concert for Sunny, dancing until she was shiny with sweat. Even when the band played "Wheat Kings," the song that Sunny cried to over and over in grade nine, when her mother was diagnosed with breast cancer, Rachel kept spinning around with a smile on her fat face. Sunny didn't care how funny Ed said he found Rachel's pieces on hanging out in the Blue Jays dugout or trying a liquid diet; she didn't care how fascinated he was by the new girl's New York pedigree. Sunny just hoped Rachel would find whatever she'd come looking for and go away.

But she was forever at hand, even when they both moved on to a city of eight million people. Sunny could hardly escape hearing about Rachel, whose circumstances were a sorry comedown from all she had left behind. Sunny had been in town for a couple of years when she ran into Rachel. They were at the same party, for *Re-Vision*, and Sunny offered to help her get published. She'd taken pity on Rachel but instantly regretted making the suggestion. Rachel had been completely ungrateful, muttering something snotty about her lack of experience with magazines that paid in prestige. If Rachel was so obsessed with money, she should have gone into private equity.

To go by what Rachel was wearing to today's meeting, her money troubles had yet to let up. She'd shown up in a basic striped boatneck T-shirt and Levi's. As the woman droned on about what was and was not "appropriate," something came over Sunny, and she elbowed Rachel in the ribs. "I didn't realize you still worked here," she whispered. Rachel gave her a shrug and went back to texting her mother. Sunny's face tensed. No good deed.

Through Geraldine, Sunny had dimly followed Rachel's progress from hotheaded twenty-five-year-old lifestyle journalist to magazine editor–slash–teen novelist. When she was browsing at the Strand one day, Sunny had flipped through one of Rachel's books and confirmed it was cheesy and childish. It certainly wasn't what Sunny would have imagined Rachel would end up doing. She never would have pictured Rachel getting married under a chuppah on Long Island, the beginnings of Cleo swelling beneath her lace wedding dress. Sunny always found it odd when people acted so determined to become, before hitting forty, abjectly normal.

She reached into her bag and found a graph-paper notebook. "Did I miss anything important?" she wrote, and slid the paper onto her neighbor's lap.

"HR reminded us not to fuck the interns," Rachel wrote back, then looked up at Sunny. Her gaze was heavy-lidded, slightly cutting. Rachel definitely hated her. Maybe it was the thrill of feeling rejected, but Sunny found herself drawn to Rachel. She was still pretty, just more guarded than when they'd been young. The woman at the front of the room went from rambling about Uber receipts and workplace conduct—"If you have to ask whether it's appropriate, you have your answer"—to the ethics of writing about friends and taking freebies. "Do not accept a trip to GoldenEye in Jamaica unless the invitation comes from James Bond himself and you have run it by every appropriate channel and it has been deemed absolutely necessary. The only favors the magazine should be accepting are those you can offer yourselves."

"That doesn't even make sense," Rachel whispered, and Sunny tittered.

"I don't need to tell you that recent events have upended the standing of the media," the woman went on. "Our president has declared us the enemy. You might not think this relates to glossy magazines, but it does. We can't afford to make missteps. Our reputation is all we have."

Sunny stopped listening. She made art, not propaganda. Which isn't to say she wasn't political. She'd marched. She was angry, in a Canadian way. But Trump had had enough victory. He wasn't going to impinge on her work.

"And while we have everybody assembled," Ceri said, "I'm going to add a few points. We're not content until we have maximized content. Make videos. Take pictures. Make sure everything you work on is alive and well on social media. We need to do more with our resources."

"Exactly." Miriam jumped in. "Don't think you can get away with not meeting your web quota. You all know how many posts are expected of you. So let's get to it."

"How am I supposed to write my column without accepting bribes?" Sunny murmured when the meeting was over. Rachel granted her a wearily amused nod.

From across the room, Miriam gestured at Sunny, moving her fingers as if trying to create a safe space between Sunny and anyone else. Sunny pretended not to notice and fixed her eyes on Rachel.

"I saw Geraldine a couple of weeks ago," Sunny said. "She came to my opening."

"I know," Rachel said. "She stayed with me. She always stays with me." Rachel's delivery was more beleaguered than boastful.

"You should have come," said Sunny. "Afterward we all went to this reggae club on Franklin Avenue." Rachel used to dance like Rihanna before there even was a Rihanna. Sunny remembered watching her out of the corner of her eye at *Province* parties and thinking that if there were one thing she could change about herself, it would be her inability to command a dance floor.

"I thought it was a private dinner for like eight." Rachel stared at Sunny.

Sunny felt a frisson of the illicit. So Geraldine was actively keeping the two of them apart. "That's strange," she said. "Because it wasn't. How's our friend doing? We didn't really get to talk."

"I think she's okay. . . ." Rachel's voice trailed off. "She had a meeting at the CBC."

"Right, she mentioned that. How'd it go?"

"I'm not sure it played out that well in the end, but she was still really excited. It was good to see her that way," Rachel said. "I'd almost forgotten what that part of Geraldine is like. You know, when she's full of possibility."

Sunny nodded. "I heard from Peter." She scratched at her throat. Sunny so rarely spoke of anything that discomforted her. "His mother just died, and he's acting really strange. It sounds like things are catching up with him and he wants to talk it out."

"They have therapists in Toronto," Rachel said.

Rachel folded her arms, and Sunny noticed Rachel's brightly colored watch. Sunny hadn't thought about Swatches since the eighties. Filing away that she would buy a vintage Swatch, Sunny stepped in closer. "I just don't want him bothering her. Or, you know, chasing after her. Not until she lands on something good." Rachel was nodding as she listened. "She deserves that much, right?" Sunny asked.

"More than anyone," Rachel agreed. "Peter has no right to come after her, not for anything, ever again. What do you think, should we poison him?"

"Have you ever sat through a dinner party with Peter? He's immune to toxins. But maybe we can steer her to safety."

"We have to try."

Sunny handed her pad to Rachel. "Give me your info."

"Do you two know each other?" Miriam had come to loom over them. She'd removed her blazer, and Sunny could see dark pools of sweat under her shirtsleeves.

"We used to work together in Toronto, back when we were babies," Rachel answered, her tone almost apologetic.

"And we still have a good friend in common," Sunny said.

"Sunny knows everyone, doesn't she?" Miriam said. "One day you'll have to share your secret with the rest of us—perhaps in a column?"

"Oh, I'd rather keep my secrets," Sunny said, then turned to

Rachel. "It was good to see you, Rachel. I'll reach out soon. We can go for tea and strategize."

"Yeah, I'd like that," Rachel said.

Sunny glanced back at Miriam. The invitation was worth it for the expression on her face alone.

# 7

The birds of downtown Toronto were chirping like mad, and children were laughing and whizzing up and down the paths of Trinity Bellwoods Park on colorful scooters, which felt wholly inappropriate given the occasion. Geraldine's group was gathered around Ernie, a dog who was about to die.

Upon learning that their nine-year-old mutt had advanced-stage lymphoma, Geraldine's boss, Garth, and his wife, Miranda, had invited Ernie's closest friends to come say their final good-byes. Garth regularly brought Ernie to the office, and Geraldine had become close to him, volunteering to slip on his booties and take him for walks whenever she felt like procrastinating instead of writing tables of contents or formatting recipes for upcoming issues.

Ernie lay on his stomach in a mound of dirt. His eyes looked glassy, and his mismatched ears hung flat against his head. It pained Geraldine to see his checked-out behavior, and she wondered if she'd made a mistake in refusing Barrett's offer to accompany her to the sendoff. Barrett had taken on an overly solicitous air with Geraldine since he'd announced he was going to be leaving. He and Katrina had found a sublet in Cabbagetown, a tiny house that belonged to a professor of musicology. If Geraldine had to overhear them discussing their excitement about the tapestries in the stairwell one more time, she might snap.

"I hear I have you to thank for the juice, Ms. Despont." Geraldine looked up to see Louise McKnight, a fellow *Province* alum, gripping a paper cup of wine. Her cheeks were flushed, though she came from Scottish stock and always looked slightly sunburned.

"I didn't know what to bring," Geraldine said. "This was my first pre-funeral."

"You know Garth, always prepared," Louise said.

This wasn't exactly Geraldine's experience with her boss, but she smiled and inquired after Louise. "Are you still at the *Globe*?"

Louise nodded with disinterest and flipped the conversation away from herself. "How've *you* been?" Her eyes drilled into Geraldine, her voice ringing with concern. Was there anybody who hadn't heard about Geraldine's crack-up?

Geraldine straightened her back. "I'm well," she assured Louise. "I've been really busy, and I've been traveling a lot, mostly to New York."

She savored those last two words. They were what kept her going, even if they were also what historically got in the way of her doing the things she knew she was meant to be doing, like responding to messages on dating apps or thinking about grasping a low rung of the Toronto property ladder. Most people couldn't even say what stood in the way of their happiness. What had she been thinking all this time, meting out her joy in quarterly visits to New York? "I'm thinking of taking a sabbatical and spending more time there," Geraldine shared.

"So long as you don't let the city snatch you up the way it tends to," Louise said, as if reading Geraldine's thoughts. "Sunny's become a real fixture there, from what I hear. Do you still see her?"

"All the time," Geraldine said proudly. "And Rachel Ziff. Remember her?"

"How could I not?" Louise chuckled. "How's that one doing? Any closer to settling down?"

"She met a really nice scientist, and they have a baby now." Geraldine's thoughts disintegrated, her head suddenly empty, her sense of connectedness to her body shot. She placed her hand on Louise's elbow to steady herself.

"Oh, for shit's sake," Louise said as soon as she fastened onto the situation.

Peter stood across the throng, his back to them, but it was indisputably Peter. Geraldine's heart tightened when she saw he was holding a leash with a pug attached. Peter was big and soft-haired and prosperous, a Labrador or golden retriever through and through. He would never buy a little gremlin with four legs, of that Geraldine was certain. So he was with a woman with a preexisting pug. She probably had microbangs and knew about bands that had formed since the late nineties. Maybe *she* had been formed in the late nineties. At least he wasn't with another, slightly superior variation on Geraldine. "I love and respect and enjoy you more than I am able to show," Peter had said when he'd started to end things, burying his face on the tops of her bare feet. "But something in me is dead." Heat rose to Geraldine's face as she recalled the scene of that night. At first she'd thought he was trying to tell her he had a tumor. It took her another moment to grasp what he was conveying, which was that she was not enough. A couple more breakups followed, until Geraldine's fuzzy sense that she was going to lose Peter was whittled down to a solid understanding that he had no use for her and the wedding was but a delusion.

Peter turned around to scan the crowd. An expression of worried hopefulness came to his face as he raised an arm at Geraldine.

She felt her breathing come up short and looked to Louise, who was now talking to Garth's younger brother. Trembling, Geraldine pulled her phone out of her coat pocket and opened up Twitter. It would calm her to watch everybody's half-baked ideas flow by. The avatars of a cookbook store in London and a stocky music critic everyone was always meaning to set her up with floated to the top. A few slots beneath them was a tweet of Rachel's. Her Twitter presence always struck Geraldine as schizophrenic. Half the time she tweeted as "young-adult writer" Rachel Ziff and went back and forth with somebody named Cassie Burkheim, who had over a million followers and seemed to spend her life attending meet-ups in horrible-sounding suburban hotels. The rest of the time, she was the Rachel with whom Geraldine was familiar, sharing hopelessly arcane observations that rarely generated much response. But now a third side was on exhibit. Three minutes ago Rachel had simply written, "@SunnyCloud can't wait."

Geraldine's throat went dry. Why was Rachel addressing Sunny? She took a slight step forward and tapped the screen to uncover what the message was in response to. She saw that the previous night Sunny had tweeted a link to a benefit for Planned Parenthood that a fellow artist was organizing. Geraldine rammed the phone back into her pocket. Only weeks ago Rachel had done her habitual thing of bringing up Sunny's name and then simpering throughout Geraldine's innocuous response. Rachel never would have followed Sunny on Twitter . . . not unless there'd been some precipitating factor. It didn't matter that they worked for the same magazine; Sunny worked from her home studio. They saw each other at company events once or twice a year, Rachel had told Geraldine. What had Sunny done to embolden Rachel to write her as if they were friends with each other? And why had neither of the two said anything about it to Geraldine? Did they not owe that to her? If only as a way to acknowledge the strain they had heaped upon her by maintaining their petty animosity for so many years, to thank her for bearing the burden. It had not been easy for Geraldine, censoring her conversation, ping-ponging between appointments with the two of them like some child shuttling between parents in the middle of a terrible divorce. Whatever it was that had magically changed the dynamic, they should have immediately informed Geraldine. They might have even waited for her blessing. Geraldine felt like such a fool. Her reason for putting off informing Sunny that she planned to give up her Toronto apartment soon was that she'd felt guilty for the hassle it would create for Sunny. She should tell her right now—in a tweet, Geraldine thought with a stab of anger.

She stood with her hands buried in her pockets and watched the guests step forward to tell Ernie how much he meant to them and how deeply he would be missed. Certain she could feel Peter watching her, she shifted to the left in order to stand behind an obscenely tall man, curling her toes toward the ground. Her sense of betrayal over her friends' collusion was consuming enough; she didn't possess the resources to simultaneously be vulnerable to the one person she'd ever truly loved. It had taken her years to get here, to believe that there might be a future in which Peter did not play a part. But whenever she saw him, which happened all too frequently given the small size of their shared city, her resolve buckled. His presence set off a slide show in her mind of the handful of men she'd tried on since. Perverse as it was to admit, not a single one had come close to making Geraldine feel as understood as Peter had.

Garth wrapped up his speech, and it was Miranda's turn to give her living eulogy. She reached down to stroke her dog's neck. "I didn't used to think of myself as a dog person. I was worried that all those late-night walks would get in the way of my social life. And they did." She paused, waited for the laughter to subside. Tears rolled down Miranda's cheeks as she kissed her dog on the snout. "It would mean a lot to me if you would all take a moment to hug one another. Even if you don't know each other, introduce yourselves and give each other a hug. Make a warm bubble bath of love for Ernie."

Geraldine seized up when she saw that Peter was making his approach. Did he seriously expect a bubble bath of love from her?

"I just wanted to say hi," he said sheepishly. "No hugs necessary."

Geraldine searched Peter, for signs of both wear and madness. But he looked the same as ever, a rumpled baron with his flared nostrils and thatch of sand-colored hair that shot out of his head like dynamite.

"What are you doing here? I thought you and Garth . . ." She trailed off.

"We've made amends. He didn't tell you? Secretive little bastard. We see each other right in this spot every goddamn day." Peter motioned around the park, then to the animal at his feet. He was wearing brown brogues with purple laces. "I have a dog now." He spoke in the rich, flat tone he used when he was being ironic. It used to thrill Geraldine to be one of the few people who knew how to read him.

"Congratulations," Geraldine said.

"I've been thinking about you. A lot." Peter stared at her a moment too long. "My mother passed."

"I know. I was sorry to hear it." She didn't bother to mention the letter she'd sent to Peter's father. Lionel Ricker had always been kind to her, asking her opinions of films and playing games of Scrabble with her on family vacations. He'd taken Geraldine to lunch shortly after the wedding that wasn't, and over a bottle of frighteningly expensive Pineau d'Aunis, Lionel had called his son a sorry fool. Now face-to-face with Peter, Geraldine couldn't bear the tension in the air; she feared she would erupt in sharp trills of laughter.

"I heard you're headed to New York soon," Peter said, and Geraldine nodded slowly, as if she couldn't believe it herself. Peter closed his eyes for a moment. "Is there any chance—would you want to get a coffee . . . or tea?"

Geraldine studied his face. The brackets around his mouth had deepened, and his skin looked weathered and golden. He was like a leather couch she wished she could curl up on and stay nestled in all afternoon, reading and napping.

"Is there something in particular you want to talk about?" Geraldine said.

"No agenda. I just miss our talking."

It took every ounce of her will not to tell him that she did, too. "I should really get going," she said, the words catching in her throat. "We should keep doing things the way we were, don't you think?" Peter just stared at her. "I mean, I'd prefer not to talk to you." Geraldine took a baby step back and watched him give a staggered-looking nod. "It was good seeing you," she said. "I'm sorry again about your mother. She was a remarkable woman, and she did so much good for the city." With that she pivoted and wrapped her arms around a woman standing a couple inches away. "Please don't let go until that man I was talking to moves away," she said. "I'm Geraldine, and that man broke my heart."

"Nice to meet you." The woman gave off a vibrating laugh, and Geraldine started shaking, too, though with tears.

# 8

Sunny was already in the café's back corner, her head bowed over a laptop, her fingers flying across the keys. The picture struck Rachel as somehow incongruous, which she realized was silly. What did she think Sunny used to compose her *Cassette* contributions—parchment and a quill?

The tables were packed together too tightly, so Rachel rotated her round hips and sidestepped over. Up close, Sunny looked positively incandescent. Were it not for the slight shadows under her eyes, her skin could be mistaken for that of a child. Rachel wished she knew Sunny well enough to ask about her skin-care regimen. She was certain it involved appointments with a woman named something like Maja, not products that could be obtained at Duane Reade.

"Hey, Sunny?"

The register of Rachel's voice betrayed her nerves. Sunny smiled coquettishly as she closed her computer and came to her feet. She was wearing mannish trousers and sneakers that looked like All Stars but had shorter toecaps and had to be bespoke. She was tiny without appearing skeletal, with bracelets of gold floss circling her wrists.

"Sorry I'm late. I'm coming from the backwoods of East Canarsie, and the trains were not on my side."

Sunny widened her eyes. "I didn't realize you lived so far away. We should have met somewhere in the middle."

"I don't live there—I was doing a school visit." Rachel unzipped her jacket and sat down, feeling something close to awe. Did Sunny really have no idea about her life? When Rachel returned from Toronto, she had lived with her parents for a spell—nowhere near East Canarsie, nearly a decade ago. Now she lived somewhere semi-desirable. The café they were in was on Twelfth Street, a block or two from Sunny's house. Rachel knew not only where but *how* Sunny lived, thanks to the pictures she'd seen on real-estate websites and in the pages of *Cassette*. She knew Sunny down to her vintage silverware and her proclivity to store spices in old candle jars. Rachel was never going to be anything like Sunny, who had a charmingly vague way about her that nobody who grew up in a coupon-clipping household could possibly acquire.

"It must be so satisfying to get to share your work with children," Sunny said, seemingly unaware of any offense she'd caused with her East Canarsie comment.

"To read to teenagers who are on their phones, you mean?" Rachel tried a grin. "Actually, it wasn't so bad. I read from something I just started working on, and the response was pretty positive. One of the girls said it was 'nasty.'"

Sunny's mouth stretched into a smile. "You've struck gold, sounds like." Rachel was relieved to see she had at least half a sense of humor. "What's it about?"

Rachel stalled, not sure how Sunny would react to hearing about a scene where a changeling named Renetrios drags a pinkblood named Freya out of biology class and back to the immortal city, whereupon he engages in battle with Roki the overlord. "It's based on Norse mythology," she said. "You know, pagans and sex and bloodshed." Sunny cradled her hands around her empty coffee mug and cocked her head to the side. "Do you want something else?" Rachel asked. "I'm going to go get a coffee."

"I'm good, but"—Sunny's eyes went beseeching—"would you mind getting yours to go? I have to pick something up, and I just remembered it's Friday. The place closes early. We can walk and talk?"

Rachel said that was fine. It wasn't until she'd been waiting in line for a good three minutes that she realized Sunny hadn't even bothered to explain what errand was urgent enough to disrupt their plan to stay indoors. As she eyed the café's drinks menu, which featured something called a Lotus Latte, Rachel's thoughts zoomed back in time. Flying Lotus was a Thai place around the corner from her first sublet in Toronto. The food wasn't too greasy, and it was popular with solo diners, which Rachel appreciated. The hostess always seated them together, at a row of two-top tables in the rear that functioned as a parking lot for the widowed and the recently divorced. Though she was several decades younger than the other lone wolves, Rachel was going through a breakup of her own. She'd been the one to end things with Joshua, by moving to another country, though he wouldn't let go so easily and continued to place tearful long-distance phone calls.

Rachel had been contentedly losing herself in a paperback of Nora Ephron's old columns when she saw her co-workers. Across the dining room, Geraldine and Sunny were laughing, their seats nearly touching. Geraldine was the prettier of the two, classically speaking anyway. Sunny was cute, with her bright brown eyes and preternaturally clean tennis shoes. Something about her reminded Rachel of a baby panda. Rachel shimmied out of her seat and made her approach.

"What are you doing here?" Geraldine's tone was happy, thankfully.

"This is my spot," Rachel replied. "Back there in the VIP section." She turned to point at the wall of shame, though a couple of loud men had come to occupy one of the tables so her sad-sack quarantine theory wouldn't make sense to them.

"Want to sit with us?" Geraldine said. An expression of what might have been violation flashed on Sunny's face, but then she spoke. "We're nearly done, and we're going to get a nightcap," she told Rachel, who felt herself ease.

Half an hour later, they took a taxi to Bloodhorse, a rowdy Queen West establishment that was all dark wood and exposed red lightbulbs. Sunny tilted her head toward the back of the room, and a man with rockabilly sideburns came out from behind the bar and removed a Reserved sign from a corner booth. He whispered something to Sunny that made her laugh and whisper something in response.

While the three of them waited in the booth for drinks, Rachel told them about Joshua's recent threat to come up and visit.

"Trouble is, he's hot," Geraldine told Sunny. "I saw a picture."

Sunny flicked her eyes at Rachel, who detected a frisson of dislike. Rachel shifted to interview mode, as she was wont to do whenever somebody made her feel nervous.

"All my life, pretty much," Sunny responded to a question about how long she'd been in Toronto. She reached over the table, dipped her pinkie in the candle's hot wax. "I grew up in Hamilton, and then I came here to go to OCAD."

"Ontario College of Art and Design," Geraldine supplied. "Most of the Group of Seven came out of there."

"I have no idea what you're talking about," Rachel said. "I'm sorry. My mother's an art teacher, so my thing growing up was hating art. Not that I actually hated it, I've just always been more of a 'word person.' . . ."

Sunny gave a slow blink and stretched her swan neck. "I have to go to the washroom," she addressed Geraldine, and slipped out of sight.

"How badly did I offend her?" Rachel asked Geraldine twenty minutes later, when Sunny still hadn't returned.

"She probably went out to the patio," Geraldine said, not answering Rachel's question.

"Without telling us?"

"Don't take it personally. She just likes who she likes."

"That's the fucking definition of personal," Rachel said.

Geraldine smiled unsurely, and the hurt Rachel had been trying to contain ballooned in her chest.

"Really, I wouldn't worry about her," Geraldine said. "She can be unpredictable. I'll still be your friend."

Now, latte obtained, Rachel returned to the table with her paper cup. A vague feeling of victory ran through her. She had cracked the nut of Sunny, all these years later. "There's something I have to tell you," she said. Sunny looked up, her expression one of interest swirled with wariness. "I have a Tom Thomson poster in Cleo's room," Rachel said. Sunny looked confused. "Remember that night we went out for drinks with Rachel and I'd never heard of the Group of Seven? I was so embarrassed. I bought a book—I still have it. So thank you for setting me straight." Rachel smiled meaningfully;

Sunny simply said that Canadian art could be so funny and started to gather up her belongings.

"You're not going to believe this," Rachel said when they were outside, wind ripping from all directions. "I got an email from Geraldine *right* while I was coming to see you. It's like she has some sixth sense."

"Maybe she does." Sunny lightly placed her hand on Rachel's elbow and steered her around the corner, onto Greenwich Avenue. "Did you tell her you were meeting me?"

"No, I didn't write back. I've barely been in touch with her at all."

"It's fine either way, so long as we get our stories straight," Sunny said. "She actually just wrote to me, too."

"Also asking you to look into getting her a job at *Cassette*?"

"Is that something she wants to do?" Sunny waited for Rachel to give a shrug. "Wow—imagine that! She wrote to me about the apartment. She's decided to move out for good. It's technically my apartment, so I get to deal with relinquishing it or finding another subletter." Sunny clenched her jaw. "I'd ask Nick to deal with it, but it wouldn't be fair to my landlord. She's got to be eighty years old, and Nick gets super aggressive when it comes to real estate."

Rachel couldn't fault Geraldine for wanting to leave Toronto. It was a fine city, but it lacked an essential electricity. In all her time there, Rachel had witnessed people arguing on the street exactly once, outside Club Monaco on Bloor Street. She'd stopped and stared, feasting on the public acrimony, water in the Canadian desert. Rachel realized Sunny was watching her, waiting for her to say something. "Did Geraldine tell you about Peter?" Rachel asked.

Sunny stopped in midstep. Apparently Geraldine had not. "What about him?" she asked.

Rachel tried to recall the exact wording of Geraldine's note. "It's like you called it," she said. "He broke their covenant of silence. He came up to her at some event in the park and tried to get her to go for coffee with him."

"She said no?" Sunny waited for Rachel to nod. "Good. He'd only discard her again. That would kill her."

"He practically already did kill her. . . ." Rachel trailed off. It was so sad, the way Geraldine's childhood, pocked as it was with solitude and deprivation, had programmed her to think that she needed somebody who could lift her into a realm where she'd be taken care of. She mistook safety for love. Geraldine's father, Bruce, was a one-time junior-ice-hockey phenomenon who drank too much and sold restaurant equipment. He spent most of his time on the road and left his family when Geraldine was three. Rachel had seen Bruce's scraggly handwriting once, on a card. "Happy Christmas! Merry birthday, G. Love, Your Pa." It was the "Your" that struck Rachel—as if he needed to remind Geraldine who he was. Was it any wonder Geraldine had been so certain that a man like Peter was out of her league and nearly ran herself into the ground trying not to lose him? Yes, he was eligible in his high-thread-count way, but a man who lacked a center of his own could not possibly provide one for somebody else.

"Peter scares me," Sunny said. "You don't know him like I do."

Rachel studied Sunny as she cast her eyes up at the sky. "Can I ask you something? Did you and Peter ever . . . ?" Rachel couldn't bring herself to complete the question.

"God, no," Sunny said. "We were just close friends."

Rachel felt nothing but acute admiration. There was no question in Rachel's mind that Sunny was lying. What was more remarkable than Sunny's acting skills were her powers of self-conviction. In order to move through the world so gracefully, Rachel figured, Sunny believed the stories she spun about herself. "Are you still close friends?"

Sunny shook her head. "Only theoretically."

"If you have his ear," Rachel said, "can't you tell him to leave her alone?"

Sunny pshawed. "Peter? He doesn't listen. I honestly don't think he knows how to. All I can do—all *we* can do—is give Geraldine the support she needs to move on before she caves in. I introduced her to a friend of mine, but that doesn't seem to be working."

"Gus?" Rachel said. "He sounds like a royal asshole."

"He's always been sweet to me." Sunny lifted her chin. "I should have thought it through more carefully. At least Geraldine knows that backsliding with Peter is not an option."

"She's finally open to growing up," Rachel said.

"And Peter isn't having it," Sunny tutted.

"That guy is such a slug," Rachel said. Most of the wealthy men she knew moved fast, all impulse and hunger. Peter was different, prone to brooding and projecting his feelings onto any available surface. When she'd first met him and he'd told her all about his issues with his overbearing father, she'd been charmed. This was true generosity of spirit, she had believed. Rachel now understood that he simply used his angst and supposed suffering—because, really, did that man know suffering?—to his advantage. It was emotional honesty at its most dishonest.

"I'm optimistic, too. Something has definitely shifted within Geraldine," Sunny confirmed, sliding in closer and absentmindedly linking her arm in Rachel's. Rachel waited for Sunny to realize her mistake, yet a third of a block later Sunny was still holding on.

"But I worry," Rachel said. "Not just about Peter but everything. What if the world isn't as open to Geraldine as we'd hope?" Now her voice became quieter. "I feel terrible saying this, especially after how long I've encouraged her to get back on her feet, but now I have this sinking feeling about her whole New York plan. Things have changed since the last time she was knocking on doors, right?"

"I don't know." Sunny frowned. "She's definitely changed, though. She's deeper—and weirder."

"And ballsier. She pretty much asked me if I would give her Ceri's email."

Sunny looked taken aback. "Really? Did you give it to her?"

"No. It's not that I didn't want to, but it's hard to imagine Ceri responding warmly to Geraldine."

"Definitely, Ceri would sniff out her weakness. I think the only person who can help Geraldine is somebody who loves her. I'm praying this Barb thing comes through."

Rachel moaned. "Barb is useless. She was able to get Geraldine the opportunity to slave over an ideas memo. And that was that."

Sunny shook her head. "Geraldine should know better than to give things away for free."

"Here's an idea," Rachel said. "Why don't I introduce her to Elinda, in HR?"

"The one with the silver bob?" Sunny sounded incredulous. "She's always such a bitch to me."

"She's just super corporate," Rachel said. "Even if she can't *do* anything for Geraldine, she would be polite to her. And it would make Geraldine feel good to know that people are having her in and that we're looking out for her."

"I've certainly tried to be good to her," Sunny said. "I barely charged her anything in rent. I hardly made any money on the deal. I hope she understands what it's going to cost to live anywhere else."

"What are we going to do?" Being helpful was something Rachel took pride in—so long as she wasn't *too* helpful. There was only so much good luck to go around, after all, and only so much space in her heart.

"I don't know." Sunny looked up at the sky as if for an answer.

When they reached Sunny's destination, an old-fashioned dry cleaners, Rachel waited outside and watched through the window as the woman behind the counter came out to hug Sunny before handing over an enormous brown paper bag. There appeared to be no exchange of money.

"Thank you so much for letting me do this," Sunny said when she came back outside. "Nick's old friend Laird is coming in this weekend, and there was a mysterious rip in the guest duvet. Nick's daughter, Agnes, has a thing for scissors."

"Better that than cutting *herself*," Rachel said, then instantly realized how weird this must have sounded. "Sorry, cutting is a big thing in the YA world." Rachel felt mist on her nose and pulled her hood over her hair. "I should head back."

"Not yet." Sunny reached out for Rachel's elbow. "You did not schlep into Manhattan to watch me run errands. There's this new Viennese bakery on Bethune. They have these pastries that are made with cardamom and ground hazelnuts. Tell me you eat nuts."

"Okay," Rachel said after a moment. She'd eat only a few bites, quickly, and bring the rest home to her daughter.

# 9

Mrs. Wang has decided to be nice and let us break the lease," Sunny told Geraldine. She was feeling less than nice herself. Tracking down her aged landlord had been more of an ordeal than she'd foreseen, and now she had to relay all the information to Geraldine, who would do her part to prolong the exchange. If Nick didn't keep an eagle eye on their finances, Sunny would just have absorbed the cost of letting the apartment sit empty an extra few months. "She says May first is fine with her, as long as you help her find a new tenant."

"Sure, I can get the word out," Geraldine said. She was speaking from work, in a near whisper.

"No, I think what she means is she wants you to *line up* the tenant," Sunny clarified. "Mrs. Wang doesn't like real-estate agents. I doubt she even has a computer. We still have over a month—it should be fine." Geraldine was being particularly exhausting. She didn't even have a plan besides putting her belongings in storage and showing up in New York. Sunny imagined Geraldine floating out of a Wednesday matinee of *Hello, Dolly!*, her hazel eyes adjusting to the splintering sunlight, the rest of her day utterly unaccounted for. Every time Sunny started to imagine what Geraldine would be expecting of her, an antsy feeling came over her.

"She got an iPad," Geraldine said, a little louder now. "One time I came up to bring her her mail and she was watching a video of Lady Di playing the piano."

"Do you think you can you find someone?" Sunny said abruptly.

"Yes. I mean I'll try. It's such a lovely apartment, and so reasonable, it shouldn't be a problem."

"No, I don't think it should." Sunny thought of the old neighborhood, with its low-slung buildings and secret alleyways. There was nothing like it in New York. There was a Laundromat in a Victorian storefront that held Friday-night socialist talks. Sunny and Geraldine had attended one, on a lark. The lecturer, a sixty-something draft dodger in a Hawaiian shirt, had taken a shine to Geraldine, who had asked a question about globalization. A handwritten four-page letter addressed to "Glorious Geraldine" had arrived at the *Province* office the following week.

"What about your stuff?" Geraldine asked Sunny.

Sunny hadn't even thought about this aspect of Geraldine's move until now. She tried to picture the apartment, with its fleur-de-lis wallpaper and faint aroma of disintegrating cork. "There's your beautiful bureau, and the pantry still has all those storage containers of *Province* issues," Geraldine reminded her. "You must want them, right?"

Sunny remembered a few of her favorite covers. There was one with Harry Potter and a maple-leaf-shaped scar. Another, for a

Valentine's Day issue, featured a photograph of a rising Montreal chef and his girlfriend having a two-person dance party in Sunny's apartment, twisting in their bare feet on top of her antique steamer trunk. Insane to think that Sunny had once lived like a grad student, making cakes in scratched-up pans and playing records on an old turntable she'd bought on eBay. She used to have Geraldine and Peter over for "picnic-style" dinners that were no more than some merlot and a baguette and triple-crème cheese.

The three ate out often, too. They would go for steak at the French bistro near Margaret Atwood's house and often went to Terroni for late dinners after the magazine's Tuesday-night close. Sunny and Geraldine had plenty of dinners without Peter, too. Once she was dating Peter, Geraldine had access to an entirely new level of office gossip, but Sunny was just as riveted by Geraldine's stories about her upbringing—the disappearing father, the collection agencies, the mother who stashed Geraldine away at her grandparents' house in Thunder Bay over holidays and summers. It was all Dickensian, thrillingly so.

One winter night Sunny had been waxing her upper lip when Geraldine called sounding frantic, saying she'd discovered a damning receipt. A three-hundred-dollar sushi dinner that had ended just before midnight, over a weekend when Peter was supposedly visiting his parents at their cottage. Sunny and Geraldine had met for drinks at a Portuguese bar near Sunny's place, and though Geraldine had cried and cried, she'd pulled Sunny aside at work the next day and told her that everything was fine. "Better than fine." Peter had explained that his brother was having marital difficulties and he'd taken him out for a rant. Geraldine shared that they had a night of sex that Geraldine could only describe as "mostly vertical."

"You want the magazines, don't you?" Geraldine repeated into the phone.

"I already have my favorites," Sunny muttered. "You can just recycle whatever's left."

"What about the furniture?"

"It would cost more to ship than any of it's worth." Sunny could hear Geraldine's hurt in the ensuing silence and had to remind herself that the possessions she was belittling were her own, not Geraldine's.

"So everything must go," Geraldine said with an air of defeat. "I'll do my best not to get too sentimental."

"We don't have time for that," Sunny said. "Just find a new tenant and we're golden."

"Oh—there's one thing I was looking for," Geraldine said lightly. "Do you still have that book of mine—the journal I made, with all my life's indignities?"

Sunny felt her jaw clench. "I need to get that back to you, I know. It's in the country. I can picture exactly where it is—on the bookshelf, right by the almanacs," she assured Geraldine.

"The material keeps on coming, I'm afraid," Geraldine tossed off the line.

She made good on her promise, lining up a couple of teachers whom Katrina and Barrett knew. She also arranged for Goodwill to take away the furniture the new residents didn't want and, despite Sunny's protestations, mailed a package containing a few belongings she said she couldn't bear to throw away. A dozen or so old magazines, a ski trophy Sunny had won as a child, and the quill-shaped medal Sunny had received at the Canadian Magazine Awards, just days after her expulsion from *Province.*

A wisp of irritation crossed Sunny as she unearthed the award from the package. Geraldine had to know that Sunny would not want this reminder of that time in her life, which had been abjectly humiliating. At the awards dinner, Sunny'd had to sit at the same table as Geraldine and Peter, who got to keep their jobs, as well as Ed, the one who'd told her that he couldn't afford to keep her. She'd given a gracious speech, reserving her anger for when she was by herself, and thrown the medal into the back of a kitchen drawer.

Even if Geraldine had been trying to be thoughtful, the gesture grated on Sunny. So rather than thank Geraldine for going to the trouble, Sunny began to compose an email to Rachel. As she started to type, she felt a quickening that only a new friendship could provide. She and Rachel had hung out a few times now, but never in each other's home. They'd met for one more coffee, and Sunny had taken Rachel to a friends-and-family breakfast at a new hotel restaurant on the Bowery. Buzzed on free lattes, they talked about their shared love of Shelley Duvall and whether there was such a thing as a "Pilates body." And, of course, they spoke of Geraldine.

"Nick and I are having friends over for drinks on Saturday night," Sunny wrote. "Any chance you can make it?"

The doorbell didn't ring until after eight, at which point everybody was seated around the table wearing lobster bibs. The drinks Sunny and Nick had hosted had bloomed into a full-on dinner party, with Nick's surprise delivery of a crate of lobsters and the arrival of not only Laird and his new wife, Reineke, but also Yves, a real-estate developer who spoke not at all and only stroked his shirt collar, and Nick's sister, Barbara.

"That must be my friend Rachel," Sunny said, feeling a flip of excitement in her belly. "I invited her for drinks. I didn't think she was going to make it." She had lost hope of Rachel's being able to extricate herself from her family duties.

"Shall we pretend we didn't here that?" Nick glanced at his watch. He was a tiny bit drunk on gin and tonics, and when he was drunk, he could be a tiny bit mean. He had already chased out a couple whom Sunny had invited for cocktails by thanking them for stopping by in that way he did that telegraphed his readiness for somebody to leave. "It's past cocktail hour," Nick said. "And we can't fit another for dinner." But Sunny was already halfway across the parlor floor.

She opened the door to find Rachel standing on the top step, bundled up in a fur-trimmed parka. Her blue eyes blazed in the March night. Next to her stood a stubble-faced man with heavy eyelids and a sleeping toddler slung over his shoulder. He was beautiful, embarrassingly so.

"Are you Matt?" Sunny said, almost in disbelief. Geraldine had spoken of Rachel's husband as a cute nerd who liked to surf. Sunny had pictured a generic-looking white man with a heavy backpack, very grad-student, not unattractive or bad but nothing to get excited about.

"My brother, Jesse," Rachel supplied. "He's been helping me out. Matt's stuck at home on a Skype call. His adviser is in China."

Sunny took another look at Jesse's eyes and pulled her cardigan tighter around herself. "I thought you weren't coming," she said to Rachel. "We actually started eating dinner a while ago—"

Rachel's face flooded with alarm. "Oh, no! I thought it was a cocktail party."

"It was," Sunny said, confused. "I invited you for drinks, but that's turned into dinner. I'm sure we can throw something together—"

Sunny inhaled Nick's oatmeal soap and knew that he had come up from behind. He placed his hand on Sunny's shoulder and pressed down tighter than usual. "What's going on?"

"You must be Nick," Rachel said. "I'm Rachel, and I'm so sorry to be butting in. I totally misunderstood the invitation. I thought you were having a party, which is why we're so late."

"I've told you about Rachel," Sunny said speedily. "The children's-book writer." She hoped Rachel wouldn't catch that she had chosen to put it this way, rather than saying she was a *teen* writer, which wouldn't interest Nick. She was protecting her friend, was all.

"It's my fault," Jesse said. "I kidnapped these two for the afternoon, and my truck had some last-minute difficulties."

"We went up to Beacon for this mega yard sale, and then we spent three hours in a frozen-yogurt shop waiting for triple-A."

"I think we've been to that yard sale." Sunny squeezed Nick's hand. "It's where you got your chess set?"

The child jerked up with a start, and Jesse cupped his hand over the back of her head, calming her and drawing her body back against his. The girl rearranged her cheek against her uncle's shoulder and went completely still. She was so beautiful, Sunny thought.

"You're all welcome to come in?" Nick's voice was pitched somewhere between politeness and agitation. Sunny could feel his hot breath on her neck. Now Laird's wife was hovering in the foyer, looking at the newcomers as if they were feral animals.

"No, no, we don't want to ruin dinner." Rachel was already backing down the stairs. "Wait, I have something for you." She reached into her tote and came up the steps to hand Sunny a brown paper bag filled with something heavy. "It's nothing," Rachel said. "I just saw them at the sale and thought you could do something with them."

"That was so sweet." Sunny brought the bag close to her chest and peeked inside. It was filled with buttons of all shapes and colors, glinting like so many precious coins. Sunny remembered the rag dolls she used to make as a little girl and wished Agnes were the sort of child who found enjoyment in the same things Sunny used to.

Before she shut the door, Sunny peered down the street and noticed a blue Ford pickup parked a few buildings away. It looked defiantly out of place on her block. She turned and went back into the dining room, where she found Nick and his sister already seated with Laird and Yves. They were working on their mushroom soup, as if nothing had happened.

# 10

Oh, goodie, an orange." Geraldine pinched the wedge out of her drink. "I don't think I've had a single piece of fruit since I've been down here."

Jeremy tilted his head quizzically. "Should we ask for more? We don't want you getting scurvy."

"No, thank you. I'm perfect. Everything is perfect."

Geraldine had been in town for less than four days and was in a slightly manic state. Here she was, in Union Square, sipping on a pale cocktail that tasted faintly of lavender while a woman she was fairly certain was Gwyneth Paltrow picked at her dinner some twenty feet away. Growing up, she'd felt a certain kinship with the actress, who also had an ugly *G* name. The blonde turned her head, and Geraldine could see it was a very birdlike woman and not the actress, though she refused to let that deflate her.

Geraldine and Jeremy had been emailing some during her final weeks in Toronto. She'd written him first to thank him for having her over to dinner, and a few more messages had followed. He was funnier than she'd previously given him credit for, and nicer, running on nerves and insecurity. He sought her approval on the tattoo design he was considering for his right arm and made her promise not to tell anybody that he'd thrown out his back while jumping rope. For her part, Geraldine had sent him an Etsy listing for sock stencils she thought he'd get a kick out of and a photo of the crowd at the goodbye party Barrett had thrown for her at a bar on College Street. There'd been a Rush cover band, and Katrina had baked a fondant cake decorated with orange flower petals.

Now Geraldine and Jeremy were perched on tall stools at the copper bar in a fake French brasserie whose ornate wall paneling reminded Geraldine of her grandparents' knockoff Tiffany lamps. Jeremy was nursing his back injury with a murky drink that came in a tumbler lined with black lava salt. He puckered his mouth every time he took a sip. The low lighting was meant to flatter, though it made him resemble a sinewy ghoul.

"You've been keeping occupied?" he asked.

"Too occupied," she said. "It's amazing what a fuss people will make when you're coming and going. I have a dinner plan every night until next Thursday." Geraldine had been working her way down a list she'd made up of everybody she'd ever met in New York and at this point had to stop saying yes to lunches if she wanted to get anything done during the day.

Her network, loose as it was, included nearly fifteen people. She still hadn't reached out to Rachel or Sunny to set up a plan. It hadn't been her intention to distance herself, yet now that she'd managed to go this far without clinging onto them, she was hoping to last until Sunny caved in and called her and apologized for not being more hospitable, which was, admittedly, a bit of a fantasy. Especially now that Sunny and Rachel had their new friendship to keep them busy. A friendship about which, unbelievably, neither of them had said a word to Geraldine. Jeremy had told her he'd seen the two of them at a party at one of Nick's hotels. Geraldine was not impressed. It would have been so much easier if they'd just gotten along with each other all this time, rather than make Geraldine play monkey in the middle. And they'd finally decided to run off together, without her. Geraldine was angrier at Rachel, of course, since she considered her to be the closest of her New York friends. Whether this closeness was bound up in Rachel's being the most available of her New York friends was something Geraldine did not wish to dwell on.

Geraldine liked to play the phone call in her head. When she told Sunny that she'd actually already been in town for a couple of weeks, staying at a hotel downtown and socializing with several people Sunny knew, would Sunny invite her over—not for the usual tea on her front steps but an actual meal? When Sunny was about to move to New York, Geraldine had done as much for her, organizing a dinner party in honor of Sunny's twenty-seventh birthday. Sunny was already spending quite a bit of time in New York, meeting with principals at design agencies, contributing postage-stamp-size illustrations to a few magazines Geraldine had never heard of before. It was clear to all her Toronto friends that they were about to lose her.

Though she was no cook, Geraldine had decided to make a classic Valencian paella. It was late February, the weather still treacherous. She'd braved the snow and gone to the posh cook shop on Yorkville Avenue and special-ordered a pan that came from Barcelona and took up the entire stovetop. She'd insisted on making every component of the meal by hand, taking two days off work to create a spread of tapas and exotic salads and saffron flan. The food had turned out surprisingly well—thanks in large part to the power of expensive olive oil and Maldon salt. This was not lost on the group, a dozen or so of Sunny's friends as well as Peter's brother, Will, and his wife, Lia, who were involved in the New York art world and whom Geraldine had thought Sunny might like to meet. Rachel had come, too, since leaving her out would have been more work for Geraldine than including her.

The night had been beautiful, all snowflakes and candlelight, and they all did their part to keep the banter effervescent. And yet Geraldine felt ignored. Then she realized that it was not simply a feeling but that it was what was actually happening. Nobody was trying to talk to her. Not Rachel, who was flirting with one of Sunny's exes, and not Peter, who was bending toward Sunny like a flower into the sun. To be clear, Geraldine's jealousy was not sexual. She wasn't even mad at Peter but at herself. Geraldine was not Sunny, never would be. Even if her paella was out of this world, she was hopelessly earthbound.

Seated at the far end of the table, watching everyone else watch Sunny cozy up to Peter's sister-in-law and talk about "the eternal problem" with Toronto's art museums, it dawned on Geraldine that Sunny hadn't said a single word to her since arriving. Were they even actual friends? Rachel eventually wised up to what was happening and shot Geraldine a look that was intended to be kind but that filled Geraldine with shame. She always defended Sunny when Rachel brought her up, but it was getting harder and harder to maintain that Sunny was just an introvert who had her own strange ways.

Geraldine managed to hide in the kitchen for a good twenty minutes, pretending to prepare dessert. She was able to pull herself together and sang during the birthday-cake portion of the evening. Sunny was one of the first to leave. When Geraldine walked her out at the end of the night, the guest of honor made no mention of how little the two had spoken, no gesture to the trouble Geraldine had gone to. She simply said the flan was excellent and landed a kiss close to Geraldine's ear.

Even Rachel hadn't known what to say. On her way out of the apartment, she'd rubbed Geraldine's shoulder. "I'm sorry she did that. That was weird." An awkward silence followed. "The food was delicious, at least."

At one thirty in the morning, while they were still cleaning, Peter asked Geraldine why she expected more from Sunny. Their conversation devolved into an infuriating fight, about Geraldine's inability to connect with how things really *were*, how some people were just one way and some people were another way and that was something Geraldine needed to accept if she was ever going to grow up.

"And the place where you're staying?" Jeremy asked now. "It's okay?"

Geraldine gave an animated nod. "It's great—and it's just a couple of blocks away from here. I can get to the Strand in four minutes, and I don't have to text anyone to make sure they'll open the door when I come home. Now I just need to make some other friends, is all. Adults can make friends here, right?"

"Friends is the last thing you should be worrying about," Jeremy said. "You have a way with people. I think I know your secret." He looked straight into Geraldine's eyes. "You ask good questions."

"Really?" Geraldine said, scrunching her nose. "I was raised to think asking questions wasn't nice. My mom was always telling me it was rude to be nosy."

"That's crazy," Jeremy said.

Growing up, Geraldine had to obtain most of her information by riffling through her mother's mail or listening in on her phone calls.

She was fifteen when she snooped on a heated call between Joanne and Bruce—she never thought of the two of them, as a pair, as "her parents"—and learned that her father had gotten a better job and was offering to pay for Joanne and Geraldine to take a vacation. "We're just fine" was her mother's refrain, words Geraldine could mentally hear her saying more easily than "I love you."

"And work?" Jeremy asked. "What's the latest?"

"I'm busy," Geraldine said. "I'm writing podcast proposals and doing some work for my old boss up in Toronto." She smiled. "You have no idea how good it feels to call him that. I'm sure the feeling is mutual. That's the only reason I can think of that he threw me freelance work."

"He wants to make sure you don't starve and come crawling back?" Jeremy said.

Geraldine nodded. "I'm doing a better job than I have in years."

A man in a tight blue suit came over and asked if they would like a table. "Up to her," Jeremy said, turning to Geraldine.

It was a shared-plates kind of place, and the menu was filled with combinations that seemed designed to intrigue rather than entice. Watermelon figured into a couple of the options. So did nigella seeds. Jeremy ordered for them both, four dishes and a bottle of Riesling that wasn't remotely sweet.

"So?" Geraldine asked. "How's . . . I'm blanking on her name."

"Renata? She saw a psychic." He winced.

"Oh, no."

"He told her she would have a son within a year, so we got to have a premature family-planning conversation. I didn't see that coming. There's a lesson to be learned there."

"That psychics are the worst?"

"The scum of the earth." Jeremy gave Geraldine an adoring look, and she proceeded to tell him her astrologer story. His name was Braham, and she'd met him at a party, shortly after Peter had left her. "He told me he *knew* Peter—they'd met at some event—and that Peter was a classic Gemini with a dual nature. Braham was off duty, so I guess he could say whatever he wanted. Then when I told him my birthday, he laughed and said of course I'd been clueless to what was going on around me. Like the whole thing was my fault because I was born on December fifteenth."

"Sagittarius?" Jeremy clinked glasses with her. "Man-horse represent."

The portions were tiny, and even though Geraldine had been careful with the wine, she felt tipsy when they went outside. The digital clock on a parking meter said it was 9:55.

"Do you know how good it feels not to have to rush back to Matt and Rachel's and worry about waking up Cleo? I don't have to check in for two whole hours."

"Wait, I thought you were staying at a hotel?"

"I am," she said briskly.

"Your hotel has a curfew?"

"It's not *exactly* a hotel. It's like a dorm-hotel. You get your own room for twelve hundred dollars a month. My friend Monika told me about it—she lived there last year when she was recording an album with the guy from Beirut." Jeremy looked concerned. "It's not sketchy, I promise," Geraldine said. "You know those hotels where secretaries and models lived in the 1940s? It's like that, but with Juilliard students and random foreigners. The girl across the hall is from Tokyo and does Japanese hair straightening."

"Can I see it?" Jeremy said.

Geraldine felt her knees lock. "Men aren't allowed above the ground floor."

"Then I'd like to see the ground floor." Jeremy's tone was more serious than Geraldine had known him to be capable of.

They walked quietly for three blocks before turning onto Third Avenue, where Geraldine stopped in front of a building. A knot of young women were smoking outside the entrance. One of them glared at Jeremy and flicked her cigarette on the sidewalk. Inside, the corridor smelled of cleaning fluid, and Geraldine bit back the impulse to gag. A security guard sat behind a window working on a Sudoku puzzle and surrounded by a bank of television monitors.

"He's not allowed above the lobby," the guard intoned.

"We know," Geraldine said sunnily. "I just want to show him the lounge. Jeremy, do you have ID?"

When no response came, Geraldine turned around to face him.

"You packed light, right?" he asked. She nodded slowly, knowing where this was headed.

"Go get your stuff," he instructed her.

"Really, I'm fine," she said stiffly.

"It's not up for debate," Jeremy said. "Friends don't let friends live like this. I'll wait out front. Text me when you're ready, and I'll order an Uber."

# 11

Rachel rolled her spiky massage balls further under her sitz bones just as her postpartum doula had shown her and waited for her computer to wake up. The machine finally made a loud spaceship noise, and Rachel was relieved that the only other people who'd shown up before ten o'clock were a couple of online editors who wore rose-gold headphones while they worked.

Rachel was going to be in the office all week, putting in more than twice her usual hours. She was covering for Miriam, who was out on a press junket funded by the Albanian Tourism Association. Ceri had been iffy on the idea but signed off when Miriam offered to tack on a weekend in Moscow to meet with a couple of czarinas for a piece on the new Russian power players. "It can be inside their closets or art collections?" Miriam had put forth. "Do them both," Ceri had told her. "And let's think of a third package. Family heirlooms? We'll blow it all out online." Ceri's delivery had been well oiled to the point that

Rachel was sure her boss was just parroting another, savvier editor in chief at the company. Ceri didn't know how to tag friends on Facebook, let alone break the Internet with a slideshow on despots' samovars.

The *New York Times* home page bloomed into view, and Rachel x-ed it out before she had a chance to see what Steve Bannon was up to. The new world order was unsettling as hell. It was also going to be *Cassette*'s undoing. Even Geraldine had figured out this much. Geraldine had taken it upon herself to put together a memo suggesting ways to "expand" *Cassette*'s "hermetic" point of view. "Would you mind looking this over and, if you don't think it's terrible, sharing it with Ceri?" she'd asked in an email, still not suggesting a specific night she could come by and hang out, as Rachel had requested. "I'm afraid if I send it to her, she'll just delete it," Geraldine had written. Her ideas were off-brand, but they possessed a looseness and relevancy that surprised Rachel. She'd nearly forgotten about Geraldine's ability to weather-vane the culture, as she'd done at *Province*, suggesting a few of the magazine's buzziest cover stories. Now, in Cambria font, Geraldine pointed out that nobody was forwarding recipes anymore, just articles about refugee kitchens and bodega workers on strike. The only socialite anybody was talking about was the president's daughter. "The age of aspiration has given way to an age of anxiety," Geraldine had written. Rachel told Geraldine an unsolicited critique might offend Ceri and suggested she bring up some of the ideas at her HR meeting instead. "I appreciate your read and your offer to get me in the door," Geraldine replied. "I know you're busy—seriously, I don't know how you do it all. I'll be here whenever you're ready to introduce us."

Rachel knew she needed to come through on her promise. She could just stand up and take the elevator to the thirty-fourth floor and walk through the proverbial door itself, but first she had to edit a travel piece on the romance of backpacking, as well as Sunny's upcoming column. This slightly terrified her; she and Sunny now texted daily, and Sunny had snuck a rendering of Rachel into a pastel drawing of pedestrians she'd just made for some museum talk she was giving. After peeking at the column—whose theme was horses—Rachel got started on the travel essay. It was good enough, with an emphasis on summer-camp nostalgia, and written by somebody named Eve Adoush. Rachel sent a new version back to the author within a couple of hours. Her main request was that Eve mention the new line of Moncler backpacks that the art director had already laid out on the page. "And maybe you could register somewhere that now is a particularly anxious moment, if you can find the right place to work it in?" Rachel wrote.

She spent the afternoon responding to emails and slipped out a little after five o'clock. She'd get around to Sunny's column tomorrow. The digital girls were still sitting in the exact same place, diligently clicking on God-knows-what. Mounds of work remained to be done, but Ceri had been out with the sales team since lunch, and Rachel was not going to miss her daughter's bedtime. Rachel could put up with anything so long as she got to hold Cleo in her arms at the end of the day.

Her phone was warm in her hand, and she refreshed her email one last time as she descended the subway stairs. There was a message from Ceri, who must have stopped by the office right after Rachel's departure. "Did you leave already?" was the subject, the body empty.

Rachel returned home to find Matt on his knees, helping Cleo use a foam bat to knock down a tower of Magna-Tiles.

"Mama!" Cleo cried.

"Hi, Schmoops." Rachel ignored Matt's dubious look—he hated that nickname—and gave them both kisses on their heads. "You two smell like bubble bath," she told them.

Matt whispered something into Cleo's ear. "How day?" Cleo asked, pride at correctly parroting her father flashing across her face.

"My day was good, little monkey." Rachel smiled. "How was *your* day?"

"Monkey." Cleo laughed. Then she yelled "Book!" and ran into her bedroom.

"We already ate dinner," Matt said.

"It's not even six," Rachel said with a light laugh.

"We're deep in the Cleo space-time continuum. I need to finish off some work."

"Okay, I got it from here. Let me just stuff my face for a second." Rachel went into the kitchen and ate the remains of the mac and cheese that Matt had made. Then she opened the fridge and filled a water glass with pinot grigio. When she stepped back into the living room, she found Matt on the couch, too lost in his computer world to pass judgment on her heavy-handed pour.

An hour later, when Rachel had delivered her daughter into a deep sleep, she came out of Cleo's room and found Matt watching a video of what looked like a psychedelic ringworm colony. She settled in next to him and let off an exhausted sigh. "Guess what Cleo wanted to read?"

"*Fe-Fi-Fo Farm*? She seems to like the goats." Matt absently cupped Rachel's knee with his hand.

"'Four goats dip into the moat,'" Rachel recited. "What does that even *mean*?"

Matt shrugged. His chest muscles contracted beneath his MIT rowing T-shirt.

"Who comes up with this stuff?" she mused, Googling the title on her phone. "So *there's* the genius behind it." She laughed and tilted the screen at Matt, who didn't appear to be interested in the old lady in the picture. "This granny was canny enough to score a book deal."

Matt gave Rachel an incredulous look. "Don't do this."

Rachel felt a catch in her throat. "What?"

"You love books. Don't talk about them this way."

"I might as well talk about them. I don't have the time to read them."

"We're all stressed out. I'm the one who only has a fifty-percent chance of tenure."

Rachel held her eyes level with his. She could feel the muscles in her cheeks pull down. "Of course you're going to make tenure, honey. Everything's going to be fine for you. Everyone loves you."

"Everyone loves you, too."

"Not in the same way. Everyone's wondering what happened to me. I peaked too early. Here I am now, with two jobs but no career to speak of and a daughter I don't get to see enough."

"You're doing beautifully," Matt said, massaging her shoulders. "You're the best mother, and you're writing a book about monsters."

"Sexy monsters." Rachel grinned.

"Smokin'-hot monsters. And when you sell it—"

"*If* I sell it," Rachel interjected.

"*When* you sell it, we can talk about your shifting to just writing, if that's what you want. People make adjustments all the time. Look at your friend Geraldine—she's applying for hostess jobs at cocktail lounges."

"What?" Rachel jerked her head toward her husband. "How do you know what jobs Geraldine is trying to get?"

"I was talking to Jeremy," Matt said.

"I don't see the connection. Did he buy a restaurant?"

"She's staying with him," Matt said.

"No, she's not," Rachel said. "We just emailed today, about a meeting I'm getting her. She would have told me if she'd moved in with my friend."

"I'm glad to hear you refer to Jeremy as your friend," Matt said.

"He took her in a couple nights ago. She was staying at a maximum-security dorm. He says it was super sketchy."

"That doesn't make sense—she's not even legal here."

"Where there's a will . . . ," Matt said, shaking his head. "Can you picture Geraldine having breakfast with Jeremy, stirring her tea and telling him about whatever show she just saw at the Guggenheim while he tries to read his phone?"

She was too stunned to reply. How had Geraldine thought it was okay not to give her a heads-up about this new arrangement? Rachel took a sip from her glass. The wine was cool, and it tasted clean, and there wasn't nearly enough of it.

"I can't believe she didn't tell me," Rachel muttered.

"It's a little strange. But she's got to be more depressed than she's letting on. Have a little empathy."

"You think I lack empathy." Rachel swallowed. "Can't you ever just agree with me without telling me how I could be more enlightened?"

"I could agree with every crazy thing you say, but then you'd be signing away your right to be taken seriously."

"So now I'm crazy? For such a nice guy, you can be really mean." Rachel worked her body off the couch and stepped over a stack of Cleo's stuffed animals and lacing toys. "And why is it just assumed that my job is to help her? Who's helping *me* here?"

"Rach, do you really want to be doing this?"

Rachel didn't reply. She locked the bathroom door behind her and slid down to the floor. With her back against the wall, surrounded by nothing but her own ugly feelings, she planted her face in her knees and began to cry.

# 12

I guess I've always had a soft spot for turtles." Sunny used her most childish voice, and the members of the audience nodded encouragingly. She got nervous and hated live events, though the feeling never seemed to be mutual.

Sharing the stage with Sunny were Yoni Subamariam, a handsome twenty-something poet whose multipart Twitter "compositions" were regularly retweeted by rappers and French intellectuals, and Monika Kull, a singer-songwriter who came from Edmonton and was filling in for a better-known musician who had to drop out at the last minute. The three of them were participating in "The New Pioneers," a conversation series the Museum of Modern Art was putting on in collaboration with the independent publishing house Predicate Books.

The events were meant to foster dialogue among visionaries in different disciplines—and, of course, to lure youngish people to West Fifty-third Street and inject new blood into MoMA's membership pool. The series had developed a reputation as a mating ground for culture vultures—Sunny's friend Jaycee was still dating a film editor she'd met at the drinks after the "Emo Emoji" chat. And so on a clear spring night that would have been perfect for jogging over the Brooklyn Bridge or drinking rosé at an outdoor table, some two hundred people had crammed into the basement screening room.

Tonight's topic was "urbanized nature." Yoni had taken Metro-North round-trip from 125th Street to Fairfield, Connecticut, and tweeted an essay about the dilapidated views and colonialism. Monika had composed a couple of haunting songs—one about drinking whiskey under a clothesline, the other about a water bug who possessed the power to remind the singer she came from another land. Sunny had created a trio of watercolors that sat on an easel off to the side of the stage and were projected, thirty feet high, behind them. There was a dusky scene from the dog park where she took Stanley, ferns framed in an Upper West Side windowsill, and snapping turtles swimming in the Gowanus Canal, unbeknownst to the group of people crossing the wooden bridge. Sunny had thrown Rachel in there just to stay awake.

"I especially love the snapping-turtle painting, because it makes me wonder what threats lie beyond what meets the eye," the moderator said. She was a design and architecture curator, and her voice was velvety and she knew it. "I'm thinking of all the hidden contours of the city, all the nooks and crannies filled with unfathomable things for us to be afraid of."

Sunny grabbed a thick section of hair and tucked it behind her ear, nodding respectfully. The moderator's attention shifted away, and Sunny eased into her Eames chair. During the production of the paintings, she had been primarily consumed with how shitty things were becoming with Nick. While she could pinpoint the most recent time she and her husband had had sex, she couldn't do the same for the last time they'd properly kissed. He was supposedly mad at Sunny because he didn't think she'd been warm enough to his sister, Barbara, during her recent visit. "Warm to her?" Sunny had objected. "She's the one who goes stiff as a board if you try to hug her."

"Did you try?" Nick grabbed his keys off the silver tray and stormed out of the house. He'd met up with Jeremy and stayed out until two in the morning. Sunny had been too proud to ask if Geraldine had been with them.

She needed to call Geraldine and set something up. Peter had been emailing Sunny to ask for Geraldine updates. Sunny didn't know how to respond, not only because she didn't know the answer. She wasn't sure what kind of response would keep Peter at bay. Sunny wasn't going to get any intel from Nick, not while they were in one of their silent fights. As soon as Nick woke up that morning, he said he had a lot of work to do and had the car brought over from the garage and drove straight to Long Island. He said that Sunny was welcome to meet him out there after her talk.

Sunny tried to stifle the panic that was rising in her by surveying the crowd. There was her editor, Miriam, a few rows back, wearing an uncharacteristically flamboyant top. Annie Reamer, a freelance writer who'd written a piece for Refinery29 on "Girl Crushes" and cited Sunny and Neko Case as hers, had planted herself in the middle of the second row. The second that Sunny spotted her, Annie gave an eager little wave.

"Is that a notion you were playing with, Sunny?" the moderator asked.

Shit. What *notion*?

The stage lights shone down on her aggressively, and Sunny

blinked hard, as if to shield herself from the scrutiny. "I'm not sure it was the notion I was playing with so much as the sense of the unnatural that surrounds us. We keep our trees in these tiny plots of dirt on the sidewalk and our dogs run around the park and dig up cigarette butts."

"But does that prevent our city from being a utopia?" Yoni chimed in, eager to bring himself closer to the center of the proceedings.

Sunny cocked her head and tried to appear to be thinking hard. "I'm not sure anywhere in this country could be considered a utopia in 2017," she said at last. This garnered a lukewarm laugh and few adamant claps.

When the houselights came back up, everybody whispered excitedly about skipping the reception in the lobby. Sunny slipped her coat on and kept stride with a younger group, who flowed west to an Irish bar on Ninth Avenue that the museum art handlers liked to go to after work. She ended up at a back table in the warm room, fielding questions from a woman who worked in the museum's development office. She wished Nick hadn't so abruptly skipped town and left her on her own. She didn't want to go home to an empty house. She shut her eyes. Everything felt crooked, and it wasn't just the noncommittal April weather and horrible political situation. Something was the matter on a cellular level. She opened her eyes and watched Monika, who was tossing her long hair and dancing gracelessly by the jukebox. The best dancer Sunny had ever seen—the best unprofessional, tipsy dancer, that is—was Rachel, whose moves managed to be both funny and sexy. Sunny remembered how she would burn with jealousy at all the *Province* parties. Now she wished Rachel were here to keep her company.

"A kir, my dear?" Sunny looked up to see Jeremy bearing down on her, proffering a magenta drink. He was in a crumpled blue suit and held a bottle of Stella. Sunny had never been so happy to see Jeremy, with whom she'd barely ever spoken. At least not about anything memorable.

Once they'd made their way through the usual hello-what's-up stuff, Sunny broached the subject on her mind. "I hear my dear friend is staying at the Jeremy Cleeve Home for Wayward Girls," she said lightly. "How's that working out?"

"Excellent," Jeremy said. "Somebody's finally using my kitchen—there's a lot of lentil action. I don't see her that much, though."

"Why not?" Sunny kept the weightlessness in her tone.

"She's out the door before eight most mornings."

"I thought she was working at a cocktail bar?" Sunny crossed her arms on the table.

Jeremy pursed his lips. "I talked her out of that. Elsa told me too many stories," he said, bringing up an ex-girlfriend who looked like a giraffe and worked in hospitality.

"What's going on with her podcasting?"

Jeremy started to say something, then gave Sunny a sideways look. "Why are you asking me? I'm sure she'd like to hear from you."

Sunny sighed. "I get the feeling she wants to be left alone." Jeremy didn't contradict her. "I'm going to call her. But promise me this—you'll let me know if you notice anything that worries you? Geraldine is a delicate soul."

"She's not made of glass," Jeremy said curtly, and squeezed himself onto the banquette next to the girl whose name Sunny couldn't remember, leaving her to sit there feeling mad at herself and at Jeremy, who had never been the one to end a conversation with her until now.

She'd pressed the matter too far and wasted her opportunity to learn anything useful. Jeremy was already wrapped up in conversation with the girl, a conspiratorial vibe lifting off them like smoke. Was the girl flirting with Jeremy, or did she understand that he was a potential donor? Sunny wondered. She took a pull on her drink—syrupy as a Shirley Temple—and glanced around the bar. Her gaze drifted to an area near the dart board, where a couple leaned against a wall. It took her a second to place the man's wide mouth and high forehead. They belonged to Rachel's brother, Jesse. Sunny realized she was staring and glanced at Jeremy. His lips were moving, and the girl—Sunny still hadn't caught her name—was nodding with fervor.

Sensing Sunny's attention, Jeremy eyed her. "Where's the old man tonight?" he asked.

"Nick's on the North Fork," Sunny said. "I'm going to meet him out there tomorrow." In fact, she still hadn't decided, but she would not let Jeremy see the fissures in her marriage.

"Maybe we can all meet up out there," Jeremy said.

Sunny went hot when she realized his "all" included Geraldine. "That would be fun," she said quickly, and rose to her feet.

No sooner had she started to step away from the table than she noticed Annie Reamer heading straight for her. Sunny couldn't play the part of Sunny the Girl Crush, not now. She glanced back at the dart board and confirmed that Jesse was still there.

"Can you do me a favor and pretend to be excited to see me?" Sunny said as she pulled up next to Jesse. "I'm avoiding someone."

This prompted Jesse's companion to turn around and survey the crowd. Annie was now bobbing her head at a writer for Artnet. Jeremy was holding the corner of a coaster against his front teeth.

"I'm your sister's friend," Sunny said.

Jesse raised an eyebrow. "I know. Sunny MacLeod. You live in a town house with cute flowerpots." Sunny felt an edge of tension. "I didn't mean that as an insult," Jesse said.

"I didn't take it as one," Sunny told him. "I'm just grumpy. I secretly hate these things."

"You hate bars?" Jesse took a pull on his beer, and Sunny realized that he and his companion weren't with the rest of the hangers-on.

"I thought you were part of the group," she said. "We're all coming from an event at MoMA."

Jesse smiled and shook his head. "Nah, we're just the Jesse-and-Caitlin event." Sunny took another look at Caitlin, trying to discern her role here. She had greasy hair and wore a phallic crystal pendant on a silver chain. She was far less attractive than Jesse, but that didn't have to mean anything. "I don't really roll with a posse," he said. "No offense to those who do." Jesse brought his beer bottle to his mouth and looked away from Sunny as he swallowed.

Sunny felt thirsty. Then she realized it was something else—a flash of heat, a quickening of her pulse. Jesse couldn't have been less impressed with her, or less attainable. She moved an inch closer to him and was immediately overcome with excitement. Jesse, however, appeared to be unmoved. Casting her gaze down to the floor, Sunny tried to remember the last time she'd wanted to bring her lips to somebody else's, or a time somebody hadn't returned the sentiment.

# 13

G, Don't be mad that I'm writing to you. I get it—the one thing worse than a public nuisance is a private nuisance. I've been trying to behave. I've written you so many times, you should see my drafts folder. That ought to count for something.

I'm not trying to upset you. My aim is not to convince you of anything. You're the one who has convinced me of everything. Nobody views it any other way—there isn't a single person who doesn't see me as the big bad wolf who fucked it all up. You, me, my family, my buddies, your buddy Sunny, we're all on the same page. I know what a disappointment I am.

Nobody understands me like you do. Even when I didn't understand myself, you got it. You knew how to deal with me. I'm not talking about how you took care of me. You gave me the space I needed. We all go through our lives looking for connection. I finally found it, and I didn't know what to do with it. I learned a lot growing up, but I didn't learn much about how to be good. Day by day I'm going through the motions of being a human being—you'll be amused to hear I even show up for work five days a week. I'm in the office right now. You should see me. The smart lights have shut off, and I'm the only one still here.

I hope New York is being kind to you. I have no idea where you're living or where you go all day, but I picture you riding the subway in the morning, holding a copy of the Times folded up the long way against your coat. I always loved that about you, that you read the actual paper. I look at the theater listings and try to imagine which shows you've been going to. Rumour has it you're moving into podcasts. I'm all for it, Geraldine.

I don't mean anything by this email. Or . . . I don't know what I mean. You know me—the same idiot you ran into at that dog thing in the park, that tongue-tied and overstepping idiot. You don't have to write back. I don't expect anything from you. I just want to store my words in your vault. Knowing you're out there makes me feel more alone but also less alone.

I'm going to be in New York in a couple of days. Obviously I would love to see you. Even if you don't want to talk about any of this, we could just go to that dim sum place with the birds' nests and talk about movies.

I'm not going to tell you I've changed. But I'm changing.

P

Geraldine was back in her happy pants. They'd been through some fifteen years of washings, and the elastic at the waistband was well on its way to giving out. This meant she had to regularly hike the sweats over her hips to prevent them from dropping to her knees, but she was fine with that. They were the most comfortable thing she owned, and she put them on whenever she needed some love.

Nothing terrible had happened, Geraldine reminded herself. She was crouched down in Jeremy's entryway, arranging a bunch of spring branches she'd picked up at the farmers' market on her way back from what might have been the most pointless job interview in her thirty-six years. Elinda Jackman, the Ffife Media human-resources honcho whom Rachel had connected her to, hadn't even pretended there might ever be work for Geraldine at her company—or even in the industry. "I'm glad to hear you're not limiting your options to media," Elinda told her, not once glancing at the résumé and the packet of sample work Geraldine had spent the morning at the copy shop assembling. "You're lucky to be starting over. No sense in shoving your way onto a sinking ship."

The words replayed in Geraldine's head as she fussed with the sprigs, repositioning them to keep the whole lot from toppling over. She wasn't feeling blue so much as tired from smiling all the time. At last she prevailed in achieving balance, by which point half of the magenta buds had fallen to the floor. She'd meant for Jeremy to come home to a cheerful floral arrangement, not the sight of his roommate down on her knees pinching up blood-colored droppings.

When the front door opened, she raised her head so quickly she felt something snap in the back of her neck. "I couldn't find a dustpan."

Jeremy waved his hand in the air. "The cleaner's coming tomorrow. I'm surprised to find you here."

"Where else would I be?"

He cut her a look, and Geraldine glanced away. She regretted showing him Peter's email the previous night. Jeremy hadn't even seemed that interested, barely looked up from his take-out sushi to offer his expert opinion—yes, Peter was trying to get something more than closure.

"You don't have to worry about me backsliding," she said. "I can't think of anything more depressing."

Jeremy didn't look convinced. "Did you write him back?"

"No," Geraldine said, and felt a swoop of shame. Well, she hadn't sent anything. She'd composed two replies, one telling him she was out of town, the other predicated on the idea that she could vanquish his hold over her with a session of volcanic sex in his hotel room.

"And you haven't heard from him?" Jeremy checked. "No *Hamilton* tickets magically appearing in your in-box?"

Geraldine touched her chin to her shoulder, a move that she'd learned from Sunny. "Just an update. He said he checked in to Hotel Marlowe."

"That new tower down on Duane Street?" Jeremy winced, as if he didn't reside in a building that had recently gone up and now blocked some other rich guy's view.

"I think so," Geraldine said, as if she hadn't walked past the hotel to scope it out earlier that morning.

"What are your plans tonight?" Jeremy asked. Geraldine kept still. She didn't want his pity. She wasn't in the mood to go out either. If she were, she would have said yes to Rachel, who must have heard that Peter was in town. How else to explain her offer to bring Geraldine as a plus-one to a book party? Geraldine didn't need to be babysat and claimed a prior commitment. She knew how to handle herself. She was learning, anyway.

"Let's go for a little walk," Jeremy said, and Geraldine couldn't think of an excuse not to.

She went into her room and changed into her third outfit of the day, a daisy-print dress and Rod Lavers. She pulled on the only low-cut socks she could find—a toeless pair meant for barre class. She grabbed her gossamer-thin scarf from the hook by the front door and stepped out into the hallway, where Jeremy was waiting, holding the elevator open.

That was another thing about Toronto. There were sidewalks, but you could stroll along them for miles and miles without ever happening upon anything worth slowing down for. Geraldine and Jeremy had barely covered three blocks, and the next thing she knew, they were drinking canned rosé from a Brooklyn winery with friendly strangers. They'd crashed a party of indeterminate determined purpose, as all parties were now. The changeable letters on the sign next to the door simply said SMILE FOR THE REVOLUTION, and Jeremy paid for their tickets, a hundred dollars each. It had to be a fund-raiser. Geraldine had attended a few "Party Line" meet-ups where people gathered to call their representatives to register their fury and discontent, but not since a legislative assistant had demanded she offer up her zip code and she couldn't recall any appropriate digits.

Geraldine and Jeremy planted themselves in the back of the room and ended up talking to a couple of women, Aya and Mitzi, whose shared style of pleather pocketbooks and knee-length dresses called to mind midcentury widows. There was definitely a flirty element to them. Geraldine looked around the crowd and wondered how many people were having great sex that stemmed from a shared sense of outrage and fear. In a couple of years, the world would be swarming with Trump babies. She tuned back in to the conversation and caught that the women were in a band together.

"What's it called?" Geraldine asked.

"It's called Rubber," Mitzi said.

"Rubber band." Geraldine nodded. "That's good. But I'm biased—I love office supplies."

Aya proceeded to explain that it was actually to do with condoms. "We're coming from a sex-positive place." She rolled up her sleeve and pointed to what looked like an elaborate bracket.

Realizing that the design on the inside of Aya's arm was meant to be a vulva, Geraldine felt her cheeks redden. "That took me a second. I've been in more of a sex-negative space these days." She suddenly wished she hadn't said anything about the state of her libido in front of Jeremy. The women were looking at her like she was a pariah. "I'm totally pro sex," she added, fumblingly. "I'm just focused on work, is all."

"What do you do?" Mitzi asked.

"I go on informational interviews," Geraldine said. "I've gotten very good at them. You should see what I'm able to accomplish in under twenty minutes."

But it was true, she'd spent the past month mastering the art of making small to medium talk and poking around for information. There should definitely be a word for it, how willing people were to email others and ask them to have coffee with her. "Coffeedump"? "Kaffenichts"? Everybody was extraordinarily charitable so long as it didn't require any significant expenditure of their own resources. Geraldine was careful not to ask for anything more than advice. Each meeting she had with a friend of a new acquaintance yielded yet another introduction to another person, sometimes more than one. She knew they were all fobbing her off on one another, waiting for her to grow exhausted of this caffeinated circle jerk. Yet Geraldine had squeezed out a few scraps of work. Through a friend of

Jeremy's, she'd met Tim, a publisher of art books who took her to a dimly lit pour-over coffee place and asked her to research emerging Canadian artists for potential monographs. Geraldine had also met Nora, who wore her hair with a Susan Sontag–ish white streak and worked at a beauty-box company. Nora contracted her to write quizzes for the website. Geraldine's compensation for a day of work was one hundred fifty dollars and two beauty boxes.

Jeremy was regaling the women with a story Geraldine had already heard, about a friend who'd had a falling-out with Jared Kushner's brother over Rangers tickets. She looked about for a place to put her drink. A man with a perversely manicured goatee smiled at her, and she hated him for it and turned away.

Geraldine ran her finger along the scarf tied around her neck. Sunny had bought it for her four years ago in Montreal, on what was supposed to be Geraldine and Peter's wedding weekend. Sunny had arranged everything: they'd stayed with an old friend of hers from art school who lived in Mile End, and she'd filled every waking minute with smoked meat and flea-market crawls and an outdoor concert—whatever it took to distract Geraldine from thinking about Peter, who'd confessed his transgressions, or started to; she could only bear hearing so much—and forced her to call off the wedding. The weekend had taken a turn for the worse on Saturday night. Sunny took Geraldine to a karaoke bar, where Geraldine had what she could only conclude was a panic attack but everybody else around her judged as indiscriminate drinking, which only exacerbated the terribleness. Bloated with shame, she returned to Toronto by Canada Rail. She'd packed in haste and left the scarf along with half her clothes on the bathroom floor. She spent the week of her honeymoon not in Sardinia but in bed, wanting to die yet too drained to do anything about it. The scarf had arrived by mail the following

Monday, accompanied by a jar of medical-grade vitamins and a picture of a short-haired cat Sunny had painted on heavy card stock. On the back she'd scrawled, "Cuddles, Strength, Onward!"

Geraldine felt a touch on her arm. Jeremy was trying to lasso her back into the conversation. "Geraldine's working on getting into podcasting," he said to Aya.

"Oh, right, you mentioned that." Aya leaned into Jeremy, and Geraldine's heart dropped at the realization that they knew each other from before. She blanched as she reviewed the events of the previous hour. She wasn't crashing a party; she was crashing Jeremy's date.

Feeling slightly ill, Geraldine excused herself to find a bathroom and listed toward the back of the room. The couples in the crowd stood out, taunting reminders of her own predicament. *Why do you always insist on making things hard for yourself?* Her mother's deflated voice echoed in Geraldine's head. Her mother had been right. Geraldine was no less alone in New York. The only difference was how much more difficult everything was here than in the city she knew. From outside, Geraldine texted Jeremy that she wanted to get some fresh air and would see him at home later. She couldn't imagine that he would be bothered.

Peter was only a few blocks away. Even on a night like this, when she felt not just alone but alone and stupid—and wholly unqualified for just about anything she put her mind to—she was in a better place than when she'd been coupled and stupid. Maybe it would help to look Peter in the eye and be reminded of what true pain felt like, the kind that pinched at your heart and never let up. Then she would appreciate the relatively Peter-free life she'd construed for herself. At least that's what she told herself as she smoothed the front of her dress and headed downtown in the evening's waning light.

She texted Peter and told him to meet her in his lobby, which gave her the illusion that she had some control. When she came into the hotel and saw him, Geraldine felt a rush to the head. He was wearing a blue blazer and he'd cut his hair too short, so his ears stuck out. His face was all tragic eagerness.

"Hi." Her arm flopped up like one of those waving-cat statues in Chinatown. "What are you doing here?"

"You mean what meetings do I have or why did I set them up in the first place?" He looked at her impishly.

"I don't mean anything," she said.

"Right." Peter nodded, and it was clear he didn't believe her. "There's a bar through that corridor. It's small, but I had them hold a table for us."

Geraldine sighed and looked around the lobby, as if somebody might spot her with Peter and tell on her. "I only have half an hour."

His gaze softened. "You don't have to finish your drink."

She suggested they take a walk instead. It seemed the right thing to do: keep alcohol out of the equation. When they got outside, purple streaked the sky and the air smelled of spring. Across the street a dog was peeing on a mound of garbage bags.

"How's your dog?" Geraldine asked.

"She didn't work out," Peter said, and she sucked in her breath.

"The dog or her owner?" Geraldine needled him.

He took a beat. "I'm flying solo."

At Canal Street they came upon a throng of tourists loading onto a red double-decker bus. Its LED sign said it was making the Brooklyn Loop.

"Shall we?" Geraldine said. Minutes later they were seated on the top level and looking down on the electric ant farm of the city. As the bus pulled onto the Manhattan Bridge overpass, Geraldine felt the weight of her body shift against Peter's. She allowed herself this, inhaling the scent of the fancy dandruff shampoo Geraldine had occasionally used when they'd lived together. When Peter wrapped his arm around the back of her seat, she pretended not to notice.

"I had no idea how much I loved double-decker buses," she said.

"I would have asked you to meet me in London."

"We already did that," Geraldine reminded him. They'd stayed in the West End, seen eight shows in six days. "We took taxis everywhere."

"And trains," Peter reminded her. Geraldine was too spent to reply. Even when she was in a state of repose at Jeremy's, she could never fully let go and relax. Her job was to fill the place with flowers and snacks, to make herself scarce when Jeremy indicated he wasn't in the mood for company and be available when he was. Staying busy when you had nothing to do was downright exhausting. Goodness, she was tired.

A snort shook through Geraldine, and she bolted upright. She'd nearly fallen asleep on Peter's shoulder. The bus had come off the bridge and was now idling outside Junior's. "Too bad you hate cheesecake," Peter said. Geraldine had forgotten what it was like to be known completely and was almost mad at Peter for reminding her of it. He removed his coat and rolled it up on his lap. He lowered Geraldine's head onto the makeshift pillow and stroked her hair. She granted herself what must have been a full minute of perfect stillness.

"Hey, can you grab my wallet?" he said. "I just remembered I have something for you."

Geraldine tensed and rummaged through his coat pockets, reminding herself that Peter wasn't the type to pull out an engagement ring. When he'd proposed to her, the execution had been sloppy—no jewelry, just a hypothetical question he'd startled her with in the middle of an argument. She came to realize that Peter had startled himself with the proposal as well, but she'd still held him to it.

"There's a new pub on Finch," he said, pulling a cocktail napkin out of his billfold. "I saved it for you."

"'The Wench and the Weasel,'" Geraldine read, biting back a smile. She'd been collecting keepsakes from the terribly named watering holes of Toronto ever since she was a teenager. "Thank you." She took a deep breath. "I think I'm going to hop off here."

Peter gave an uncertain laugh. "We're in the middle of nowhere."

"Please. It's just Brooklyn," she said with surprising force.

"Let me—" Peter moved to stand up.

"No," she said, putting her hand on his shoulder and holding him back. "I'm glad I got to see you, Peter." She had no idea what she'd meant by that, or if it was even true. Summoning her will, Geraldine rose to her feet. She started toward the steps at the front of the bus, even though the driver had said in at least ten different languages to stay seated while the vehicle was moving.

# 14

The weekend's marquee event: a Saturday-morning birthday party at Underhill Playground in honor of Cyrus, the baldest and most senior member of Cleo's Summer Babies playgroup. Born in early May, Cyrus was technically a Spring Baby, but his mother, a plucky public defender named Jean, had abandoned her original Spring Babies support group for the superior one that she met while strolling in Prospect Park at the end of her maternity leave. Rachel's Summer faction comprised some very cool women, and the group had been Rachel's lifeline for a while there. The mothers used to assemble every Monday, Wednesday, and Friday, like so many patients showing up for psychoanalysis, and the rest of the time they'd email nonstop about naps and nipple butters and admittedly-insane-but-this-is-a-safe-space suspicions that their babies had Zika. Now that everybody was back to work, they liked one another's pictures on social media and convened for the occasional baby-free Tuesday-night drink.

Rachel wondered, somewhat nervously, what time Geraldine would show up. After a confounding streak of Geraldine's brushing off Rachel's attempts to get together, hardly even acknowledging the HR meeting Rachel had gone to the trouble of setting up for her, Geraldine had written to say she was sorry she'd been "tricky to pin down" and was going to be in Rachel's neighborhood on Saturday.

Rachel and Cleo were over by the jungle gym, as was Cyrus's father, Nate, an engineer who dabbled in triathlons. Across the Tot Lot, Matt was helping Jean secure a piñata—it was either a horse or a pig—to a tree branch.

While Nate bragged about carb-consumption privileges, Rachel nodded, feeling somewhat jet-lagged, having woken up before dawn to work on her *Monsters!* novel. She'd written two pages that weren't awful—as she had the last session, and the one before that.

"You should join us on a Tuesday morning," Nate was saying. "We only do one loop around the park."

"I'm scared to ask what you do on Thursdays." Rachel felt something inside her skitter, and it took her a split second to realize why. Straight across the playground stood Geraldine, her strawberry-blond hair glowing in the diffuse May sunlight. Rachel could feel the tendons in her neck tense. She should have just asked Matt to do the party by himself so she and Geraldine could have coffee and a proper catch-up on neutral ground.

Rachel turned to face Cleo. "Here, honey," she said, handing down a sippy cup. As she tended to her daughter, Rachel snuck a look at her old friend. Geraldine was dressed chicly, in a color-blocked jacket and extravagantly flared jeans. Rachel recognized neither piece.

"Heeeeeey you," Rachel said in a cheerful tone as Geraldine came to a full stop. Both of the dads Rachel was standing with regarded Geraldine with low-level animosity. Geraldine gave an unsure blink as she surveyed the park. Rachel felt protective of her guest and sick with herself. She'd been so selfish to suggest a birthday-party drive-by, not thinking that it might embarrass Geraldine to be the only adult here who wasn't attached to a baby.

"Rachel, it's so nice to see you in your element," Geraldine said, gesturing at the scene. The party suddenly felt less cute—the children, dressed in haphazard layers, weren't actually playing together, and the Bloody Mary pitcher on the grown-ups' table was untouched.

Geraldine's hair was shot through with waves, and she'd done some complicated flicky thing with brown eyeliner. Rachel felt a burst of self-consciousness. She'd applied her makeup while brushing Cleo's teeth and had on supposedly stylish "Mom jeans" that, when worn at ten thirty in the morning to the playground, deserved no quotation marks.

"Thank you for being game and coming to this," Rachel said after the other parents slid away.

"Are you kidding?" Geraldine said. "I love kids' parties. And this is the perfect prelude to the thing I'm going to."

Rachel didn't take the bait. She just nodded pleasantly.

"Cleo looks so big in her overalls. I brought her something," Geraldine said, handing over a stuffed purple bunny. The buttons on its face were set in a sad line. "It's from this store down the block from where I'm staying."

"You mean Jeremy's?" Rachel said.

Geraldine gave an untroubled nod. "The owner is this incredible Italian woman who makes stuffed animals from recycled clothing." She pitched her body toward the top of the play structure, her arm outstretched. "Hi, Cleo!"

"Not now," Cleo said, and made a stop-sign gesture before shooting down the slide and taking off toward the playground gate.

"I'm sorry," Rachel said. "'Not now' is her new thing." She took the bunny from Geraldine and followed after her daughter. "She says it even if you try to give her a cookie."

"Don't worry about it," Geraldine replied. "I know it's kind of ugly. I guess that's what I liked about it."

"Oh, she'll be in love with it by nap time. We'll be back soon!" Rachel called at the assembled people. Cleo zigzagged around the grounds, from tree stump to semiprivate boot-camp session, her unsteady gait a perfect symbol for the conversation her minders were carrying out. Rachel was curious about so many aspects of Geraldine's reality: *What are you doing for money? Are you and Jeremy sleeping together? Why don't you need me anymore?* Instead she tried to be a good listener, something she knew she was lousy at.

Geraldine's story was coming together in a piecemeal fashion: She'd unofficially quit but officially changed the terms of her position at Blankenship Media in order to relocate to New York and interview for jobs. "Garth has decided to call it a medical absence, which no doubt is some way to label me crazy, but it saves my position in case this doesn't work out," she said.

"I'm sure it will," Rachel said, even though she still had no idea what "this" was.

Geraldine dug her hands into her coat pockets. "So I actually saw Peter," she said sheepishly, and watched Rachel for a reaction.

Rachel tried to bring surprise to her face and filled with guilt. She should have tried to see Geraldine in early April, as soon as she'd arrived. She'd let more than a month pass. "You're in touchy touch?" Rachel's mouth stretched into a flat smile.

"We've been talking a little, but it's not like that." Geraldine smiled. Rachel's gaze toggled between her friend and Cleo, who was reaching for the Snack Catcher of cheddar bunnies in her mother's bag. "We've just been talking a little bit," Geraldine said. "His mother died, and he's going through a crisis."

"He's been going through a crisis as long as we've known him." Rachel rolled her eyes in a way she hoped was gentle. "Have you two been seeing a lot of each other?"

"No, no. Just once, when he was down here. Don't look at me like that—we just went on a touristy double-decker bus ride. Nothing stupid."

"If you say so." Rachel wasn't sure if she fully trusted Geraldine's report. Peter was going to hound Geraldine until she caved, she was sure of it. "Tell me about your meeting with Elinda!" Rachel said, eager to change the subject. Cleo was watching in apparent fascination as a pigeon rammed its beak into a cheddar bunny on the ground.

"You know . . . she was very nice. She said she has nothing, though."

"I'm sure she doesn't. And even if she did, I doubt you'd want it. It's a seriously weird time in magazines," Rachel said.

"I'm seriously up for weird."

"By weird I mean it's a shitshow."

"I'm sorry you're caught in the middle of the industry's nosedive," Geraldine said, and Rachel recoiled. She hadn't been trying to elicit pity. "You're going to come out of whatever is going on," Geraldine went on. "Maybe you're just meant to be writing books."

"Thanks, G." What else could she say? "And what, may I ask, are you meant to be doing?"

"Do you remember the children's book *What Do People Do All Day?*" Geraldine watched Rachel shake her head no. "Maybe it's a Canadian thing. My reality has become a lot like that, meeting with anybody who'll talk to me about their path. I'm learning a lot."

"Sounds deep." Rachel couldn't tell if her words came out sounding barbed. A flock of pigeons were hobnobbing perilously near Cleo.

"I guess it is, sometimes," Geraldine said. "I shadowed Art Gumbel the other day." She watched Rachel for a reaction. "You know, the podcaster?"

Rachel shook her head. "I bet Matt does. He's suddenly become obsessed with podcasts."

"Art is pretty big. He's going to start letting me sit in on his sessions. I think I might want to get into podcasting. At least explore it." Geraldine gave a shrug and looked at the ground. "So yeah, that's my business plan. If you can call it that."

"I'm sure it will work out," Rachel said. "You're not going to be living off your savings indefinitely."

"Oh, I have some work." Geraldine laughed. "I'm writing a style piece for *New York*." Rachel almost asked her to repeat the name of the publication. She'd tried to contribute to *New York* not long ago and had gotten them to accept a pitch on the slew of models who'd become birth doulas. Her editor had sent her article back with the directive "Think on the page," and though she tried and tried, the story never saw its way to any page. "It's for online," Geraldine added. "We'll see how it goes."

"What's it about?"

Geraldine bit her lip. "Can I tell you when it comes out?"

"Sure . . . I wasn't going to steal your idea."

"That's not— Okay, don't laugh. It's about vulva tattoos." Rachel's expression must have betrayed what she was imagining. "No, not tattoos on their vaginas! Just drawings of vulvas girls are getting on their bodies. It's a thing."

"Good to know."

Geraldine watched Rachel. "You okay?"

"Yeah, sorry." Rachel looked up at the sky. It was blank, just a couple of cotton-ball clouds in the distance. She'd promised herself she'd keep things light, but the words were already there, at the tip of her tongue. "I just— Why didn't you tell me what you were up to? I mean, to move here and . . . not hang out with me? You didn't even tell me you were staying at Jeremy's."

Geraldine bent her head forward. "I know, I'm sorry. I just wanted this time to be different. I always come and follow you around, and then I have to go back home before I have a chance to try anything on my own. You know what I mean?"

"Sure," Rachel said, feeling sore.

"And you don't tell me everything either." Geraldine raised her eyebrows. "I heard that you and Sunny are BFFs."

Rachel should have been prepared for this. "Who told you that? Jeremy? It's not true. We've just been thrown closer together at work. There have been all these meetings, and I had to edit her last column."

"It's not an accusation. I've always hoped you two would get to know each other. We should all get together."

"Right. That's always been a recipe for fun," Rachel said, and the two smiled awkwardly.

"Maybe things can be different," Geraldine said. "Jeremy and I are talking about having cocktails on his roof. You're both invited."

Before Rachel could respond, she heard somebody warble her name. A jogger appeared, running in place and panting. The woman was tall and wearing a bright green Adidas tracksuit and a Mets hat. It took Rachel a second to make out the face in the brim's shadow. "Marina?" she said. "No way!"

Marina Goksenin was a college classmate of Rachel's who had always been miserably brilliant and was now officially recognized as such: She was a staff writer at the *New Yorker* and wrote about women and ISIS. Rachel had always liked Marina, who was so authentic. In college, when everyone else was listening to Modest Mouse and Cat Power, Marina had a radio show where she played Gregorian chants. "I thought you were doing a fellowship in Austin?" Rachel said.

"So much has changed," Marina said in her manic way. "I'm in love! With a woman!"

"No way . . . congratulations." Rachel introduced her friends and watched Geraldine's face fill with recognition when she heard Marina's full name. She and Rachel listened raptly to Marina's saga of late-blooming lesbianism. "It's the wildest thing. I feel weaker than ever, in a happy way. I'm not officially telling anyone yet, but I never see you, so it's fine. We just bought a strap-on. It's bright purple."

Blushing, Rachel glanced down at Cleo. What was it, National Genitalia Day?

"My lesbian friends in Toronto all say nobody buys realistic ones," Geraldine offered.

Marina grinned. "Phallorealism is dead."

Rachel picked up her daughter and hugged her close, like a human Stuffy. "This is my daughter, Cleo," she told Marina, feeling banal but also proud.

"I like your shoes," Marina said, reaching out to squeeze Cleo's tiny moccasins. They had ants printed over a gingham background.

"We're here for our friend Cyrus's birthday party." Rachel pointed across the park and noticed that everyone was gathered around the piñata. "Apparently it's assault time. We'd better head back."

"I'll say good-bye here. I should go to my thing," Geraldine said to Rachel. "I'm sorry it's been too long. Let's see each soon, for real." She stepped forward to give Rachel a hug. "And I'll let you know about the party."

"Cool. And we should catch up," Rachel said, peering over Geraldine's shoulder at Marina.

"Seems like you're pretty caught up," Geraldine said, and laughed.

"I'm easy to find," Marina said. "I'm on anything but Facebook."

Rachel sang "Hurry, Hurry, Drive the Fire Truck" to Cleo as they made their way back to the birthday celebration. Once she was inside the Tot Lot, Rachel carefully locked the gate behind her. She took one last glance across the way and saw that Geraldine and Marina were still talking to each other. Geraldine had better hurry up or she'd miss her plan, whatever it was.

# 15

Jesse,

Hi hi. Sunny here (your sister's friend, with the flowerpots). I hope this finds you well and that you don't hate me for leaving you with that art collector at the bar a few weeks ago. I couldn't tell if you found him amusing or revolting, but he clearly thought the world of you and your mastery of Tupac lyrics. Well done, rap genius.

I'm writing to ask for your advice. I've agreed to do a project for my friend's gallery. It's a series of painted wooden picture frames. I'll be doing the painting, but I need to find somebody who can help me with the construction. It will be a very limited edition, so not too big a time commitment, but I do need someone terrific. If you know of anybody who you think might be willing and able, I'd appreciate any and all ideas.

Thank you in advance!

Sunny xx

It had been too easy. Not the writing part—words came slowly to Sunny, whose dyslexia had somehow eluded the faculty at Ryerson Hall. But veering her path into Jesse's had been about as challenging as making an almond-butter sandwich. In her early days in New York, when she still made a living helping execute other people's visions, her schemes had required a bit more guile and inventiveness. Creative directors who sat in cubicles at branding companies had only so much pull, even ones as pretty as she was. But Sunny had become a master at toying with the desires of others. Jesse had responded exactly as she'd imagined: He wrote back twelve hours later, perfectly respectable for a carpenter whose website was just a landing page and who probably used his computer only to send invoices. Her project "sounded interesting," he replied, and he was "happy to chat whenever."

Last Sunny had heard, her oldest and closest gallerist friend, Servane Klein, was taking a break from her husband and staying in Malmö. So Sunny reached out to Lawrence Irving, a lovely older man who had a space in Chelsea. He specialized in estates but didn't limit himself to them. Last summer he'd shown miniature landscape drawings by a handful of contemporary artists. Sunny's piece had sold fastest, and for ninety-five hundred dollars, the highest sum. When Sunny outlined her latest project, Lawrence's only question was when she would have the pieces ready.

Now here she was, biking down the streets of Red Hook, her stepdaughter's strawberry-red knapsack hugging both shoulders. The energy that had been bubbling through her for the past three days quickly propelled her past the derelict buildings and old-timey bourbon shops. It had been some time since Sunny regularly came to Red Hook. The neighborhood seemed more or less unchanged, an oasis of cobblestone streets and community gardens. The area's only downside was its lack of public transportation, but with a Fairway and a wine shop and even a tiny bookstore, it was essentially custom-built for somebody who could work from home all day. Somebody like Sunny, but with a stronger pirate streak.

Sunny turned onto Pioneer Street and searched for the address Jesse had given her. She knew she was upon the Collective when she heard Prince's "I Would Die 4 U" blaring over what sounded like a pack of chain saws. As she came closer, she saw that Jesse's building was an enormous garage, the double doors raised all the way to expose a pair of banana-yellow industrial fans, taller and mightier than some aircraft. A girl-woman stood outside, talking on the phone and drinking a moss-colored juice. She had on paint-splattered jeans and a leather jacket with a Hillary button the size of an apple. Sunny locked her bike to a metal post across the street and felt her giddiness drop into dread. She cursed her own outfit, a white sweater and a full skirt with X-ray blue roses. It was from Dries and had seemed sort of steampunky when she'd selected it.

Clutching her helmet protectively against her chest, Sunny slithered into the brick building. The Collective was far bigger than it appeared to be from the outside, extending to the other end of the block. Four or five guys wearing headphones were stationed haphazardly throughout the space, like so many files on a cluttered desktop. One used an electric-pizza-cutter-like tool to shave down a metal sheet, while another, perched atop a ladder, spray-painted an enormous plaster palm tree a blinding silver.

There was no sign of Jesse. Sunny was considering texting him when a hand suddenly pressed against her shoulder. It took all her self-control not to jump when she saw who it was.

Jesse was radiant. His cheeks were pink, and his white teeth called to mind a baby shark. "Hey," he said. "I ran out to get us water." He held up a black deli bag. "They're doing construction on the street, and the pipes here are all sketchy."

A faint tattoo of arrowheads cutting through a thin blue line ringed his left bicep, and there were none of the coarse hairs that sprouted out of Nick's shirt. Sunny felt dumb with lust. It wasn't too late to say the project had just been canceled.

But Jesse showed her around a little and told her that his workspace was in the back. She followed him into the sawdust haze. His workstation was surprisingly organized, with tools arranged as neatly as her kitchen spices. An early-career seminude Rihanna poster hung—ironically, she supposed—on the wall, and a set of carved wooden pieces were splayed across the table. "I'm making a rocking chair." He handed her one of the bigger pieces. "Old-growth fir."

"It's beautiful," she said.

Jesse nodded and pulled out two stools. "Aren't those knots bananas? The fir is from this tree farm upstate that's pretty much the only place I use at this point. The client wants me to stain it super dark, and it kills me."

"Don't do it." Sunny accepted her bottle of water. "You have to tell the client you won't."

Jesse tore open a bag of pretzels. "I dunno. She's this rich woman in Connecticut, and she refers all her friends to me." Sunny felt a flicker of jealousy, then reminded herself she was being crazy. Jesse was a carpenter who was making her a set of frames. That's all this was.

"So here we are, Sunny." Jesse pressed his palms against his thighs and leaned in toward her. "What's the plan?"

Sunny pulled her sketches out of her backpack and spread them across the table.

"Hey," came a woman's voice. Sunny looked up and saw the juice drinker from outside. "I'm going to go get lunch. Need anything?"

Sunny felt discombobulated as she stared at the visitor. She had crazy cheekbones and long limbs and was objectively beautiful, in a way Sunny had never been as a young woman.

"Have you eaten?" Jesse asked.

"I'm good," Sunny said, glancing at her phone to confirm it was way past lunchtime. It was 3:07. She'd suggested meeting in the afternoon, her favorite portion of the day, when all the free-floating stress that pulsed through the city did so less toxically. It hadn't occurred to her that none of these rules would apply here. She thought of Nick, who was home with a cold and probably watching European soccer and eating the zucchini loaf Sunny had baked that morning.

"Here's what I'm thinking," she said, and began walking Jesse through the plans, telling him about the fairy-tale theme. She felt herself turn serious, a pose she particularly liked to use when she was feeling shy. Jesse could match her intensity, and for the next twenty minutes they spoke about nothing but dimensions and materials and quality. She was starting to truly believe in this project.

The drawings she'd made were loose and pretty, rendered in black ink and pink and gray oil-paint sticks. There were some doodles on the pages, too, princesses and castles and medieval torture devices that would feature on the pieces. Perhaps she'd gotten a little carried away preparing for this meeting. But it had been more absorbing than the post on her morning rituals she was required to "contribute" (more like donate) to *Cassette*'s website.

Sunny's phone buzzed on the table. It was a text from Nick.

We confirmed for Santorini?

Their marriage had been less fraught of late, for all the wrong reasons. Sunny's mind was occupied, and he didn't seem to notice. She made them seasonal soups and salads, and they sat eating them in near silence at the kitchen table. He seemed not at all unhappy and not at all aware of her emotional whereabouts, which didn't exactly do wonders for her respect for him.

Sunny looked up and saw that Jesse had registered everything.

"My husband," Sunny felt compelled to say. "An old friend of Nick's has a family place on Corfu, and he invited us to visit for August. I was supposed to figure out plane tickets, but I'm dragging my feet."

"Sounds terrible."

Sunny gave a light laugh. "Fernando is sort of the last person you'd want to be stuck on an island with."

"You should do it," Jesse said. "Greece is paradise. Even if the Elysian fields are made up."

Sunny raised her eyebrows. "Have you been?"

"No, but I studied classics in college. I still read the *Iliad* every few years." The corners of his mouth tugged upward. "Thanks for looking so surprised."

"I didn't—" Sunny started, feeling flushed. "I never read the *Iliad.* I hear it's epic." Sunny waited a beat. "That was a joke. Epic?"

Jesse granted her a smile. Not a fill-the-space smile but the kind that told Sunny she was definitely all right by him. She looked away, even though doing so betrayed her nerves. They went back to discussing the project, and Sunny dropped in that Nick would be gone for much of May. It didn't come out sounding brazen, but something in Jesse's expression told her he wasn't unhappy to hear this. Maybe she needed to do this to save her marriage. She forced herself to look Jesse squarely in the eye. What would Rachel do if she knew where Sunny was? Thank God they had other things to text about. Apparently Peter had taken Geraldine on a romantic double-decker bus ride on his trip to New York. Sunny still didn't know what to think about that.

"You got any plans this Saturday, MacLeod? My parents are organizing an outing to L&B Spumoni Gardens. We do a pizza party every year around my birthday."

Sunny smiled. "I love pizza parties." She also loved the way he'd said her name and wished he'd do it again and again.

"It's super casual. I'm sure Rachel would love to have you there. She and I usually go dancing afterward. She likes this cheesy Russian lounge called Visions on Fort Hamilton."

"You definitely don't want to see me dance." Sunny was beginning to suspect that Jesse liked her, too, and she didn't know what to do with all this potential for recklessness.

"Sure we do." He tilted his head and watched her.

She honestly didn't know what to say. Everything was becoming so confusing. What had she even come here for? Certainly not to make work. She'd put herself in front of Jesse like an offering and never stopped to ask what she would do if he indicated a desire to accept it. What an idiot, letting herself become so wrapped up in getting the optics perfect. And now he was sending signals but using a code nobody had taught her. All she was sure of was that whatever she felt, it was real, and it scared her.

And so she did what any grown-up woman with a decent husband and a lovely home and a terrible urge to blow it all to pieces would do: She rose from her chair and pretended she had somewhere else to be and ran the hell away.

# 16

Geraldine was on her rooftop chatting with Rachel and their former boss, Edward Simonov, whose visit to New York coincided with Geraldine and Jeremy's Summer Awakening. The party wasn't exactly packed, but that's only because the apartment's terrace ran the length of the entire block.

"Sheryl with her siestas." Ed's chest vibrated with laughter. "I'll never forget the time she came to the lineup meeting with the keyboard imprint on her forehead. You've got to respect a woman who isn't afraid to take a nap at her cubicle."

"She was always hungover, wasn't she?" Rachel said. "I didn't get it at the time—I just thought she was vitamin-deficient. What happened to Sheryl anyway, G?"

"No idea." Geraldine sighed. She should have known better than to tell Ed to swing by the party. He'd called her a couple days ago to let her know he was going to be in town for a reunion. Edward had been a visiting fellow at Columbia's journalism school—for only a year, when Geraldine and Rachel were still in diapers. He'd studied under William Shawn, and a few of his classmates were now "Timesmen," as he was prone to reminding those who would listen.

Much as Geraldine liked Ed, who'd been *Province*'s editor in chief, his presence at her party blurred the line between past and present. The fantasy that she'd been kneading in her mind all week was that of Rachel and Sunny dropping by and seeing her inhabit her new existence with vibrancy and grace. She wanted them to meet her new contacts and friends, or at least recognize that she had them. That wasn't her primary reason for inviting the pair, of course, but it had kept her spirits high as she'd sorted out wine cases and crudités in the days before. Geraldine scanned the crowd. Her friend Sylvie had said she'd be there "on the dot," but was nowhere to be seen.

Fifty or so people milled about, and conversation had long ago risen from hum to wild babel. The evening sky glowed majestically, and the air stood still. Sunny was on the rooftop's north end, nearly at Canal Street, looking as though lit from within. She was talking to Jeremy and Christian the yogurt kingpin. Geraldine wondered if Sunny would begrudge her for borrowing from her cabinet of acquaintances. Probably not. How could Sunny possibly keep track of all her cabinets?

Geraldine caught the eye of her downstairs neighbor Kiki and waved. "There's the wonderful Kiki," she told her group. "She's this divorce lawyer who lives on the third floor. And that's Veronica Hayward," she said, pointing beyond Kiki's shoulder. "She's an editor at *New York*." Geraldine had written her vulva post for Veronica and was working on a new batch of ideas to send to her.

"I thought she just got laid off," Rachel said. Geraldine watched Ed smile knowingly. His world was nothing but layoffs, like a tree shedding leaves. Geraldine could feel herself tense. She had not spent the better part of the past week putting this party together to bemoan the state of a terminally ill industry.

"I don't think so. We emailed yesterday," Geraldine said, trying to keep her impatience from coloring her voice.

Rachel was studying the crowd, in her cravenly anthropological way. A moment later Geraldine watched Rachel's eyes light up and Ed's face stiffen at the sight of Sunny coming toward them.

"Happy housewarming," Sunny said. She had on a white tunicky thing, and Rachel was wearing a slate-gray tank dress. The two stood close together, reminding Geraldine of a pair of salt and pepper shakers. "What a perfect night to be up here, among the lanterns and lemon trees," Sunny said.

"All Geraldine's doing," Jeremy said, inserting himself into their conversation. Geraldine smiled at him, grateful for the recognition. She'd purchased the trees and dragged them in herself, rather than pay the delivery fee.

"I hear you have the domestic goddess sleeping beneath my painting?" Sunny said, grinning up at Jeremy.

"You're in the room with all of Jeremy's toys?" Rachel said.

"We cleared it out a bit," Geraldine said. She was surprised Rachel hadn't already nosed around the apartment. She'd set everything up for Rachel and Sunny's benefit: her work papers, a tasting menu from the River Café pop-up on Kenmare, and a notebook page with "Tues = Deadline!" all in fake disarray on her desk.

"Ed Simonov," Ed said, extending a rough-skinned hand to Jeremy.

"Oh, sorry," Geraldine said. "Ed, this is Jeremy, my generous roommate. And Jeremy, Ed is my old boss." An expression of confusion came to Jeremy's face. "He was the editor in chief," Geraldine supplied before she had to hear Peter's name.

"He's *all* of our old boss," Sunny said.

"Nobody could ever boss you around, Sunny," Ed said with a cool tilt of the chin. Geraldine remembered how he'd never liked Sunny, and that was back when he made five times as much money as she did. Sunny disliked Ed just as much, if not more. He'd been the one to let her go.

"What brings you here, Ed?" Sunny smiled, unfazed.

"Columbia's j-school reunion," he answered. "Even if I can't work in real journalism anymore, I can still *stand* for it."

After being on the wrong side of one too many magazine cutbacks, Ed now ran the communications department for the Canadian Teachers' Federation. He was dressed more or less the same as ever, in sneakers and a worn-out madras shirt. His dark hair had moved slightly back on his forehead, and he'd switched over to laceless Converses, which depressed Geraldine for reasons she couldn't totally understand.

Geraldine now noticed that Sylvie had shown up, and a flicker of excitement went off. She would lure her over. Ed took a pull from his beer bottle, then turned it upside down to confirm that there was nothing left.

"I'll get you another," Rachel said, before Geraldine could.

"I'll join you," Sunny said. "I want one of those pink things I saw somebody drinking. . . ."

Watching Rachel's and Sunny's retreating figures, Geraldine tried not to imagine what they might be talking about.

"I've got some good dish for you," Ed said.

"Oh, yeah?" she replied. Sylvie could wait a minute.

"Strange times," Ed said, skipping over any sort of personal update and cutting straight to Toronto media gossip. He had updates about a shakeup at the *Globe and Mail* as well as about his friend Brett, a CBC muckety-muck who was about to go work for the Trudeau administration. "Their man in New York is coming back up," he reported.

"You mean Tom Newlin?" Geraldine said. Ed nodded, and Geraldine crumpled inwardly. Tom had recently reached out to say he was still thinking about their talk, and he'd like to set up another meeting, if she was still interested. Geraldine played with her dress's spaghetti strap and tried to fight off the tide of disappointment coming in. She was going to have to wait until somebody else was appointed at the CBC, legendary for its bureaucracy, and start all over again. Tom was not her only option, she reminded herself. The party was brimming with interesting people she might work with one of these days.

"And your headlines?" Ed asked.

Geraldine twisted the cameo ring on her left pinkie. "I was supposed to be developing something for Tom, actually. I hadn't realized—"

"Oh, Ger," Ed said. "I feel like such a schmuck."

"No, don't, I'm glad you told me," she said.

"You can always come back up. It's not so bad. We got a Shake Shack."

"I love their custard," Rachel interjected. She'd returned with the round of drinks she'd promised. Ed grabbed for his fresh Peroni and went right on talking. "I have another update that will make you feel better," he said. "I saw Peter the other day, at a book signing. He's not looking so hot. That Montreal chick he was dating got fed up and left him."

"And took the dog." Geraldine tried to sound jaded. "I heard all about it." In fact, that the woman was from Montreal and had been the one to leave was news to her. Geraldine reminded herself that she had things going on that Peter didn't know anything about. She'd met and made out with a French tourist a week ago, and Art Gumbel, the podcast guy, had just made her a modern-day mixtape, in the form of an email whose subject line was "Variety Hour." It contained links to his favorite podcast episodes across all categories, with a couple of sentences introducing each show he'd selected.

But Geraldine was unable to keep her thoughts from boomeranging back to Peter, to the broken-up look in his eyes as he'd watched her from the top of the bus. When he'd smiled down at her, she'd felt a sense of fullness that had eluded her for years. He'd checked to make sure she'd made it home safely, and they'd texted late into the night. They were still texting a bit, leaving open the possibility of... what? He couldn't seriously think there was a chance. She knew there wasn't a chance. The idea alone of having to tell Rachel and Sunny that she'd let him back in was embarrassing enough to knock the fantasy right out of her.

"You okay, Ger?" Ed said.

Geraldine exhaled heavily and told Ed she'd be right back. "My friend Sylvie keeps giving me the save-me look," she told him. In truth, Sylvie appeared perfectly content standing with a cluster of punky feminist types. "Ger Bear!" Sylvie said when Geraldine joined them.

Sylvie Benghal was Marina Goksenin's girlfriend and, crazily enough, had become the person Geraldine saw the most in New York. Sylvie was about to start her master's in urban science at NYU, and she'd already quit her job working for a city councilwoman, which meant she had the time to go on walks with Geraldine during the day. Marina worked all day, nights and weekends, too.

Sylvie was wearing a denim skirt and a cropped purple T-shirt that exposed the faint brown trail of fur on her abdomen.

"You look amazing," Geraldine told her. "Come with me and meet my old friends, okay?"

Sunny, Rachel, and Ed were peeping out at the view. The setting sun reflected gloriously off the water, and honeyed light filled the streets below.

"Everybody, this is Sylvie," Geraldine announced.

"Hi, Everybody," Sylvie said, and Rachel and Ed turned around to wave. Sunny craned her long neck over the balcony. "Something about this reminds me of the Thames."

"The one in London, Ontario?" Ed cracked, and Geraldine couldn't help laughing.

"Canadian humor is the best," Sylvie said in her beautiful rasp. Geraldine could tell she'd meant it sincerely, or at least warmly, but her comment elicited looks that were the equivalent of sharp elbows from Rachel and Sunny.

"How do you guys know each other?" Rachel asked Sylvie.

"It's sort of a long story," Geraldine said abruptly, not wanting to get into the short story in which Rachel played a significant part.

Sylvie declared she was going to check out the fire-pit situation, and Geraldine promised to meet her there in a minute.

"How old is she?" Rachel sounded pointlessly scandalized. Geraldine ignored the question and told her crew she was going to check up on the other guests. "Anyone want to come with?" she asked. But the gang said they were about to go, and Geraldine did not press them to stay. She was ready to actually have fun rather than spend any more time trying to convince her old friends that she was having fun.

After saying her good-byes, Geraldine settled into a spot on the outdoor couch next to Sylvie, among Jeremy's college friends, banker types who weren't actually bankers. With her legs curled under her seat, Geraldine stuffed herself with handfuls of popcorn while Sylvie and strangers talked about an Ayahuasca-like drug that wore off so fast you could take it during your lunch break at work. "Why *wouldn't* you want to go to Peru, though?" somebody was saying.

The gas flames flickered mesmerizingly, and Geraldine fell into something of a trance until Sylvie tapped on her shin. "Earth to G-Wiz," she said in her scratchy tone.

Geraldine realized with a start that members of the group were suddenly inquiring about her, and Sylvie had stepped in to field the questions.

"She's going places," Sylvie said. "We had our auras photographed in Chinatown, and hers is this blazing tangerine. That is some lit energy."

"You know me, Agent Orange over here," Geraldine cracked, her lame effort at concealing how wonderful it felt to be enveloped in Sylvie's affection.

An hour or so later, the remaining guests migrated down to Jeremy's living room. The Rolling Stones played on the speakers, and Sylvie got everyone to shimmy around a little bit. The last guest left slightly past one, and Geraldine stayed up until past two helping Jeremy clean, which meant she cleaned while he trailed after her with a garbage bag and kept her company.

Geraldine woke up the following morning with an unearned hangover—she'd never even reached the state of tipsy—and got next to nothing done all day. She knew she shouldn't go out that night, but she hated to cancel plans. So after a brief nap, she trekked out to Brooklyn, where Sylvie and Marina were expecting her. Kiss Kiss Bang Bang lived up to the hype: The club was crowded, even at the ripe hour of nine thirty, and there were lots of teenagers and even some white-haired people. Nearly everyone was dancing, Sylvie and her pack very much included.

The music's bubblegummy blips and bloops washed over Geraldine. Paul, a friend of Sylvie's who worked as a butcher and was deep in the food scene, grabbed her shoulders and sprang up and down, as if he were riding a pogo stick. She mirrored him and came to feel deliriously disconnected from the Geraldine of earlier in the day. A few songs later, they all went out to the garden to get drinks.

"I hear you're making a podcast!" Paul screamed, not yet acclimated to the volume drop.

"I was supposed to develop one," Geraldine said. "The CBC is trying to break out of the 1970s and wanted ideas for shows. I have a couple I'm working on."

"What are they?" Marina said.

"Give us your best pitches," said Sylvie. "Pretend we're in an elevator."

"I panic on elevators," Geraldine admitted. But everybody was staring at her, and she felt compelled to go on. "I was thinking about something to do with neighborhoods. Everyone loves New York, but the picture has become so macro. What if I zoom in and focus on a different city block and tell the stories of the residents?"

Paul made a buzzing noise. "Bo-ring."

"You might as well do that in Toronto," Sylvie pointed out. "Why would the CBC pay you to do that?"

"Or I could do a spotlight on Canadian expats in New York. You know, like interviews with Graydon Carter and—"

"Rachel Ziff?" Marina laughed. She'd recently confided in Geraldine that Rachel's constant #amwriting updates had driven her to mute her old college friend on all social media.

"Rachel's not Canadian," Geraldine reminded her. "She just lived there for a minute."

"I met Rachel last night," Sylvie tossed out. "She has great tits."

Marina gave Sylvie a playful shove and fixed her eyes on

Geraldine. "Great Canadian Runaways sounds like a sinking proposition," she said. "There's no way that's what people want."

"Don't think about what people want. What shows do you like?" asked Kim, Paul's boyfriend. He was handing out beers. Geraldine knew she shouldn't take one given how sick she'd felt all morning, but she did anyway.

"There's so many," she responded, telling them about her latest discoveries: a pair of teenage best friends who recorded conversations about the ins and outs of attaining and maintaining popularity at their Chicago private school, and a show by a guy who worked in a senior center and dabbled in life-extension hacks. "These people are crazy. Maybe I need to be more insane to make a podcast that works."

"Or maybe you should make a podcast about them," Paul said. "Interviews with these kooks."

"Right, and then mix in the big names to draw numbers," Sylvie added. "Even the most basic celebrities have started podcasting, too."

Marina's eyes were narrowing, the way they did when she was thinking hard. "Has anyone done this yet?"

"I don't think so," Kim said. "I'm the worst insomniac," he added, to establish his credibility as an expert on the matter.

"The pod people," Sylvie said, raising her bottle. Her voice was a revelation, like the sound of sand and glitter. "If you don't do it, I will."

"No," Geraldine said, the euphoria spreading through her body so rich she could practically taste it. "You'll do it—with me."

# 17

You're focusing on the wrong thing," Cassie said, deflecting an aspiring writer's question about whether Cassie planned to switch agents in light of her recent Hulu deal. "You should be asking Rachel how she writes characters that make you sob. The business stuff is boring."

It was a little after six. Rachel had arrived at the Marriott in Chestnut Hill in time to throw her duffel on the hotel-room floor and wash the Chinatown bus off her face before the cocktail reception. The YAtopians had colonized Grimbles, a faux-British pub half a flight above the hotel lobby, with ornately patterned carpeting and gaudy chandeliers.

Cassie Burkheim was among the front rank of YAtopia participants–only two others, Lavinia Dallal and Emily Pike, would have their own Spotlight interviews. Lavinia and Emily weren't even staying at this hotel in suburban Philadelphia. Cassie could have asked her publisher to put her up across town with them at the Four Seasons, too, but it wasn't her style. Cassie had always had a bit of a mentor complex, adopting aspiring authors as if they were starving kittens. She was doing the rounds to promote her new book, *Court of Mourning Star*, and had invited Rachel to crash in her hotel room.

"You owe it to yourself," Cassie had said when she suggested that Rachel tag along. "You're about to have a big comeback."

"How can I come back when I was never—"

"Will you stop with the past? You're so close to all that being so far away. I'm telling you, all your books will be back in print by next Christmas." Rachel had been sharing batches of her new project with Cassie, who said she was blown away. "You really should show face," Cassie insisted. "The bloggers will love rediscovering you. Plus, room service."

Rachel had been there barely ten minutes and was already ruing that she had to return home a day earlier than everybody else. There was little chance the writers whom she and Cassie were talking to were old enough to drink. They looked like goth babies in their all-black ensembles that covered everything but the tops of their soft, chubby breasts. It felt undeniably good, soaking up their rays of adulation.

"Rachel's new book is off the hook," Cassie said.

Rachel glanced down, trying to conceal her grin.

"I'm telling you," Cassie went on. "The Maker scenes—"

"The Markers," Rachel reminded her friend. She'd come up with the idea while coloring with Cleo. Magic Markers were not the most literary of influences, true, but the Markers scenes were shaping up nicely. Markers were celestial beings that protected runaway children. Their gifts came at great cost; they marked the destinies of others. After escaping a snatcher—a vagrant that came after vulnerable girls—Desdemona, who'd been Marked, returned home under cover of night to find her mother bawling. She would linger in the shadows and learn about her younger brother's incurable illness.

"Can I take a selfie?" the shorter girl asked Rachel, who tried to think of something funny to say. All this flattery disarmed her, though, and the best she could come up with was "Of course."

It was Rachel's first time away from Cleo since becoming a mother, and she was determined to squeeze the next nineteen hours for all she could. At the dinner session, she barely touched her martini glass of bacon and chive mashed potatoes. She couldn't help running around the banquet hall and accosting familiar faces, reminding them that she still existed. Either her fellow writers were nicer than she remembered, or she'd been spending too much time in the company of people who weren't that nice.

Rachel came to find herself four inches from Barry Manski, a fifty-something father from Long Island who wrote and illustrated the middle-grade Fart Academy series. His books were huge at summer camps. He was also, Rachel remembered too late, a huge pervert who had a habit of staring at women's crotches while exchanging pleasantries.

"Rachel," Cassie said, pulling her friend away. "Your phone's blowing up. Your husband is trying to get ahold of you."

Rachel's heart lurched. What could be the matter? She then realized, with an easing in her chest, that her phone was in her pocket. "You scared me," she whispered to Cassie. "Next time say it's my mother."

"No next time, Rachel," Cassie whispered. "You didn't come here so people could talk about how Barry Manski molested you."

"Are you kidding? I wouldn't go near him with—"

"Nobody cares about what you would or wouldn't do. Do yourself a favor and keep your distance."

Rachel bit the inside of her cheek. She hated feedback. But Cassie was right. Success in the YA world was contingent on favors. She needed to lubricate her relationships with all the women and gay men in the room, not invite speculation as to whether she was flirting. Rachel felt her phone vibrate. "Matt must have sensed us talking about—" she said, then saw it was a message from Geraldine, the latest in a group text Geraldine had initiated after Sunny and Rachel had left her rooftop party. You should have stayed, Geraldine had written, beneath a photo of people dancing in Jeremy's apartment.

I'm at a dinner with your colleague Miriam, came Geraldine's latest message. She says hi. ☺ Rachel stared in disbelief at a blurry photo of Miriam seated with one arm around Geraldine and another around Ceri. They were all wearing silky dresses, and the mammoth floral centerpiece in the corner of the frame confirmed that they were at a fabulous event. Rachel didn't know what bothered her more: that Geraldine was swooping in on her life or that she was trying to play it off as perfectly natural.

"What?" Cassie peered up at Rachel, whose face must have been showing signs of distress.

"Nothing," Rachel said, trying not to care that Geraldine was canoodling with her bosses. She wondered how Sunny would react, to see her world tilting off its axis. Rachel took a sip of her drink. It tasted warm and soapy, and she didn't know how to respond. Fake spazziness, she decided, and typed OMG hi guys! Sunny's bubble opened and filled with the three dots that meant she was composing something. But then it vanished. She, too, was at a loss.

The following morning the group of authors showed up at the Rhea Greenbaum Jewish Community Center and buzzed about the reception hall, signing books and mingling with young readers. To look at the writers, one would have had no idea they'd stayed up till two drinking greyhounds and screaming over Taylor Swift. When it came time for presentations, Rachel found a seat in the back of the theater and took in panels on world building and strong girls. At last came Cassie's Spotlight interview, and there wasn't an empty seat in the house. Cassie ticked off her usual boxes—her childhood spent on military bases, her Diet Dr Pepper–fueled revision process, her lucky socks.

When asked to list her favorite contemporary writers, Cassie rattled off the Lavinias and the J. K. Rowlings. "And watch out for Rachel Ziff," Cassie said. "Literally, watch her. Right over there in the stripes." Rachel felt her cheeks go crimson and wondered if Cassie came to so many of these that championing Rachel was a way to cut through the boredom.

She wished she didn't have to leave before the panel was over. She ordered an Uber at the last possible minute and slithered toward the auditorium's side door as inconspicuously as she could. "Bye, Rachel," Cassie said into the microphone. The crowd turned to Rachel, who gave a sheepish wave and ducked out to the sound of clapping.

The sense of hope that Rachel brought home with her was only to last a few hours. Monday morning, when most of the YAtopians were still in Philadelphia and embarking on a full day of school visits, Rachel was firmly back in her real life, watching her colleagues smile uncomfortably at their boss in an over-air-conditioned conference room. They were meant to be brainstorming "way outside-the-box" ideas.

"Substance, relevance, charm!" Ceri gave a hopeful look around the table. "That's what readers come to us for. What can we give back to them?"

"Why don't we go around in a circle and throw out ideas?" suggested Miriam, who'd recently been promoted to the role of Ceri's deputy. Rachel didn't have any suggestions. All she could think about was the picture that Geraldine had texted her and Sunny. Had Geraldine told Miriam and Ceri that Rachel regularly worked on her novel at the office? Or had she not come up at all? Rachel couldn't figure out which was worse. She could feel perspiration along her underboobs and clamped her arms tight against her sides.

"Who wants to start?" Ceri asked in a clipped voice. She had let her colorist paint her bangs in discordant gold tones that split right down the middle of her forehead, a new look that gave her the effect of resembling two half people. She had no natural flair for fashion, which she made up for by wearing bold prints and daggerish heels. The eight staffers present, Rachel included, were dressed in more muted versions of Ceri's office armor. Squeezed around the table in their screeching patterns, they looked like mismatched throw pillows. Only the contributors who had been called in, Jenny Drappen and Sunny MacLeod, dared to wear simple tops and delicate jewelry.

Sunny had been acting different with Rachel, holding herself at a slight remove that Rachel felt in the gut. Sunny's temperature had dropped, as if she'd never lent Rachel her Criterion Collection Mike Leigh DVDs or gone dancing at that bar in Flatbush with Rachel and her brother's friends earlier in the month. Rachel had barely seen Sunny and Jesse speak to each other that night, but now they were engaged in some "collaboration" to do with woodcuts and myths. Rachel glanced across the table at Sunny, as if she could erase the growing distance with a smile.

"Seriously, where are the big, juicy ideas?" Ceri said. *Cassette* was coming undone, and no ideas, no matter how box-shattering, were going to fix that. Ad pages were dwindling, and morale was a joke. Rather than replace the two senior editors who had left in the past month (one to work at a podcast incubator, the other to apprentice at an urban farm in Lisbon), Ceri had decided that her assistant, Jenna, a girl whose mother attended college with the holding company's CFO, should take a stab at editing text. This meant Rachel would take a stab at babysitting Jenna, who did little to conceal how busy she was with law-school applications and couldn't write a photo caption to save her left foot.

Rachel wondered if she could afford to walk away. That would be the classy thing to do. When she was a new hire and Ceri was still the executive editor, Ceri had given Rachel the best assignments and absurdly generous word counts. More recently she'd gamely put up with Rachel's request to go part-time after Cleo's birth. But Ceri was a wreck now. She worked past seven most nights and had developed a habit of plucking out strands of hair from the crown of her head.

One of the younger staffers, Deirdre Fan, was talking about a rare genetic mutation that expressed itself as double eyelashes. "A lot of celebrities have it. There are also serious circulatory risks," Deirdre said. "The headline could be 'Killer Lashes.' And the slide show would be very sexy, of course."

Ceri folded her arms and nodded in the way she did when she wasn't remotely moved. "Aren't people more interested in politics these days? I know we're not *Mother Jones*, but we can do things the *Cassette* way."

Farrah Berlinski, an associate editor who was exceptionally talented at turning the interns into her personal slaves, suggested a piece on the next wave of urban planners. "They're politically engaged on a local level and a very attractive bunch to boot." She slid a collage of photographs down the table. Serena DiCamillo, the online editor, made a point of examining the faces before it made its way to Ceri.

"I like that idea," Sunny piped in, and Ceri's expression turned from nothing to something.

"What else?" Ceri said. "What have you been thinking about, Rachel?"

Rachel's lungs inflated in her chest. Her preparation for today's meeting had consisted of trawling on social media in the ten-minute window between cleaning up after dinner and unpacking from YA-topia the previous night. Her conditioner had exploded inside her bag, so she hadn't had much time. Despite Ceri's pep talk, most of what people were talking about—the president's love affair with Putin, the Comey firing—simply wasn't adaptable for *Cassette.* "This is a little out there," she started, "but I've heard that a number of young women are getting tattoos of vulvas. We could assign an essay on body politics."

"Anything else?" Ceri said.

Rachel looked down at her notepad. She hoped that from where Ceri was sitting, her doodles looked like notes. "And another idea I had was aura photography. I heard that Marina Goksenin is super into it. We could ask her to write about her obsession."

Ceri sighed. "Rachel, Marina Goksenin has already turned down two assignments from us."

"Only one," Rachel corrected her boss. "The other idea fell through when we realized that Ama Yaalezar was dead."

Not long ago Rachel had suggested they ask Marina to interview Ama Yaalezar, the feminist Iranian sculptor on whom Cate Blanchett's latest role had been based. Only after the pitch meeting did Rachel learn that the profile subject was eternally unavailable, which everyone had found hilarious at the time.

Rachel glanced over at Sunny, fishing for a smile or any sign that things were not as bad as they seemed. Sunny maintained a serene expression, her head cocked at a respectfully adoring angle toward their leader. Ceri brought her fingertips to her forehead. "We'll all have to keep thinking," she muttered. "Thank you, everyone." The group sat perfectly still while their boss rose from her seat and walked out.

Defeated, Rachel gathered her papers and tried to hold her head high as she walked toward the door. Weren't meetings something you were supposed to get better at as you got older? She slowed by the doorway and glanced over her shoulder and caught Sunny's eye. Rachel made a *Coffee?* gesture, jerking her hand up toward her mouth. But her miming skills were all wrong, summoning instead a sorority girl downing a Jell-O shot. Sunny shook her head in an apologetic no and pointed at Ceri.

Rachel tried to affect a look of indifference and shuffled along with the meeting attendees. She felt terrible, too terrible to just park herself at her cubicle and start working. So she texted Matt. Worst meeting ever. Ceri stared thru my ideas. He responded quickly, reminding Rachel that his zebra fish had a higher emotional intelligence than Ceri. Idk, I'm sad about Sunny, too. She's acting weird . . . like we're strangers. It felt good to cast her feelings into words, even if she knew that Matt didn't understand her infatuation with Sunny.

Love hurts, babe.

Rachel suspected that Matt was a little jealous. She pushed her phone into her back pocket. Her husband's reply was mocking but true.

# 18

Jesse had this thing he did with his tongue. He'd stick it out ever so slightly and slowly run it along his upper lip when he was thinking. It was delicate and carnal and just about the most adorable thing Sunny had ever seen.

She'd picked up this habit of his, and other ones. Like drinking iced ginger tea and listening to Kendrick Lamar while she worked in her studio. She was also back to touching herself, all the time, something she hadn't done since her teens. The night she'd gone dancing with Jesse and Rachel, he came up from behind and wrapped his hands around her hips and drew her in close. It had lasted only a second, and yet. Sunny couldn't stop fantasizing about what would happen if she gave in to the magnet pull of her infatuation and appeared in front of Rachel's building the next time Jesse was babysitting his niece. She'd nearly forgotten what it was like to be exploding with lust.

Her transformation was a positive one, save for a single thing. It went against everything she and Nick had come to be. Of course, they'd made the in-showers and on-the-beach circuit in their early phase. Now they stuck to their bed, where they lay on top of each other like two slices of processed bread. Nick looked at his share of sexy pictures on Instagram, and who knew what else on the dark web or whatever it was called. He regularly joked about wanting Sunny to become acquainted with her inner sex goddess, but were she to suddenly do that, how could he not take it as a betrayal? He'd sniff out the catalyst. So she served her enthusiasm in neat little packets, two or three sessions per week, a few innovations, performed cautiously.

Early on Tuesday morning, Sunny flicked her tongue at a patch of flesh that tasted sour and salty, like a premium tequila cocktail. She was working on her husband's inner thigh. Nick moaned and reached for her shoulders. "Stop, stop. I'm not going to last," he said. She wriggled up the sheets and looked into his eyes. "Let's not use anything," surprising herself with the words that came tumbling out. "I just had my period . . . a little while ago."

"Well, that sounds scientific." Nick chuckled.

Sunny rounded her back and kissed his earlobe.

"I do love you, darling," Nick said, and for a second she thought he might cave in. "But I love my sleep, and my sanity, and our marriage . . . and your body just the way it is." He leaned over to kiss her right breast. "Babies are evil ninjas in disguise."

"I was just . . . suggesting something different."

"Sure you were."

Sunny glanced down at her tummy, which was developing a slight paunch. She tried to affect indifference. Nick kissed the back of her neck. Her eyes fluttered closed, and she searched for Jesse in her mind. He was here with her now, and her body moved like hot wax.

Nick was too stunned to say anything when it was all over. He watched his wife shimmy into a pair of cotton underpants and walk across the bedroom. Sunny sensed him sizing her up. Perhaps he was onto her.

After her shower she found Nick napping contentedly. She oiled her body and put on her embroidered dress, then filled a duffel bag with enough items to last a weekend. The invitation had said "comfortable clothes to sweat and surrender in." She'd figure out what that meant when she got there.

Sunny prepared her breakfast of apricot muesli and coconut yogurt, threw her purse and duffel over her shoulders, and came into the bedroom to kiss Nick good-bye. He was awake, reading Elvis Costello's autobiography. She shook her head and smiled. Peel off the outer layer of a real-estate developer whose carefully considered utterances could intimidate the canniest of billionaires, and there lay an addle-brained teenager who simply wanted to sing in a rock band.

"You've got a lot going on there, darling." The left corner of his mouth twitched mischievously.

"I know, I look like a bag lady." Sunny smiled. "I'm meeting Geraldine at her thing, and then I'm going to work at the studio. In Red Hook."

"What's Geraldine's thing again?" It was so like Nick to presume that he'd forgotten something. Sunny hadn't brought it up—Geraldine had only invited her yesterday. Sunny had accepted immediately. It had seemed so much more appealing than the dinner the two never got around to scheduling. And Sunny had more time, now that the editor for her cookbook project had been laid off and the whole project was pushed back indefinitely. At least Sunny wasn't expected to return the advance. It wasn't a lot of money, but she took pride in her contributions to the account she shared with Nick.

"It's The Big Chill, that meditation series," Sunny said. "Geraldine said Aaron Loeb wanted me to come."

Aaron Loeb was a kid from Los Angeles who'd started out as a club promoter and was now organizing mass meditations that moved from one location to the next. A recent Sunday Styles article focused on a five-hundred-person Grand Central Terminal takeover. Sunny had found it pretty impressive. "My hunch is he wants to collaborate on something," she said.

"He seems very kumbaya," said Nick. "Maybe the collaboration is between you and Geraldine and getting you two together again."

"What are you talking about?" Sunny was taken aback. "Did Jeremy say something?"

"No," Nick said. "But you never mention her."

"I just saw her, at that party on Jeremy's roof."

Nick wasn't listening. "I like Geraldine. She has a funny way of cutting through the chitchat. I like her more than that Brooklyn mother, Rebecca?"

"Rachel," Sunny said. "She's my friend. Watch it or I'll turn into an annoying Brooklyn mother myself."

"I never said anything about her being annoying." Nick raised his eyebrows and visibly savored his victory.

The crowd streaming into Odile's was a determined-looking bunch, with clothing cut to reveal ropy, yogurt-fed limbs. The restaurant's tables and chairs had disappeared, though, and in their place were fifty or so yoga mats. Sunny had been to Odile's countless times for breakfast meetings. Sage and eucalyptus scented the air, and trippy, minimalist music played on the speakers. She had to admit the jarring mix of intention and location kind of worked. "Where do you think I should get changed?" she asked Geraldine.

"You're perfect the way you are."

Sunny looked to see where the voice came from and found a woman who appeared to be in her early forties, who had on black harem pants and a gauzy purple scarf wrapped at a diagonal around her torso. "I'm Margo."

"Sunny." Sunny extended her hand, which Margo accepted in a two-handed clasp.

Margo paused for a meaningful stare. She smelled of citrus. "Good to *see* you, Sunny."

Sunny settled onto a mat next to Geraldine's and sat in awkward silence. Finally Margo came to the front of the room and lit a candle. "How's everyone doing?" she said. "You ready to move ecstatically?" The group cheered. Sunny rearranged her body. It was difficult to sit cross-legged in a dress. "It's great, you'll see," Geraldine whispered.

Margo folded her legs in a way that reminded Sunny of an insect. "Let's make some beautiful energy," she said. "Now, rest your eyes. You are here. *Be* here. Welcome yourself into the place you need to be."

Sunny watched her neighbors settle into their new dimension and finally let her own eyes float closed. She was breathing deeply, following the teacher's cues, except for the one about connecting with her sacred self. She wasn't sure where to find that. She remembered the Moroccan chickpea stew that was still in the back of the fridge and must be going bad by now. She needed to throw it out.

Margo's voice was musical, and she laughed freely. "Put your arms over your head and clear the space of your fears," Margo said. "Think of what's holding you back and shake it all away. Nobody's watching you. Find your strength and be free."

Sunny couldn't resist looking over at Geraldine. Geraldine was snaking her arms overhead and smiling beatifically. Strength and resilience emanated from her body, and it occurred to Sunny that Geraldine resembled a warrior preparing for victory.

"You are so much bigger than the darkness," Margo said. "Shake it all off."

Sunny closed her eyes and tried to tune in to her demons and desires. But by all objective standards, she wasn't wanting for anything. This baby fixation that was rearing up was just her id's way of keeping things off balance. She'd never been a follower—why would she want to be like everybody else and force a little alien to pop out of her body and suck her dry? She could barely keep up with her career given all the caretaking that Stanley and Agnes and Nick required. What if she had a baby and it had her learning disabilities or some horrible rare syndrome nobody could diagnose? What if it grew up to reject her? No. No good could come of motherhood.

When it was time to stop moving, the tops of Sunny's arms were sore. "Do you feel the change in the energy?" Margo asked. Sunny couldn't deny the sparks of what Margo would probably call awareness. "You are letting go. Now it's time to nourish yourself. I want you to look within and think of what you need. Is it acceptance? Happiness? Forgiveness?" Margo paused. "What's your word?"

Sunny stole a glance at Geraldine, whose skin was glowing as she swayed on her meditation pouf. She seemed undeniably content. Sunny felt something inside her lift. What did it matter if Geraldine wanted to drift back to Peter? Maybe they were fated to be together. Peter had misbehaved, over and over, but who was Sunny to impede Geraldine's happiness and say he wouldn't reform? Or maybe he already had. It had been years since Sunny'd been close with Peter.

A new song came on, sung by a woman with a feathery voice. She repeated a chant that sounded like "Jonathan, he's so hung." There were bells, and Sunny detected the sound of children playing in the background.

The week before, Sunny had gone for her annual ob-gyn appointment. She'd brought up the subject of egg freezing. "Are you asking for yourself?" Dr. Yu had sounded incredulous. She examined Sunny's chart, her brow furrowing. "I thought you told me babies were out of the question."

"They were, but . . . maybe my husband and I aren't ready just yet. I think we might need a few more years. Or a year?"

The doctor's frown had a tragic tint to it. "Ideally you'd freeze in your mid-twenties. If you think you're going to be ready for a baby in the foreseeable future, you've got to start trying right now. You're thirty-seven, and you have a partner. Don't wait."

"Hold on to your word," Margo said. "Don't let it slip away."

Sunny still hadn't found her word. Was it "baby"? Or "Jesse"? She tried to make a selection, but an image of an infant Jesse was what filled her mind. He was somewhat perverse-looking, this baby, with Jesse's arrowhead tattoo and eyes that blazed wildly. He reached his arms out to Sunny. There was a rippling deep inside her, and it hurt. Something wet landed on her palm. She was crying. She tilted her head back, as if that could stop the tears. "Hold your word in your heart," Margo said. "Tell the universe you are ready."

"Thank you, Margo. That was beautiful." A man rose from a mat in the back of the room and came to join the leader. He had broad shoulders and stoner eyes. This must be Aaron, Sunny realized. "And I want to thank all of you for finding the time to come." He padded across the room, the gleaming wood floor creaking beneath his bare, golden-haired feet. Aaron stopped here and there to hug attendees, men and women alike. "You are all here for a reason," he said, pulling

Margo in for a burly embrace. "Honor your reason," Aaron said, and Sunny felt overcome with a sense of bright weightlessness.

The sound of a gong reverberated through the room, and Sunny wiped the back of her hand across her eyes. She saw that Geraldine was watching her. "Aren't you glad you came?" Geraldine whispered. Sunny wasn't the only person whose eyes were smeared with tears, but that didn't help lessen the shame that engulfed her.

# 19

Barrett insisted on picking Geraldine up at her place. It was opening night for the New York Documentary Film Festival, and Barrett, who was now working for the *Toronto Star*'s editorial page and gathering ideas for his Reel Real op-ed series, had invited her to come as his date. On top of his chivalry, Geraldine sensed a streak of the protective little brother in her former roommate. It wouldn't have totally surprised her if he'd colluded with her mother—Joanne had always been such a fan of Barrett's, eyebrow ring notwithstanding.

Barrett came straight from the movie theater where he'd bunkered himself all day. He was bursting with excitement, words bubbling out faster than Geraldine could follow. She had never thought him to be brilliant when they'd lived together, but clearly he was. Had she been that depressed? Barrett was dressed in cargo shorts and vintage Reebok Pumps, a lime-green all-access festival badge hanging around his neck. It had been four months since Geraldine had seen him, and she was hit with raw emotion and the faintest whiff of artificial butter as she hugged him at the door.

"You live here?" Barrett craned his neck into the loft. "For real? This is some *Million Dollar Listing* ridiculousness."

Jeremy gave a dramatic throat clearing from his place on the couch. He was on his iPad. "Hi." He waved. "Don't worry, I'm not a sociopath. I just have violently good taste."

"I told you about Jeremy," Geraldine said, slightly blushing as she introduced her current and former roommates. "He's my patron saint."

"Slumlord with benefits," Jeremy said, then realized he needed to backtrack lest Barrett get the wrong idea. "Geraldine keeps things civilized around here. Without her there'd be no conversation or flowers," he added.

"Plants, mostly," Geraldine said, and excused herself to change into something a little mellower than the silk dress she had on. "You guys both have English mothers!"

She kept her bedroom door open so she could eavesdrop on their conversation. Barrett was overcompensating for his prior faux pas by praising the apartment's "ambient light." By the time Geraldine came back out, in a batik jumpsuit she'd found at a thrift store with Sylvie, the two were discussing a documentary Barrett had seen earlier in the day, about an extreme mountain climber's gruesome death in the Amazon Basin.

"I like him," Barrett said on the elevator ride down. "You could do a lot worse."

The door opened, and Geraldine didn't move. "Jeremy and I aren't together. You know that, right?" She was getting sick of insisting on this to everyone, sick of the two responses it invariably garnered.

Either people didn't believe her or they looked at her as if she were the world's biggest fool for believing that something so good could come for free. Then again, she'd sooner hear unsolicited commentary about Jeremy than about Peter, who was coming back to New York and wanted to take her to Nantucket. He'd gone to a charity auction and bid on a three-night stay at a beachfront home. "You'll be supporting a good cause," he'd tried. She'd said no, it probably wasn't a great idea, but they both knew she'd left the possibility open, just a sliver. The hinges on Geraldine's door were broken, so it was never going to close completely.

It was spitting rain, and they walked closely under Barrett's umbrella, catching up on his new gig and Geraldine's eternal search for one. "My friend Sylvie and I recorded a couple of episodes of a podcast. Have you heard of Art Gumbel?"

"Of course. That interview he did with Sylvester Stallone and his yo-yo dieting was unforgettable. Why?"

"I met him through a friend, and he's been helping me out with equipment and editing software," Geraldine said, trying to sound nonchalant about her brush with nerd celebrity.

"You're a podhead, that's awesome," Barrett said, bouncing along. "Can I listen?"

"Not yet. I don't want to put them out on my own until I get confirmation that none of the distribution companies I'm talking to want it. There's this California entity that seems pretty shady, and Barb is low-key helping me navigate the CBC."

"The old hometown bureaucracy." Barrett smiled.

"It's insane," Geraldine said. "I'm not sure how they ever put anything out when nothing ever gets done behind the scenes. I've had meetings, but all anybody wants to talk about is who should get cc'd and bcc'd on emails."

"Sounds about right," Barrett said. "They should rebrand as the bcc."

Geraldine laughed. "I know I really should get a proper job. I was trying to when I first got here, but everyone told me I'm either overqualified or underqualified," she said. "You can tell my mother to get the guest bed ready."

"You could get married and stay here forever," Barrett said.

"Like that wouldn't be hard to pull off."

"Easy peasy. You're the coolest person I know."

Geraldine rolled her eyes. There were many words she'd use to describe herself, and some were nice ones, but "cool" was not among them. And did wife seekers even want cool? Didn't they want pretty? Or rich? The one exception she could think of was Nick, who had chosen Sunny. They'd married the same summer as Rachel and Matt, in the lush garden behind their friends' home in the Hudson Valley. Sunny had seemed so solid and beaming in her mauve wedding dress, as if she'd unlocked the cupboard to human contentment. Yet now that Geraldine had witnessed her having a near breakdown at that meditation event, it was hard to think of Sunny as entirely cool, or of her and Nick as remotely happy together.

Barrett gave Geraldine's shoulder a squeeze. "Everything's going to be fine," he told her. "If things were squared away, life would be less interesting."

They came upon the boutique hotel where the party was being held. The red carpet in front sat sodden and empty. A lone photographer had taken refuge from the rain under an awning. Geraldine steered Barrett's rigid body onto the carpet and smiled determinedly. She had fantastic teeth. With visible reluctance the photographer took their picture and asked for their names.

The party was on the "lower penthouse" level, aka the second floor, and it was surprisingly packed. The crowd shared an earthy affluence that Geraldine concluded must be common to documentary filmmakers, lots of platform sandals and layered ethnic necklaces. Barrett knew some of the other badge wearers and brought Geraldine over to a circle of them. They were eating lobster rolls the size of baby carrots and discussing the festival's buzziest film, *The Payback*. Geraldine gathered it was about a woman who'd bullied Ivanka at summer camp and who volunteered at the Trump campaign in order to apologize to her in person. Geraldine slipped away.

Standing at the bar five minutes later, she still didn't have a drink. She couldn't bring herself to be as aggressive as those being served. While she snacked on curried cashews, she watched the party play out in the mirror behind the bottles. All the banquettes were filled, and a tall woman was walking around with a blatantly old-fashioned VHS video camera propped on her shoulder. Geraldine located Barrett and his crew where she'd left them. Everything in her body went full stop when she saw that Barrett was chatting with Sunny. It didn't make her proud to feel this way, but was there nothing in the city that Geraldine couldn't have to herself? She'd taken Sunny to the meditation event, even though Sunny never asked Geraldine to be her date to anything. Geraldine didn't even want a drink anymore.

Feeling deflated, she pivoted and came to face a pair of women who appeared to be in their late fifties. One of them had the most beautiful earrings made out of what looked like ancient coins. Geraldine realized that this was Elinda Jackman, the HR woman from Ffife Media.

"Elinda?" Geraldine tried. "It's Geraldine Despont; we met a few months ago."

"Of course," Elinda said, as if it were slowly coming back.

"Are you in film?" her friend asked Geraldine. She was dressed more corporately, with a scarf jauntily tied around her neck.

"I just know a few people here," Geraldine said, glancing over at Barrett and Sunny. They were laughing with the woman carrying the video recorder. Elinda's companion continued to stare at Geraldine, waiting for her to explain her existence. "I'm sort of a free agent." The words sounded silly and made her smile.

"You're an agent?" Scarf Lady raised her eyebrows.

Geraldine shook her head. "Right now I'm making a podcast."

"Are you?" Elinda said. "That's very interesting. What is the focus?"

"It's called *Pod People,*" Geraldine said. "The host is this girl—I guess I should say woman?"

"Girl's fine by me," Scarf said.

"Her name is Sylvie," Geraldine said. "She's the most hilarious person I have met in New York. For the show she interviews the best podcasters. The idea is every week you have a built-in audience."

The women were clucking in approval. "And who's distributing?" Elinda asked.

Geraldine tried to still the self-doubt fluttering within her. "I'm in talks with the Canadian Broadcasting Corporation."

"Are you?" Scarf said in an impressed tone.

"You should be in talks with me, too," Elinda said brusquely, handing Geraldine her card: ELINDA JACKMAN, CHIEF STRATEGIC OFFICER AT FFIFE MEDIA. Geraldine felt a quickening. She hadn't received a card at their previous meeting.

"We're undergoing a lot of changes, all exciting," Elinda said. "We're moving forward, developing our brands off the page. Some of them are adaptable. Some less so . . ." She frowned. "You must be relieved we didn't find you a job at *Cassette.*"

"*Cassette* was good," the other woman allowed. "It really captured a moment."

Geraldine felt thick-brained. She'd been so busy chasing after the moment, she hadn't heard anything about its passing. "They pulled the plug on *Cassette?*" she asked.

Elinda let Geraldine's question evaporate and turned to her friend. "I should introduce her to Doug." She looked back at Geraldine. "You'll call me tomorrow. And don't say anything about the magazine to anybody—it's all still in flux."

Geraldine's confusion lifted, and a gauzy sadness came to take its place. Rachel had a baby to feed and a husband who earned only in the upper-five figures. They needed Rachel's income. "I should go back to my friends," Geraldine said, and assured the women she would be discreet. As she came up to Barrett's side, Geraldine tried to push thoughts of Rachel out of her mind.

"Geraldine—there you are," Sunny said. Her tone was untroubled; she must not have seen whom Geraldine had been talking to.

Geraldine leaned in for a kiss and attempted to block out the guilt pressing in on her. Even Sunny, who didn't need *Cassette*, wasn't going to be thrilled when she learned the news. Geraldine could feel Elinda's card turning moist in her palm as she tightened her fist around it.

"Miss MacLeod!" A man in silver accountant-chic glasses grabbed Sunny by the elbow and slotted her into a new conversation. To go by the look Sunny shot at Geraldine, she was disappointed not to get to talk further. A moment later, though, Sunny was performing animatedly for a ring of attentive strangers, a supernova in a distant galaxy.

# 20

What's the holdup, Rachel?" Miriam's tone was sharp as a thumbtack. Rachel x-ed out of her email so a layout of Sunny's column bloomed on the screen. It was about wabi-sabi, the Japanese art of imperfection. Rachel swallowed and sat up. "I'm sorry," she told Miriam. "I'll have everything in by lunch, promise."

"Everyone's in the conference room. It's very important." Miriam walked away, her strides heavy with determination. Now Rachel saw that the workstations around her sat empty. She'd been dimly aware of a mass migration, but she'd assumed it was somebody's birthday and that her colleagues were just marching toward a box of esoteric doughnuts in the kitchen.

Rachel grabbed her phone and sprinted to the room where she was supposed to be, the blisters on the backs of her feet flaring up in her rubber flats.

"Hi, Rachel," Ceri said in an eerie tone, then lowered her head and folded her hands together, which she did when was she was trying to compose her thoughts. She was wearing Buddy Hollys—it was the first time Rachel had seen her in glasses. "As I was saying," Ceri said, "I am aware you all have so much work left to do on this issue."

The staff looked slightly dumbstruck. Rachel ducked her head and settled into a spot in the standing area in the back of the room. Something major was going on. It had been two weeks since the last surprise all-staff meeting, where Ceri had laid out the "tangible assets plan," which was a fancy way of saying everybody had to come up with ideas for *Cassette*-related books and kitchenware and other merchandise. Today, though, nobody was passing out memos that were still warm from the copier. Midtown sunlight slashed through the windows, washing out the enormous photograph of Depression-era construction workers that hung on the wall.

Ceri cleared her throat. "I am so proud of *Cassette*, and all of you should be, too. I believe the magazine has only become finer over the years, and we saw a seven-percent uptick in sales over the last year, which is quite significant in this economy." The stench of fear rose up through the room. "I take great pride in what we do as well as what we don't do," Ceri said. "Our readers look to us for good taste and integrity, and we deliver on both counts. There are plenty of places to find reality stars and beauty looks. What *Cassette* has is the sharpest and liveliest in art and design and ideas. We bring our readers the inspiration to live if not their best, then certainly their better, lives."

Ceri's words were turning to slush. It wasn't until Rachel heard "The issue we are closing will be our last" that she truly came to attention.

Everyone erupted into a chorus of gasps and omigods. "Are we going entirely digital?" Deirdre asked.

"To be honest, I don't know what the company has planned for the brand," Ceri said. "I won't be a part of *Cassette*'s next stage. Not my choice." She paused to accept the stunned looks. "The magazine will continue to operate until a week from Friday, so we will finish the September issue. HR has assured me they are going to do their best to find a place for all of you after that."

Rachel's phone vibrated. It was a text from Matt, who was in Toronto of all places, meeting with a former mentor about a collaboration. Flight's on track. Will pick up your ketchup potato chips and be home for dinner. All the love. Rachel eased and returned her focus to the front of the room. "Elinda Jackman, whom many of you will remember from human resources and who now runs Ffife's strategy, is here to answer your questions," Ceri said. "If you have any questions for me, Miriam will give you my personal email address."

Rachel hadn't met with Elinda since she'd first interviewed with Ffife, over six years ago. She barely recognized the woman who stepped forth from one of the room's wings. She had a silver bob and coin earrings that told a story of summers on boats in the Adriatic Sea. "Thank you so much," she said with an uneasy smile. "You're welcome to stay, Ceri."

Ceri made a point of not meeting Elinda's eye as she surrendered her chair. Ever the dutiful lieutenant, Miriam rose and accompanied her boss out of the room. Elinda wasted no time and spoke crisply about new media-consumption patterns. The company would be prioritizing its digital initiatives, of which there were several, and she assured those assembled before her that there would be ample opportunities.

"So you're saying you still have jobs for us?" somebody asked.

Elinda clasped her hands together. "We are working on creating new positions, and once they are formalized, you will have priority status."

"But we're getting laid off?" challenged somebody.

"Technically, yes."

"Fuck me," somebody behind Rachel couldn't resist saying. Other members of the group were yelling over each other, about how *Cassette* was their family and how screwed they would be under Trumpcare. Rachel felt a creepy numbness through it all. She tried to imagine what Matt would say when she told him she'd lost her job. He was going to freak out. Money was already tight, and there was no way Rachel was going to get hired over her many soon-to-be-former colleagues who hadn't spent the last three years being pregnant and leaning out so they could dabble in literary juvenilia. *Monsters!* was far from a sure thing. What was she going to do? Her brain fired blanks.

The final two weeks at *Cassette* were electric. The dress code crumbled to ratty T-shirts and jean shorts, and everybody ate meals together, loudly. As her colleagues began to shift into characters from her past, Rachel felt a warmth toward them that had heretofore eluded her. She was suddenly fond of the magazine, now that it was about to be pulped. Sunny, too, seemed to be upset about its unraveling, far more than she really needed to be. She'd scrapped the column she'd been working on and decided to weave together a personal tribute to *Cassette.* Sunny had been emailing Rachel pdfs of mementos from the magazine's heyday. There'd been one picture, taken at a book party Rachel was fairly certain she hadn't been invited to. Wearing a block-print turtleneck dress Rachel recognized from the

*Province* days, Sunny chatted with what looked like Salman Rushdie while Jane Jones, the magazine's former editor in chief, stood a few feet away. Sunny was in her early thirties, still smoking cigarettes at parties. In the picture she'd clasped her hand over her mouth as if she'd just heard the most scandalous thing ever. "This was the night I met Jane and made my big move," Sunny wrote to Rachel. "I was so nervous." Rachel enlarged the picture until Sunny took up the whole frame.

Nobody had seen Ceri since the big meeting. She was rumored to be licking her wounds at a Union Square ceramics studio. Being the lone Jewish mother on staff, Rachel stepped up. She brought in her portable speakers and filled the office with the sounds of The New Pornographers and Beyoncé, and tried to help everybody keep their minds off the virtually nonexistent job market.

On the final day of *Cassette*, after all the pages had shipped and desk drawers been emptied, the crew walked the twenty-odd blocks to Ceri's place on the Upper West Side. Ceri appeared too stricken to do more than sit in an enormous chair and receive condolences as her former team filed into her home.

"You're going to be fine," Rachel said when it was her turn.

"They lit my house on fire." Ceri spoke through a clenched jaw. "You'd better not go back and work for those pillagers."

"I don't think you have to worry about that," Rachel assured her.

HR hadn't come through for anybody yet, and only two people had jobs lined up—Gretchen DiCambria, a video editor, had found a maternity leave to cover for at BuzzFeed's investigative unit, and Melinda Silver was going to work at her father's landscape-design firm in Boston.

Rachel moved along and piled a plate high with tortilla chips and guacamole. She milled around with a group of assistants before giving in to the pull of Sunny and joining her on the floor. Sunny was sitting alone on a sheepskin rug, picking at a miniature pesto-and-mozzarella sandwich. "I can't believe this is what it took for all of us to have a party," Rachel said. "Remember those Friday drinks they used to have at *Province*?"

"Saturdays, too," Sunny said. "You'd think none of us had any friends outside the office. We couldn't get enough of one another."

"You could get enough of me."

"What can I say? I was stupid." Sunny gave a weary smile and looked up at the people staggering around the room. Everyone was talking about how weird it was going to be to wake up on Monday morning with nowhere to go. "Another chapter of our lives, over."

"I'm not sure you get to count *Cassette* as one of your chapters," Rachel said. "How many other projects do you have going on?"

"Nothing terribly amazing." Sunny sounded sad and drifty. "You must be kind of happy. You get to focus on your writing."

Rachel dug her heels into the carpet. She'd negotiated pretty well for herself and was making as much as some of the junior staffers, plus benefits, for only two days of work a week. Now that Rachel and Matt were down an income, Matt was lobbying for a move to a rental in Fort Lee, New Jersey, which was closer to Columbia's campus than where they lived now. Rachel wouldn't hear of it, but she couldn't come up with a counteroffer either. "You know I wasn't working at *Cassette* for the fun of it, right?" Rachel sighed. But Sunny wasn't going to understand, not really. With Nick on hand to bankroll her artistic adventures, her earnings added up to pin money.

"You need to get away so you can finish your book and get a movie deal." Rachel rolled her eyes, but Sunny kept talking. "Why don't we go to my house on Long Island next week? You can write, and Matt and I will take care of Cleo."

"I wish. Matt has to be at his lab. His fish don't travel."

"I have an idea." Sunny pulled her phone out of her bucket bag and typed something, staring at her words for a moment before pressing SEND.

"What did you just do?" Rachel said.

Sunny smiled. "I asked your brother to come out with us. He and I can finish our project when Cleo is napping. I'll cook for you."

"Jesse?" Rachel said doubtfully. "I thought you were done with that project. Anyway. He's too punk to go to anyone's country house."

"We'll see." Sunny pulled her knees under her chin, forming a basket around her legs with her long, tapered fingers. "You should come, no matter what."

# 21

Everything ok? Nick's text had come in over an hour ago.

Morning, bunny, Sunny typed back. It was still dark, and she could make out the sounds of baby talk and kitchen-cabinet doors opening and closing. Everything's good. I'm hiding out in bed. They sure get the party started early. Can u bring an extra pair of earplugs?

Should be some in my nightstand.

Sunny rolled over and investigated his drawer. A near-empty sheet of licorice menthol gum, a napkin scrawled with numbers he'd totted up in crimson ink, and a pair of foam nubs.

Found them, she texted back. Miss you.

Sunny briefly considered going downstairs to put on coffee for her guests. The machine was Danish and always gave people trouble. The next thing she knew, it was nearly nine and the predawn cool had dissipated. It was going to be insufferably hot today. She could hear the clanging of dishes and the murmurs of conversation coming from the kitchen. Sunny stretched her arms overhead and reached for her phone. Nick had written again.

Miss your tail, too.

She smiled and slipped on a cream tank top and a pair of paint-splattered cotton shorts. She considered putting on a bra and decided not to bother. Her breasts weren't big enough to require support. The smell of coffee and buttered toast hit her before she reached the stairs and saw Rachel standing over the kitchen island, carving stone fruit into pieces too tiny for Cleo to choke on. Jesse was splayed across the couch, bopping his niece up and down on his knee. He was wearing a flecked gray T-shirt and cargo shorts, and Sunny could make out his biceps even from this far away. She couldn't help thinking about Nick, who treated his body as if it were something he inhabited, mummifying his joints in protective covers when he played basketball on Sunday mornings at the Y. Given the age difference, it wasn't fair to make comparisons, but Sunny suspected that Nick had always been this way, like a convalescing prince. She averted her eyes, as if she could quiet Jesse's vitality.

"Georgie shouldn't return to the mothers," Jesse was saying to his sister. "He needs to go to battle and suffer another loss. Hey, I got it—he fights the cloud keeper and then after a bloody victory realizes it was his mother he killed." Jesse raised his arms in victory. "Boom! There's your bestseller."

Rachel popped a peach segment into her mouth. "Are you crazy? He can't kill his mother. He already lost his father, and his sister's memories are frozen."

"Life is hard," Jesse said. "What do you think, Cleo? Should Georgie murder his mama?" Cleo tilted her head and let off a squeal.

"See?" Jesse extended his legs, swinging her ceilingward and causing her to break out in a fit of giggles. "She knows what's up." Only now did Jesse glance at the staircase and notice Sunny.

"Morning," Sunny creaked. "Sorry I slept so late."

"I'm glad we didn't wake you up," Rachel said. "At the ungodly hour of six-ten, Cleo was determined to sing every song she's ever heard. Now we're workshopping." She gestured to a plate by the stove. "And eating Jesse's famous blueberry pancakes."

"I am a full-service operation," Jesse said. "I tend to children and neurotic writers. We saved you some."

Sunny was a bore about her morning muesli and coconut yogurt but didn't want to call attention to herself, so she helped herself to a pancake and bit right into a blueberry. It bubbled onto her chin.

Rachel laughed. "I'd offer you a paper towel, but I have no idea where they are."

"Under the sink," Sunny said.

"Nope, over by the TV," Jesse said. "Cleo and I made a paper-towel castle."

"Way to be green," Rachel chided him. "I'll replace the roll," she told Sunny, then gulped the remains of her coffee. "Now's your last chance to weigh in on a potential matricide before I disappear for the next five hours. Do we kiss Georgie's mother good-bye?"

Sunny wiped her face with a dish towel. "Everybody likes a good killing," she said. "Off with her head!"

Jesse nodded agreement.

Sunny watched Rachel wash a few dishes and then go over some ground rules with her brother before disappearing behind the house with her thermos of coffee. Sunny took her time fixing herself a mug of Darjeeling tea, packing the loose leaves into a silver tea ball, and brought it out onto the porch. She squinted at her geraniums and saw they looked dry, possibly beyond the point of rescue. The screen door screeched open. Out came Jesse, carrying Cleo. He had a crooked scar on his right ankle, Sunny noticed.

"If you want to go into town, we should do it soon," she said, holding her gaze at the cloudless sky. "It's going to be crazy hot." She realized she'd been rehearsing the line. In one of her stupider fantasies, she and Jesse stood on either side of Cleo at the Greenport Carousel, their hands sharing a metal pole. She'd always liked playing house, ever since her mother gave her her first Madame Alexander doll.

"Actually, Cleo and I have plans to go swimming at Doug's," Jesse said. "Do you want to come?"

Sunny turned to look at him squarely. "Who?"

"Doug the neighbor. He was out with his dog earlier, and we started chatting."

"Are you serious?" Sunny said. "Did he know where you were staying?" She visored her hand over her eyes and looked at the gray roof poking through the treetops across the street. "That man hates us."

Doug and Austin, who'd moved in across the road and were trying to repurpose their classic suburban clapboard three-bedroom into a mini-estate that belonged on the South Fork, forever adding piles of crushed bluestone to their driveway, had become Nick and Sunny's enemies. It had started with trees—they were cutting them down or installing them in the wrong place, Sunny couldn't remember, but Nick loathed whatever choice they'd made with the trees—and so now everything they did was wrong. Doug and Austin had invited Nick and Sunny to their housewarming, a tasting of local wines, and Nick had refused to go. Then they all ran into one another while trying to buy sandwiches at the Smile in SoHo, and Sunny had moved to say hello. But the pair had feigned cluelessness and walked right past them.

"Tell you what," Jesse said, hiking his niece higher up on his hip. "I'll help you fix that door, and you can help me make sure this little lump doesn't drown."

Jesse and Sunny were no more equipped to get a toddler ready to go for a swim than prepare for a rocket launch, but they were determined not to bother Rachel and expose their combined weakness. It took them some twenty minutes to find Cleo's swimming diaper, another five to pretzel her limbs into her bikini. By the time they made it across the street, the sun was beating down so hard the only thing any of them would need a towel for was modesty. Jesse peeled off his shirt and set to slathering sunblock all over Cleo. Doug was under an umbrella and alternating between reading the *Wall Street Journal* and taking in the visiting Adonis. Doug turned to Sunny and asked, "Where's your husband?"

"He's in the city. He's coming tonight." She dug around her bag and found the snow-pea-print dish towel she'd painted herself. "I brought you something." Doug accepted the gift without much interest. "It was really nice of you to invite us," Sunny said. "We'll have to have you guys over soon."

"No need, I'm not a tit-for-tat type," Doug said, gazing with visible pleasure at Jesse. He leaned back in his chaise and closed his eyes.

Sunny jumped into the pool and joined Jesse and Cleo as they goofed around with an inflatable flamingo. Sunny held Cleo aloft while she splashed her uncle, who pretended to sink to the bottom of the pool each time water sprayed him. After one particularly glorious detonation, Cleo turned to make sure Sunny had seen it all. The joy on the girl's face was practically too much to behold.

Doug eventually said something about having to make a call and disappeared, leaving his three visitors to play around. Golden light poured in through the treetops, and sounds of joy reverberated through the space around them. Sunny didn't notice that Rachel had come to sit under the umbrella until a tube of sunscreen flew through the air and hit Jesse's head.

Sunny felt a flash of embarrassment. "How did you find us?"

"I can make out my daughter's voice from a mile away," Rachel said, and Sunny dipped her head under the water.

"Get back in your writing shed," Jesse instructed his sister. "You've got a family to feed."

"I did two thousand words," Rachel told them. "I'm all about quantity, not quality. Say Cheetos!" She raised her phone to eye level and took a couple of pictures.

"What are you waiting for?" Jesse cried. "The water's perfect!"

"I don't have a suit," Rachel protested.

"Captain Underpants it up," Jesse instructed.

Rachel was focused on her phone.

"Please tell me you're not posting this?" Sunny said, wringing out her hair.

"No, I'm enjoying Geraldine's latest update. There's a photograph of a Bloody Mary in a lobster-shaped glass. She's in Nantucket, apparently. On a restaurant deck overlooking the ocean, to be precise."

Jesse whistled. "Well done."

"She used to visit there with Peter, didn't she?" Rachel said.

"I think so," Sunny said. "But Geraldine and I talked about Peter at that meditation thing she took me to. She didn't seem that interested—she was way more into Sylvie and Marina. My money's on it being a girls' weekend."

"Maybe." Rachel gave a weary sigh. "We're definitely not her girls anymore." She rested her phone on her lap and watched her daughter ride Jesse's shoulders. "Somebody needs her nap. I'll take her in. Why don't you guys go eat something delicious?"

Jesse motored through the water and delivered Cleo to her mother, then turned to Sunny. "You hungry?" His lips were red and perfectly defined, like the bottom of a toy boat. There was no way she could be alone with him. Besides, she had work to do—she was supposed to be illustrating an essay on Japanese bathhouses that she still hadn't read all the way through, for a Russian-funded luxury magazine. And she'd also promised herself she would come up with a few ideas for a fall project, something to make up for the *Cassette* checks she could no longer count on. But Rachel was watching, and Sunny feared that her friend could detect the way her synapses were firing in proximity to her brother. So Sunny just said, "I'm starving," and suggested she take Jesse to a place called Gino's. "They have delicious fish tacos." She looked up at the house to find Doug peering down on them through a window and was relieved to see his mouth moving, which meant that he was still on his phone call and she didn't have to do more than wave good-bye.

You're a fine driver," Jesse said, trailing his hand out the open window.

"I never said I wasn't." Sunny switched lanes and turned off the miniature highway in one uninterrupted swoosh. "I grew up in the suburbs." She loved weekday driving in the country, with its nonexistent traffic and the sense, however false, that everybody she passed was a local and not a fellow jerk from the city.

They were heading north, toward Orient Point, where the beach was rocky and never too crowded and where she liked to bring books to read over a single afternoon. It was undeniably lovely out here, and it became more so with every year. Most of the people Sunny knew who had children stayed for entire months, if not the whole summer. This all still felt slightly unnatural to her. Where Sunny grew up, second homes were cottages, not vast estates, and were never flaunted. Her family was one of the better-off ones she knew; her mother made a decent living in human resources at a financial-planning firm, and her father was vice president of a consumer goods company that had an enormous piece of the antibacterial bathroom-soap market. Displays of wealth were not something her household condoned, though; they ate frozen President's Choice pizza and still shared the family cottage with the rest of the MacLeod clan. Her parents started taking exotic trips once the children were out of the house. Sunny didn't grow up wanting for anything, though she certainly hadn't been spoiled. It wasn't until she was out of school that her father slipped her a not-insignificant check—or "water wings," as he'd called it—to help her get started out. An additional infusion came several years later, when she moved to New York.

When Sunny and Nick purchased the house on Long Island, she had mollified her conscience by stating that she planned on renting it out on VRBO. It would pay for itself. She wasn't rich. At least she didn't feel rich. So she'd tricked out the place with British shelter magazines and stocked the fridge with local sparkling wines, in hopes of earning five-star reviews. The inquiries about availability had started immediately. But when the second set of guests had called hourly with questions about hot water and which towels were to be used where and then left the house smelling of warm buttermilk, she'd admitted that the enterprise had proved more trouble than she could tolerate. She'd given in to just being one of the haves.

Sunny was dismayed to find the parking lot outside Gino's nearly full. The private waterfront lunch she'd been envisioning was now more likely lukewarm tacos eaten from take-out boxes. She slipped into the spot nearest the dumpster, and they entered the restaurant through the screened back door. There wasn't an empty seat in the house, and a few people were waiting by the front door. Jesse approached the waitress, and a moment later he motioned to Sunny to follow him to a two-top by the window.

"What did you say to her?" Sunny asked as she settled into her seat.

Jesse feigned confusion. "I just asked for a table." He gave her a smile that made her cheeks go hot. She ordered for them both—steamed mussels and fish tacos and fresh rainbow slaw and a basket of fries.

Jesse ate voraciously, nearly wordlessly, slowing down only after two of his tacos had disappeared. "What's next?" he asked.

"We should go to the fish store," she said. "Nick can grill dinner."

"Not what I meant. What's next for you?"

Sunny straightened her back. "I don't follow."

"Where do you see yourself in the future, a little further down the line?"

"I'm not really good at strategizing."

"I respectfully disagree," Jesse said. "You seem to have a distinct talent for figuring shit out. What are you doing in five years?"

"Hopefully I'll still be making art."

Jesse planted his forearms on the table and leaned forward. "And what about the other stuff? Any collaborations with Nick?"

Sunny laughed when his intention clicked. "You mean am I going to have a baby?"

Jesse nodded and fed himself a handful of fries. "I see you playing with Cleo. You'd be good at it. My mom was really into crafting, before it was considered cool. She used to bring home art supplies from school. I remember one Easter we made chickens out of pipe cleaners and pom-poms that ended up big enough to ride on. We put them in the front windows."

Sunny wasn't totally following. "Is this something you think about for yourself, having children?"

"There's still a lot of bourbon to be drunk and books to be read, ideally simultaneously." Jesse shrugged. "But sure, it's something I might be talked into one day."

Sunny could sense her throat closing in, and she waved at the waitress. "Can we have two glasses of rosé?"

She realized she must have eaten next to nothing; she was feeling the wine's effects before she'd finished her glass. Jesse drained his like water and drove them back to a quiet house. Once they were inside, Sunny looked at her watch. Half past three. Nick was still hours away. She remained in the kitchen while Jesse checked the bedroom upstairs that had been assigned to Rachel and Cleo.

"They're fast asleep," he reported when he returned.

Jesse stepped closer, and Sunny was sure she could hear her heart beat in double time. A deviousness radiated from Jesse's eyes as he removed the sunglasses from her grasp and took her tiny wrist in his hand. The light outside was remorseless and stark, but this space that they shared glowed. Sunny saw tiny wrinkles around Jesse's eyes that she'd never noticed before. An unfathomable stillness followed. Then Jesse placed his hand on the small of Sunny's back and leaned in so close she could catch the scent of his deodorant. Rum and sunshine. He brought his forehead to touch hers.

"I should . . ." Sunny struggled to find words. "Nick is going to be here soon."

"Right." Jesse's touch lingered, and Sunny dug the heels of her hands into the kitchen counter to steady her body. He cupped her cheek in his palm, and a heat rose up from within as he kissed her, and kissed her some more.

# 22

Geraldine adjusted her headphones. They were German noise-canceling earmuffs, and the leather was so new it made her ears itch. She closed her eyes and focused on the clip. Art Gumbel was sparring with Quentin Tarantino on *That's Entertainment!*, Art's dishy podcast about the film industry. Geraldine had heard this bit twice before, once while meandering through Gourmet Garage selecting yogurts and, more recently, when she and Sylvie were preparing for today's interview with Art. He had kindly agreed to be one of the pioneer Pod People.

Art had recently dared to show up on the set of Quentin Tarantino's new film, a manga adaptation, and tell the director he thought Japanese comics were overrated. Tarantino had launched into an evaluation of his interviewer's "melon-ball" intellect. The director had done his homework—Art made a living as the head writer of an esoteric Netflix cartoon about a high-strung watermelon who worked as a nursery-school crossing guard and was in several kinds of recovery.

"Zing!" Sylvie gave a hyena laugh. "I could listen to that a million times."

Art took a sip from his water bottle and shot Geraldine a smile through the recording booth's window. "Can we not?" Art appeared to be blushing.

"I don't know what I would have done if that were me," Sylvie said. "I legit think I would have cried."

Art wiped his eyes and shook his head. "You noticed I didn't disagree with him," he said. "I peaked at eighteen, no question. If I ran into my old self, I think I'd be intimidated."

Geraldine felt an easing in her chest. Art was playing ball. He got it. Even though the concept of her show was that young Sylvie, an aspiring podcaster, seeks the advice of the best in the business, the episodes came to life in the digressions. Geraldine often figured into these moments. In addition to producing the show, she played a character on air, the producer who interrupted Sylvie to supposedly steer her questions on track, only to further derail the conversation with commentary and musings. On tape Geraldine was an exaggerated version of herself, all floaty thoughts and heavy heart.

Folding in the Canadian sidekick had been Sylvie's idea, and Geraldine had to admit it was brilliant—and certainly more fun than any of her previous jobs. She excelled at lunching with potential guests and watering the social-media garden. It was the recording sessions, though, that she relished. There was none of the skim milk of chitchat. Instead she asked strangers their thoughts on important issues: Do You Believe in Love? What Is Friendship? Where Do You Stand on the Life Span of Shower Curtains?

The numbers were showing promise—the "engagement metrics"

especially, whatever that meant. Ffife Media, their distributor, had just offered to record an additional ten episodes. Geraldine was also working on a memo for Elinda, who was gung ho on revamping all of Ffife's digital offerings. Elinda was waiting for Geraldine to name her "consulting fee" so she could receive compensation for her opinions on newsletters and premium content. Feeling steadier than she had in some time, Geraldine had resumed her apartment search and had found a one-bedroom to sublet on the Lower East Side. It belonged to an NYU undergrad Sylvie used to babysit in high school who was about to go study rhetoric in Barcelona for the semester.

"Why do you say you peaked at eighteen?" Sylvie asked Art. "What were you doing then?"

"I took a gap year," Art said.

"A what?" Sylvie let off a guffaw. She was a big laugher to begin with, and when they were recording, her laughs came even easier.

"It's a year between high school and university," Geraldine piped in. "They're big in Canada."

"I love how she says 'university,'" Sylvie teased her sidekick. "Ger Bear keeps it classy around here. All right, Artie, you were saying, your gap year?"

"Right," Art said. "I got an internship at my father's friend's animation studio. He didn't give a fuck what I did. I went in once a week. The rest of the time, I stayed home and watched movies."

"Sounds profoundly educational," Sylvie said.

"It was. I wrote down the dialogue of everything I loved and could remember whole scenes. I was a walking party trick. Now I can't remember my phone number."

"I still haven't learned mine," Geraldine said. "But it's still kind of new. . . ."

"I'd say you're doing pretty well for yourself, Art," Sylvie said. "I saw someone wearing a T-shirt with your face on it the other day."

"It was probably a *Riverdale* shirt," Art said. "Archie is my celebrity lookalike."

"If I weren't gay, I'd do Archie," Sylvie said. "Not to make you feel objectified!"

The two kept at it for the next twenty minutes, occasionally landing on clips from Art's podcast and mostly moving out into conversational corkscrews. Sylvie managed to get Art to tell her about a fender bender he'd gotten into in Echo Park following an interview with John Travolta. "I've never been so paranoid in my life," he said. "Every time I saw a dude in sunglasses driving a car behind me, I was sure the Scientologists were trailing me. I had a panic attack on the highway, and I signed up for tae kwon do classes the next day."

"Oh, my God, that reminds me," Sylvie said. "My doctor told me I need a hobby."

"This doesn't count?" Art said, gesturing at the recording equipment.

"This is an important professional endeavor," Sylvie proclaimed. "He said it has to be something meditative. My doctor's really into beekeeping. I bet Geraldine has some good hobbies." Sylvie and Art looked through the window.

"I'd like to learn to sing," Geraldine said without thinking.

"In a band?" Sylvie said.

"At a piano bar," Geraldine admitted. "Not that I can carry a tune. A few years ago, I got really into touch typing."

"What the . . . ?" Sylvie said.

"It's strangely addictive." Geraldine laughed. "At least it is when your wedding has been called off and you need something to obsess over." She watched Sylvie break out into laughter and felt a warmth spreading within. She couldn't believe what she'd just said. She'd tried therapy a few years ago, with a compassionate man on St. Clair East, but she'd found the exercise of marinating in her own sadness so dreary. Ffife Media's recording studio, with its foam walls and mini fridge stocked with mini Poland Spring bottles, was far more curative.

"Is touch typing the remedy for a broken heart?" Sylvie asked.

"No. But learning that he's not completely over me was more helpful," Geraldine offered, her goofy tone the vocal equivalent of jazz hands. She needed to make it clear that she wasn't being completely sincere. It occurred to her that Peter might listen to the show or that somebody he knew might alert him to it, but what difference would that make? He'd already beaten her in the public-humiliation department. And what she was doing was healthy, using humor and perspective to insert a wedge between Peter and herself.

Their weekend in Nantucket had been more fun than she cared to admit. Peter had held true to his promise not to get heavy, so they just ate kettle chips on the beach and fooled around in the dark. It had been surprisingly airy. No deep talks about what had gone wrong four years ago, no tears. The problem was the funny feeling that lingered. When things went unsaid, Geraldine was learning, that didn't make them not exist.

While Sylvie and Art discussed his fondness for the paper hats on servers at old-school Hollywood delis, Geraldine glanced over at the assistant producer, Janelle, who was at the mixing board. She shot Geraldine a thumbs-up. They had enough material and could call it a day.

Since Art was Geraldine's friend, it fell to her to walk him to the elevator. "Thanks again for doing this," she said. "Now that we've got you on board, nobody's going to turn Sylvie down."

"Why would they?" Art replied. "You're hilarious in there, the two of you. It's like hanging out with the millennial Odd Couple."

"Except I'm barely a millennial," Geraldine said. "I've been thinking of myself as the Harry to her Sally."

Art just studied her face. "What you said in there, was that true? You got stood up at the altar?"

"Not literally." Geraldine gritted her teeth. "He called it off three weeks before. Or he made me call it off, which was the right thing to do—in retrospect."

"One of my friends just canceled his wedding. He wasn't feeling it."

"Oh, I was feeling it. And he was feeling half of Toronto." Geraldine experienced a jolt of energy. "It's fine, really. I moved into my old friend Sunny's apartment. She came back up from New York to take care of me. I'd cry in the morning while she fed me toast with butter and marmalade. I still can't eat marmalade without getting sad. Other than that I survived."

Realizing they were stalling at the elevator bank, Geraldine finally pushed the button. "Hey," Art said, "if you're not doing anything on Saturday, I was going to go to the Quad. They're screening one of the great Polish films, *Knife in the Water*."

Geraldine was caught off guard and felt relieved when she remembered she had a conflict. "I'd love to, but I have this birthday party to go to. It's for an old frenemy." She surprised herself with this word. Usually she just called Rachel a friend. Was she using this other term to make it clear to Art that she would rather see somebody she didn't like than spend an evening in the dark with him? It wasn't that the idea repulsed her. But Art had been such a good friend. She didn't want to mess up things with him.

"Cool, I look forward to hearing about it," Art said. "Maybe next week?"

Geraldine squinted. Did he not get the hint? "I'm not— Oh!" she gasped. "You mean on the podcast."

"The show," he corrected her, as the doors closed in. "See ya, Sally."

"Harry," Geraldine muttered, and stood there until she could no longer hear the whoosh of the carriage.

# 23

Being the one who knew about things—or at least the one who wasted time finding out about things—Rachel usually set the agenda on her and Matt's rare grown-up outings. But today was her thirty-seventh birthday, and Matt had researched and plotted their adventure. Their secret schedule lived on a piece of graph paper that she'd watched Matt fold into quarters and stuff into the back pocket of his shorts.

The first activity of the day had been driving to Syosset to drop Cleo off at Matt's parents' house. They weren't due to pick up their daughter until the following morning. Rachel wasn't sure she had enough charm in her to last a single meal, let alone a full day, but she was determined to try.

Matt brought her to a restaurant in Chelsea. It was a vaguely Mediterranean place, with dusty rose and ocher walls that appeared wan in the bright sunshine. The host seemed to be expecting them and seated them at a table under a pink Lucite chandelier.

"Look familiar?" Matt asked. He leaned back, seeming proud. "I believe a seminal conversation took place at this table," he added. "A young man was trying to stop staring down his date's shirt and impress her with his Neil Young knowledge."

"Seriously?" Rachel grinned. Moon Kyoto, the popular Japanese restaurant they'd gone to on their first date, had mysteriously gone out of business when they showed up for their six-month anniversary. "How did I not realize that?"

"Do you think if we get two Sapporos in you, it will have the same effect as it once did?"

Rachel smiled at the memory. Back when she'd met Matt, her fantasies were about sex. Her dreams were now of stillness. Well, that and money. But weren't they the same thing? Their credit-card bills were piling up, and they needed to buy a twin bed and fall and winter clothes for Cleo. Rachel could use some new clothes herself. And their bathroom towels were getting thin. Rachel was haunted by an image of white-haired versions of Matt and herself in old age, sharing a can of tuna fish for dinner like a pair of doddering cats. She was a public-school kid and had managed her way through college on scholarships and loans before a decade of sharing apartments that might as well have been communes. Even when she and Matt moved in together, they lived in a two-bedroom Hell's Kitchen walk-up with an organic chemistry grad student from Puglia. He had the biggest crush on Geraldine, Rachel remembered with a spot of fondness.

"Do you ever hear from Tomasso?" Rachel asked. "Is he still around?"

"He's tenured in Düsseldorf," Matt said. "Why?"

"Never mind." Rachel sipped her beer. "How's everything been going in your lab?"

Matt cocked an eyebrow. "Why don't we talk about something you find remotely interesting? It's your birthday."

"Just because I don't entirely understand what you do doesn't mean I don't find it interesting."

Matt grinned, looked appeased. "My zebra fish are losing their minds. The imaging is confirming what we thought—there's definitely something going on in the parietal lobe. And in the meantime, Granola and Dr. Feingold are doing it."

Rachel nearly choked on her beer. "Granola" was their nickname for Magnolia, a scoliotic grad student with waist-length hair who had tried to foist herself upon Matt right before he and Rachel got married. "Isn't he, like, seventy?"

"Seventy-two. I overheard him call her 'luscious.'"

"That's horrible. He could get fired."

"And I could get fucked. You're only as good as your adviser's reputation."

Rachel's stomach lurched. It had been over a month since she had lost her own job, and she'd heard too many reports through the *Cassette* grapevine to bother looking for any sort of serious employment herself. All anyone had to do was Google her to see she was the mother of a young child and had written books with such impressive titles as *The Girl from Freak Street* and *Angie Stevens, 32A*. In the eyes of employers, she might as well be a registered sex offender, but one with work-life boundaries, which was worse. "You're not actually worried about losing your job, are you?" Rachel asked.

Matt gave a chagrined shake of the head. "No, but I should be looking around. Thank God she hasn't touched my research."

"I don't want that woman anywhere near your data."

Matt gave a crinkle-eyed smile. "Hey, I should probably tell you about this other thing that happened."

Rachel fixed her husband with a stern look. "What thing?"

"Nothing like that. Phillip is really into my last paper, and he wants me to lead a weekend intensive for his group . . . in Toronto." Her husband's former mentor, Phillip Lippman, had left his post at Columbia for a swankier department chairmanship that demanded zero teaching at the University of Toronto. "He said we can all come up as the university's guests."

Rachel let off a choke-laugh. "He's not trying to entice you up there, is he?"

"Babe, I think I can handle a weekend without signing on any dotted lines. And you'll come and enjoy a few nights in a hotel. We can leave Cleo with my parents if you like."

"But can't it be a city that isn't Toronto?" She gave him a quarter smile. "There are so many places we haven't been to yet."

"Don't think of it as a place, then. You can just lie in bed and watch movies."

Rachel suddenly saw the trio of waiters headed her way with a treat. The flame looked slightly ridiculous atop the dessert—birthday candles were the culinary equivalent of a feather boa. "Matcha cake?" she exclaimed when they placed the dish before her. "They serve this here?"

"Today they do," Matt said.

Rachel gazed up at her husband. So maybe she didn't want to devour him the way she had the last time they were here, but she wanted to keep him, wanted to take care of him. Marriage had turned out to be an ocean of terrifying and wonderful feelings. She'd only been in lakes before. Lakes and puddles.

"Make a wish," Matt told her, and she obliged.

They passed the next three hours doing very little, as exotic an activity as Matt could think of. It was a beautiful day, with a generous sun and a hint of green-apple scent in the air. After visiting a couple of galleries and the tiny bookshop that Rachel loved, they went up to the High Line, where they joined the stream of tourists walking hand in hand past the wildflowers and cordoned-off patches of grass. When they'd reached the southern end of the path, Matt glanced at his watch and pulled Rachel toward the stairway.

"Where are we going?" She was giggling with exhilaration as they clopped down to the street. "Do I need to change?" Her hair was a mess, and she could make out the smell of sweat rising off her sailor-striped dress.

"No, you're perfect," he promised.

Surprise!" the room chorused.

Rachel tried to feign disbelief as she and Matt walked into Jeremy's living room. A bunch of her mom friends had made it. So had Cassie Burkheim, as well as Alexandra Lustig, her college roommate with whom she was on the phoniest of terms after a massive falling-out they'd had over a guy in their early twenties. She spotted Sunny and Jesse over by the kitchen island, eating crudité kabobs.

"I can't believe you're all here!" Rachel offered the room, manufacturing the biggest smile she could. She accepted a drink from Jeremy and embarked on the process of dutifully kissing everybody hello. She was still buzzed on her and Matt's blissfully unproductive afternoon and wished she could be alone with him on this rare Cleo-free evening, not surrounded by people who would expect her to string words together in interesting combinations.

Rachel was in the middle of greeting Alexandra and also Claire, from her mothers' group, when Sunny joined them. Sunny was struggling to finish chewing something and pointed at her mouth. Geraldine darted over to them. "Happy birthday!" she said, taking Rachel in for a hug. Her hair was damp, and she smelled amazing, like Snapple iced tea mixed with cloves. "I'm so sorry I can't stay for dinner."

"That's okay," Rachel said, vaguely startled. "I didn't even know there was dinner until just now."

"I'm not sure it's *a* dinner," Sunny said. "I overheard Jesse and Jeremy discuss the pizza order."

"Well, that makes me feel better. I had pizza for lunch," Geraldine said in a skittish tone. She was eager to leave. Rachel stood motionless, the tension between Geraldine and herself palpable. She would have preferred it if they were in a fight.

"Let me introduce everybody to everybody before Geraldine disappears," Rachel said.

"I love that name," Alexandra said to Sunny. "And your dress." Rachel looked at Sunny's outfit—a boxy short-sleeved shirt and trousers—and realized Alexandra had been addressing Geraldine, who had on a smocklike garment with flared side pockets.

"It's great," Rachel agreed. The fabric's bold purple-and-yellow print reminded her of an expensive tablecloth. "Geraldine lives here with Jeremy," Rachel said to her friends, by way of explanation.

"That's almost over," Geraldine said. "I'm moving to the Lower East Side."

"You are?" Rachel could feel her eyes grow.

Geraldine nodded in a way that was livelier and more self-possessed than Rachel remembered her being capable of. "I'm actually headed there now. I need to meet the super. His name is Baz." She laughed.

"Stay for a few more minutes?" Sunny said.

"Yeah, don't go so fast," Rachel added. "How has the rest of your summer been?"

"It's been fun. I've been working on that podcast I told you about, which is finally coming togeth—"

"I just listened to it the other day," Rachel said. "You're practically the star of the show."

"I'm the tragicomic relief." Geraldine cocked her head.

"Don't sell yourself short," Rachel said. "That bit about not recognizing your father at the airport when he came up to you just about killed me." She watched Geraldine lower her eyelids. "Sorry, I'm not trying to upset you."

"No, it's fine." Geraldine wagged her head. "It's just weird to think about people I know listening, is all."

"How could we not?" Rachel said. "It's fantastic, totally addictive. And I get to keep up with you! You were out in Nantucket, right?" she asked Geraldine, innocently enough.

"I didn't talk about that, did I?"

Rachel felt her misstep. "I saw your Instagram."

Geraldine's lips curled in a sphinxlike smile. Rachel shot Sunny a desperate glance. Their Peter suspicion had just been confirmed. But Sunny maintained a blank expression while Geraldine was saying something about a Malia Obama sighting. God, Sunny was good at pretending.

"Were you with Peter?" Rachel's question cut Geraldine's soliloquy short.

Geraldine looked startled. "Yeah—I mean, I wasn't *with* him. We're not back together or anything."

"How's he doing?" Sunny said, her voice as level as if she were asking after a family pet. "I haven't seen him in so long." Rachel watched in horror as the two chatted about Peter's funny way of doing everything at the last minute and his new environmental foundation.

Geraldine sighed. "Okay, I really should get going," she said.

"Thanks for coming—or staying around to say hi," Rachel said lamely. If Geraldine wanted to pull away, what could she do?

"I brought you that salty caramel ice cream you like, so don't let Jeremy forget to put it out," Geraldine said.

Rachel shook her head as she watched Geraldine scurry out the door. "What the fuck?"

"She seems to be doing great," Sunny replied.

"Did we not just have the same conversation?" Rachel asked with blunt force. "She just said she's back with Peter, basically."

"Did she?" Sunny said. "It's what she wants. It's all she's ever wanted, isn't it?" Sunny dug her hands into her pockets and let off a barely detectable sigh. "I don't think we're giving Geraldine the credit she deserves. She's all grown up. And she knows what Peter is all about."

"So do you," Rachel said, shutting Sunny down. Within moments Sunny had shouldered her way across the room, where she and Jesse were now laughing about something on his phone.

Rachel glided a few steps over to Claire, Cassie, and Alexandra. They were talking about one of Alexandra's clients, something to do with taxi medallions. Geraldine's perfume lingered in the air. It had taken a turn for the less sweet. Rachel detected fig, maybe a bit of black pepper. She was determined to figure out what brand it was and hoped it wouldn't be weird if she bought a bottle for herself.

# 24

What's up with this bowl of old grapes?" Nick called from across the house. Last Sunny had seen him, he'd been seated in an armchair they usually reserved for movie watching. He'd been working something out on a legal pad.

"I don't know what's up with it," Sunny shot back. "Maybe it's going to check out that new AcroYoga studio later on."

"I always said you should get into cartoons," Nick called out.

Sunny finished tidying up the kitchen and gathered her phone, water bottle, and keys and tossed them into her bucket bag. "Okay, I'm going." She came over to kiss Nick good-bye. He still hadn't budged. "Good luck, with whatever that is." She gestured at his tornado of scribbles.

"And to you." Nick looked up at Sunny with incredulous eyes, the way he used to when they were falling for each other. He reached out to graze her knee with his hand. "You look beautiful, standing in front of the window like that."

Sunny glanced down. "Can you see through my dress?"

"No." Nick gave a heavy-lidded smile. "When will you be back?"

"Not too late." She made it as far as the doorway, then turned around and ran up the staircase. In her studio she found a small rectangle of paper and a silver Sharpie. She dashed off a picture of a man and a woman hugging and wrote "I love you" underneath. The message was lame, counterproductively so. She was trying to cover her steps, not underscore the lack of feeling she had for her husband. Only after adding a bunny did she feel satisfied enough to take the note into the master bedroom and tuck it under Nick's pillow. She was just going to be gone for the day, but Nick always napped after lunch when he was in the country. Her Jesse obsession had a strange effect on their marriage: It made her want to take better care of Nick.

"Bye!" she called out. "I'm really going."

Sunny was relieved not to see anybody she knew on the bus and curled into her seat with her hand gripped around her phone. She examined her to-do list, a mix of shows and books she'd heard about and tasks she needed to take care of. Among the latter was write to Peter. He'd emailed again, and she'd been putting off responding.

Dear Sunny, I'm organizing a fund-raiser concert at the Tarragon in early October. You're welcome to come. I was hoping to use one of your Lake Ontario images for the invitation. There's something else I'd like to run by you, on the phone. Are you up for a call? Anytime this week should work. xP

The email had come in four days ago, and Sunny knew she should just address it before it blew up.

> Hi, Peter! Sorry for the delay, things have been slightly nuttier than ever. I'm flattered you asked, and you're welcome to use my work. I've been out of the city, but I'll send you some high-res options when I'm back at my desk next week. Is that enough time? xxxS

Sunny reread her composition, feeling hamstrung about how to address the important part. His request for a call had to be about Geraldine, and she didn't see why she had to become involved. I can ring you tonight, she added. Peter was a stubborn guy, and if he was determined not to leave Geraldine alone, there was nothing Sunny could do about it. Honestly, the only reason Sunny would say anything at all would be to appease Rachel, who was beginning to drive Sunny crazy with all her inquiries. Rachel's obsession with keeping Geraldine away from Peter was getting weird. It wasn't as if Rachel and Geraldine were terribly close these days. Why did she have to make Sunny feel as though she were eternally in trouble? Sunny looked out the window and saw the blocky towers of LeFrak City. The realization that the jitney was already in the city filled her with a tingly energy. She pulled her knees into her chest and twisted her hair around her fingers.

Half an hour later, she showed up on the block where she was supposed to be meeting her former *Cassette* editor. Miriam had reached out about her new start-up and wanted to see if Sunny might be interested in coming on board in some capacity. Miriam was already waiting outside the Le Pain Quotidien in Chelsea, waving at Sunny with a doggish enthusiasm. She had on a horseshoe-print wrap dress that belonged inside an office. Her only concession to her unemployed status was a pair of clogs.

"Liberation suits you," Sunny lied.

"Do you want to go inside? Or we could sit in the park?" Miriam said.

"Do you mind if we go in?" Sunny said. "It's so hot."

The notion of taking a business meeting on a park bench depressed her. Besides, she liked having the emergency exit of a waiter to signal to for a check. If this meeting could last only five minutes, that would be perfect. Sunny had booked a seat on the 4:40 bus back.

Their waiter was an older man who appeared overwhelmed by his job. They told him what they wanted, then spent the next fifteen minutes talking about the perils of online shopping and Ceri's Facebook suicide and all the money Ffife was pouring into its new podcasting arm and Sunny's rediscovery of Elizabeth Bishop—everything but Miriam's new project. This was part of the game, pretending to be close friends who would be having this coffee in the middle of the workweek even if Miriam didn't have commissioning power.

"So before I forget to tell you, it's a newsletter," Miriam said when their avocado toasts arrived.

"What is?" Sunny feigned confusion.

"The thing I'm working on." Miriam salted her food. "It's going to be smart writing for feminists who aren't, you know, babies. And it's not about babies either. It's about style and life—but not lifestyle, because that is so tired. Just substantial, honest takes on the things smart women like us care about. What publication can you think of that does that?" Sunny was rendered silent. "I'm thinking of calling it

*The Moment*," Miriam went on. "It's a play on the word that everyone in magazines uses when something is cool."

"Like roller-skating is having a moment or boleros are having a moment?" Sunny said.

"Exactly. And it's also a euphemism."

"For hot flashes?" Sunny was joking, but Miriam simply nodded. "Don't people hit menopause in their late forties?" Sunny asked.

"Perimenopause starts about ten years before." Miriam pushed her glasses up the bridge of her nose. "It's not a menopause magazine. Think of it more like something for all the women who are exiting their fertility windows."

Sunny could feel the sweat collecting under her arms. She willed herself to calm down. Work is work. Connections are connections. "Who's backing it?"

"It's not like that," Miriam answered. "It's going to be a grassroots effort—all you need is an email account to blast these things off. But if I have the right names involved, I think it can attract attention and go places. Think of all the companies who'd kill to spend ad dollars to reach women like you and me. Well . . . women like you."

Sunny balled up her napkin under the table and glanced around the room until she spotted their waiter. He was far away, crouched over a computer in a posture that suggested lower back pain. Sunny wondered what he used to do for a living.

"So?" Miriam said brightly. "Would you be up for contributing?"

"Sure!" Sunny bluffed. "I'll think of something that will be good."

"Honestly, you can draw a turd on a napkin. I really don't care." Miriam's eyes registered Sunny's offense. "I mean, it can be anything so long as it's coming from you."

Sunny caught the waiter's eye and found slight relief in the knowledge that she would never have to see Miriam again.

Mtg done. See you soon, was all she texted Jesse from the cab, imagining Nick reading over her shoulder. Her texts came up on her iPad, and Jesse was mindful of this, too.

She wasn't even sure she wanted to be near him. Making out was the last thing she felt like doing. Jesse was thirty-four, and though they'd never talked about it, she was certain that postadolescent, nowhere-near-menopausal nymphs littered his romantic past—maybe even his present.

Kk, he wrote back. Will show u the bindings.

What were they going to do when their project wrapped up and they had no excuse to see each other? Come up with some other pseudocollaboration? Maybe she could do an apprenticeship in the workshop, then turn it into a comic. Sunny fiddled with her seat belt and gazed out the window.

By the time her car eased up outside Jesse's studio, she'd pulled herself together. Jesse's studiomates, used to her coming by, waved hello. She walked faster than usual across the cement floor and ran down the ramp to Jesse's shop. He had on a blue face mask, and he was using a tremendously loud belt sander to smooth a strip of white oak. It took him a moment to notice she was watching from the doorway. He turned the machine off, and the silence that followed felt piercing. He came up to kiss her but stopped when he read her face. "You okay?"

"I'm fine. I don't want to talk about it." Sunny leaned up against him and let him wrap her in his arms. She let off a satisfying exhale and looked up into his eyes. The whites were so bright. They reminded her of the keys on the piano she'd practiced scales on as a girl. "I'm starting to feel better," she told him.

"Good." Jesse bit his lip and sighed.

"What?" she asked.

Jesse took her hand and pulled it to his chest. "I can't stop thinking about you. It's fucking scary."

"Oh," Sunny said stupidly, and stood motionless. On the one hand, she was so happy. On the other, she was terrified. This could all turn catastrophic. Maybe it already had.

"You're a terrible liar. You're not feeling better." Jesse said. "Let's go get you sorted out."

Cisco's was a dump, one level removed from a motorcycle bar, and it was impressively crowded for this early on a Wednesday afternoon. Sunny waited on a bench in the back of the room while Jesse got their drinks. He came over with two bottles of Budweiser and a pair of shot glasses filled with clear liquid.

"They were out of rosé," he said to Sunny. She rolled her eyes and gulped from the glass. She shivered at the toxic taste and took a swig of beer. "There you go," Jesse said. He sat next to her, close. "So what happened?"

She relaxed and told Jesse everything about her morning—leaving out only the menopause.

"Sounds like a real opportunity," he said. "Drawing turds on napkins, for free."

Sunny leaned back against the wall. "I guess I had a good run."

"It's not over," he said. "You just have to evolve."

She frowned. "Didn't Trump just outlaw the word 'evolu—'" Sunny suddenly stopped speaking. Geraldine came through the door. The figure was far away and in silhouette against the daylight pouring through from behind, but it was unquestionably Geraldine. A guy stood next to her, and when Sunny's eyes adjusted to the light, she noticed he was cute, and with a strong jaw. The pair hovered by the jukebox and consulted with each other, their body language fluttery and nervous. Sunny shielded her face with her beer bottle.

"What?" Jesse asked.

"Geraldine's here," Sunny said, sinking lower in her seat. "Don't look."

"Are you sure that's her?"

"Yes, totally," Sunny said in a low voice. "Is there a back exit?"

"She didn't see anything scandalous. We're working together and grabbing a beer," Jesse reminded her. "She's heading our way," he said in an undertone. He rose to his feet and gave Geraldine a hug. Sunny copied him, pretending to be surprised.

"What the heck are you guys doing here?" Geraldine asked. "I thought you were on Long Island."

"In town for the day," Sunny said quickly.

"My shop is nearby," Jesse said.

"We're collaborating," Sunny clarified. "What brings you to Red Hook?"

"My friend and I were taking a walk," Geraldine said, pointing toward the entrance. Sunny narrowed her eyes, pretending to be having difficulty fishing out the tall, boyish guy among the day drinkers on their barstools. Geraldine must have read the awkwardness in her face. Instead of motioning for her friend to join them, she said, "I should probably get back to him."

Geraldine crossed the room and said something to her companion that made him put his hand on her back and plant a kiss on the crown of her head. Sunny was fascinated by this version of Geraldine, the one who kept a lover in every port. Sunny's sense of disorientation gave way to one of relief. Peter wasn't going to destroy Geraldine. If anything, Geraldine might bring ruin on him.

There was no need to call Peter, no wolf to defang. She wished she could call Rachel and explain what she'd witnessed, but the Jesse factor made that impossible. Sunny lifted her beer to the back of her neck. Her skin prickled at the cold, and she let off a slow exhale. It was the first time she'd felt anything close to pleasure all day. She scooted a couple of inches closer to Jesse and leaned into his golden, solid body.

# 25

There's something I think we all want to know. What's your secret?" Linette Alvarez widened her eyes and pursed her lips around the straw jutting from her cup. She was drinking a supersized passion-fruit iced tea that she'd requested in the green room, requiring one of the Brooklyn Ideas Festival volunteers to bike a mile to the nearest Starbucks.

"You're looking at her." Sylvie pointed at Geraldine, who was seated in the swan chair next to her. "Geraldine Despont is my magic canoodles."

Most of the questions were for Sylvie, so Geraldine had little to do but adjust the cross of her legs and follow their chatter, interrupting every so often in order to earn her spot on the stage and not seem as nervous as she was. As an interviewer, Linette was pleasant enough, with intelligent eyes and one of those oversmoked voices that had helped her secure a place at the top of the ranks of American public radio. Their conversation would air on Linette's nationally syndicated NPR program the following week. Geraldine tried not to think about this.

"Allow me to rephrase," Linette said. "I know why *I* enjoy listening to you, but I'm curious to hear your thoughts about your unique appeal. You broke the top ten on iTunes last week—no easy feat." Geraldine's neck warmed as the audience applauded, and Linette resumed speaking before the clapping died down. "Take your most recent episode, for example. You interviewed Petra McGill, of Shits and Giggles. I don't care about celebrity gossip, but I couldn't stop listening to your conversation. How do you do that?"

Geraldine surveyed the crowd. Two hundred fifty tickets sold, according to the festival president. The cheap seats blended into the shadows, and there were too many rows to count. It sort of scared her.

"I don't know," Sylvie said. "Talking. That's the thing, right?"

"The thing." Linette knit her brow.

Geraldine glanced down at the microphone pinned to her blouse. "It's the medium that people love," she said. "We all crave intimacy, and podcasting provides that. When Petra came on, she got into her anxiety disorder. The way she described what happens to her when she has a panic attack—I could slip into her skin and feel one coming on myself." Geraldine paused as she gathered her thoughts. "The human voice is extraordinary."

"Some people might say it's the most ordinary thing ever," Linette countered, with the ease of somebody who'd spent the last three decades playing devil's advocate on issues from modest fashion to gun control.

"No, it's not," Geraldine said. "Conversation has become so rare. Not contrived conversation, where the three of us are on a stage in

Gowanus pretending to have a natural exchange in front of hundreds of paying strangers, but real . . . you know, conversation." This basic conviction, that what people really wanted from their media these days wasn't to feel smarter or more informed but simply to connect, had been the cornerstone of her memo for Elinda. It had been what had inspired Elinda to create a new job for Geraldine, overseeing the revamp of Ffife Media's "third layer," which is what they'd agreed to call materials that did not live on a printed page.

"Some very sexy paying Brooklyn strangers," Sylvie added, earning a round of cheers.

"They certainly brought their A-game," Linette said, elbowing in on Sylvie's banter. "But seriously, there is such a thing as the art of an interview. There's a balance one has to strike between spontaneity and purposefulness. When you sit down with someone, be it a life hacker or a manic-depressive comedian, what is it that you're going after?"

"It's simple," Geraldine said. "I just want to connect." Linette glanced down at the notes in her lap.

"And I fear we're not one hundred percent succeeding on that front with you," Sylvie added with a laugh.

Linette looked startled, then gathered her composure. "That is something I've noticed you two do a lot—unpack a conversation while it's happening."

"And you want to unpack that? Okay." Sylvie shrugged. "I have no experience doing interviews. I've worked in city politics, and I did nude modeling in college. Geraldine has more experience in the bigger sense—"

"By which she means I'm eons older," Geraldine butted in.

"And wiser." Sylvie said to her partner, and turned to Linette.

"There's this thing she does, which you may have noticed. She seems like she's playing for laughs, but she's actually—"

"Taking risks," Linette filled in. "I can definitely hear that. There is an authenticity to your contributions that is shocking, Geraldine," Linette said.

"The new shock jock is a polite Canadian," Sylvie said to the crowd. "Don't you love it? In Trump's America civility and honesty are revolutionary and heroes are from Manitoba."

"I'm actually from Toronto," Geraldine said.

"Toronto, Manitoba, and all of you who came to Gowanus," Linette said, glancing at her wristwatch. "Let's hear it for Sylvie Benghal and Geraldine Despont, extraordinarily talented host and producer of *Pod People.*"

After the talk a festival assistant led Linette and her guests to a pair of tables in a back room with a skylight and ivy-covered walls. "You can sign your books here," he told them.

"Oh, shit—were we supposed to write one?" Sylvie asked playfully.

"We don't have any merch," Geraldine told him.

"I'm just following protocol," he said twitchily.

"The people want you." Linette gestured at the crowd queuing up in two lines. The meatier cluster, Geraldine realized as she took her seat, was for the Pod People. They were mostly interested in talking to Sylvie, but a couple of them walked up to Geraldine, who gamely answered questions about distribution channels and posed for selfies. A white-haired man who had his arm in a sling simply wanted to tell her that he grew up in Ottawa and had been a Beaver Scout. Another, dressed in all black and platform boots, wanted to take her to task for something she'd said a few weeks ago, about how she hated horror movies. "Watch this and then see if you still stand by that," he said, pressing a DVD into her hand. She expected it to be a film he'd made and was trying to promote, and she was heartened to see it was *Diabolique.* Sylvie, who'd been watching the entire interaction, turned to Geraldine when the guy meandered away. "I wouldn't even know how to watch a DVD if my life depended on it," she said. "Thank goddess for all my older women."

Nobody else came to take the man's place, so Geraldine pulled her phone out of her bag. Peter had texted: hi. His persistence was impressive, Geraldine had to give him that. Peter was in Scotland, attending a film festival. He was thinking about making a documentary on a New Brunswick farmer who was obsessed with the nation's endangered microbats. Geraldine and Peter had been in regular touch. He was working on her to come up to Toronto for his fundraiser. She wasn't sure, she kept telling him. She wasn't even sure she wanted to see him again, she kept telling herself.

She was dating, for the first time in her life. She'd gone out with John, a book critic whose big shaved head she found both repulsive and weirdly sexy. And there was Duncan, a tenants'-rights lawyer who wore secondhand blazers that smelled of her grandfather's tobacco. And she and Art had been hanging out, a lot. His conversation had the most vitamins. Plus, he was a gentle and talented kisser. It was all fun in theory, fun in the moment, too. Yet summer had nearly passed, and she worried about how much longer this three-ring circus could go on.

"Which one of you is the one who killed her pet turtle?" came a voice. Geraldine looked up and bit back a smile when she saw it was Art. They hadn't seen each other in a little while, but with the exception of Wednesday they'd spoken every night this week. Two nights ago she'd fallen asleep with his voice in her ear.

"Art School!" Sylvie exclaimed.

"You didn't tell me you were coming," Geraldine said.

"You guys were really good," Art said.

"Please tell me you didn't buy a ticket," Geraldine said.

Art didn't answer. "You smoked out the competition."

"I'm not sure I believe you, but thank you," Geraldine said. "I'm not used to these things." She looked through the arched doorway into the main space. The projection over the stage said that the next event was a conversation on technology and voter suppression. A girl who wore her hair in Pippi Longstocking braids bounded over to breathlessly profess out-of-control fandom to Art. "Let me take a picture of you two," Geraldine offered. Looking at Art through the iPhone viewfinder, Geraldine felt her heart quicken. She wasn't proud of herself for feeling this way, but it turned her on to see him through Pippi's eyes.

Ten minutes later Geraldine and Art were winding down a desolate stretch of Nevins Street in search of a place to get drinks. "I feel bad I didn't say good-bye to Linette," Geraldine said. "I should send her a text."

It wasn't until she'd composed her message that she realized she didn't have Linette's number. She closed the window and noticed that a photo was attached to Peter's text from earlier. It was a cluster of women who appeared to be ninety years old drinking pints at an outdoor pub. "I think this is what Sylvie means when she says 'hashtag goals,'" she muttered, and turned the phone to Art.

"What's that?" he asked, and she regretted showing it to him.

"No idea. My ex is in Glasgow and sent it."

"That Peter guy? He's texting you?" Something inside Art appeared to go inert.

Geraldine grabbed the phone and mumbled a few words about how she and Peter were on friendly terms now. She remembered some of the things she'd told Sylvie on tape and felt pinpricks of shame. No matter what she was wearing, Peter used to ask her to brush her hair and change into a cardigan when they visited his parents. He berated her while cleaning up after dinner parties for her proclivity of being too honest in group conversations. Art had heard all about it, along with thousands of other listeners.

"Moving on is dangerous," Art said. "That's when we swoop back in."

"He sent me a picture of an old lady, not a sext," Geraldine said, frustration flattening her voice. Art wouldn't dignify her with an answer. She was glad when they came across a restaurant, a self-consciously chic New American spot on an otherwise unhappening block. A few groups eating early dinner took up the tables in the front of the restaurant. Geraldine and Art settled at the bar and ordered a couple of Cokes. She wished she could erase the last five minutes, wipe out the weirdness setting in between them.

"So I might be going to L.A. soon," Art said, in what she couldn't help suspecting was an attempt at retaliation for her daring to be in touch with Peter.

She raised her chin. "To visit your family?"

"It's a work thing. Someone wants to produce a live-action movie of *Furious Curious*, and they're making noises about me directing it." Art folded his hands together on the bar. "Actually, I'm the one who's making noises about directing it."

Geraldine forced a smile. She had no claim on him. "That would be huge," she told him. "This would be your first film?"

"Yeah . . ." Art trailed off. "So I'll be out there till February."

"It's happening for sure?" She took a sip of her drink and felt a wave of sadness.

"Nothing's signed yet, but it's looking very likely." They were silent for a moment. "I didn't realize he was back in the picture," Art finally said. "He hurt you. You know that, right?"

"That was a long time ago. We're just friends."

"Uh-huh," Art said.

Geraldine fiddled with the corners of a cocktail napkin and felt a stirring of indignation. Why was everyone convinced that cutting off Peter was the only answer? Her mother had done that to her father, more or less, and look where it had gotten her.

"People don't change," Art said at last.

"Isn't that a bit reductive?" Geraldine asked. "What's the point of being alive if you can't change? I've changed!"

"People grow. That's different. But once an asshat, always an asshat."

Geraldine frowned. "Are we British now?"

Art's cheeks went pink. "I was really into Monty Python in high school."

Geraldine laughed in spite of herself. Who was this guy? Why couldn't she fall in love with him? Or send him on his way and let him make some other woman happy? The only friend of hers who knew Art was Sylvie. They'd all hung out a couple of times. Sylvie was a huge fan of Art's, but she was a lesbian and loved him in the way you love people you're happy to run into on the street.

Art was now murmuring in a strange accent about land and cows. "What's the deal?" Geraldine said. "If we keep hanging out, is there a saturation point where you will cease to get weirder and weirder?"

"Depends how you feel about prog rock." Art reached across the bar and helped himself to an olive from the garnish basin. Geraldine was about to ask for one when he deposited a green sphere on the cocktail napkin in front of her. "You're welcome."

She inserted the olive into her mouth and glanced at Art. She wondered what she would make of her companion were she not straining to look out at him from under the fog of Peter.

# 26

Rachel tossed a bowl of romaine with lemon-dill dressing and finished the salad with a handful of sprouted sunflower seeds, the super-salty kind that Cleo liked. Jesse, her supposed cohost, remained in the next room with their parents. Joseph and Phyllis Ziff were talking about Rachel's Uncle Roger, who'd just undergone bariatric surgery.

Joseph could no longer hear very well in restaurants, which was a shame considering how much time he still spent on Chowhound. Rachel had offered to cook his birthday dinner. She wasn't going to suggest that her parents host their own party. The one time she'd been to her brother's apartment, for his housewarming, there'd been nowhere to sit, just a card table groaning with beer bottles and girls slung all over the place.

Rachel came out of the kitchen and circled the table, depositing salad on everyone's plate. She pinched a couple of extra avocado cubes out of the serving bowl and dropped them on Cleo's high-chair tray. "You serve with your fingers?" her father chided. "No wonder the girl sucks her thumb."

"I'm not sure I see the connection, Dad," Rachel said. "Or why it bothers you. Her dentist said not to worry about it until she's four."

"You're lucky you're such a cutie patootie," Joe said to his granddaughter. "You're going to end up looking like a walrus. And your mama's going to have to shell out some big bucks for your braces."

"Have some salad, Joseph," Phyllis said. "The dill is wonderful."

"Don't mind your grandfather," Rachel told Cleo in mock exasperation. "And, Dad, you know how sexist you sound, right?"

"And I was about to ask you if you baked me a cake."

"Just roast chicken, olive orzo, and hors d'oeuvres." Rachel rolled her eyes. Truth was, she felt comfortably happy in a way she did only when she was with her family. No matter that her father was now sixty-eight, it was just like old times.

The pistachio-lemon cake was delicious, and they ate in near silence. "All right, tell Matt we say hello," Joe said, pushing his empty plate away. "Mom and I should get going." They had tickets to a South African dance concert at the Brooklyn Academy of Music.

"Matt sends his love," Rachel said. "He's sorry he couldn't be here. I told him to bring back those Nanaimo bars you love." Her husband was in Toronto, visiting Phillip Lippman for a second time. Phillip's department was trying to persuade him to take a fellowship for the spring. He'd assured Rachel that he was only going up there to tell Phillip no in person. She wasn't worried. But he wasn't home either.

After she'd said good-bye to her parents for the thousandth time, Rachel peeked into Cleo's bedroom. Jesse was reading a book about a dog birthday party, and Cleo had already begun to assume child's pose on top of her sheets.

Rachel started to clear the dishes, then wandered over to the window. The last light of the day blanketed the block, casting gothic shadows on the sidewalk. She wondered when their rent would go up again and what she and Matt would do when it did. Maybe her novel would work out. Rachel had told Josie that it would be ready before she could actually have it ready, and she was killing herself to deliver it when she'd promised, out of fear that her agent would lose interest in seeing it before she could truly deliver. On top of that, Rachel was killing herself to find supplemental income. She had spent her past three days submerged in what was called "content generation." She'd written an appreciation of Abraham & Straus, the downtown Brooklyn department store her mom used to take her to, for a package J.Crew was planning on "Lost New York." Sunny had hooked her up with the gig, which was nice.

"She's out," Jesse said triumphantly when he returned. "I fell asleep for a few minutes, too." The sky had gone deep blue. Rachel realized she must have been standing there for a good while.

She entered Cleo's room and stroked her daughter's cheek. Something had started to happen to Cleo's face, or maybe her ears? She looked different from the way she had at the beginning of the summer. Rachel hated nothing more than when people told her that children grow so fast, but it was true. They did. Rachel pulled the blanket over her daughter and tiptoed back into the living room, where her brother was washing dishes. "Dad seemed happy, right?"

"He loved it," Jesse said.

Rachel fished a plastic take-out container out of a drawer and packed it with the remaining chicken and orzo.

"I was going to eat that," Jesse said.

"Matt's back tomorrow," she said. "He can have it for lunch."

"You pack his lunch?"

Rachel felt flush with embarrassment. "Your girl gang doesn't do that for you?"

Jesse shook his head and wiped the lid of a pot. "Why do you have to typecast me? It could be girl, singular."

Rachel felt a little bad. "Sorry. Are you going to tell me you've narrowed in on somebody?"

Jesse's smile went crooked. "I'm falling for someone, Rachel."

"Seriously? I don't think I've ever heard you say that."

"It's a little delicate." Her brother was considering his words slowly. "No-judgment zone, right?"

"Zero." Rachel felt a glimmering inside. She loved gossip even more than wine.

"She's married."

Rachel's head dropped forward. "Do you even *know* married people?"

"It's Sunny."

Rachel laughed. "Sorry, sorry. Everyone's in love with Sunny."

Jesse's face broke into a sad smile. "No, Rach. Sunny and I . . . we've been seeing each other."

Rachel wanted to respond but couldn't bring herself to speak. She and Sunny had spoken two days ago, when Rachel had called to tell her about the launch party she'd gone to for Miriam's newsletter. They'd gossiped about the *Cassette* veterans, and Rachel had told Sunny what Geraldine had said on her latest podcast, about how she'd spent an afternoon shopping for a dress. She was going to Peter's fund-raiser, there was no question about it.

"Like, in a nonplatonic way?" Rachel's voice croaked and she watched her brother nod. She heard a ringing in her ears. It was dull and unrelenting. "What do you want me to say, Jesse?"

"You don't have to say anything." Jesse fluttered his lips, looked around the room. "I just thought I should tell you. Not telling you seemed wrong somehow."

"'Wrong somehow,'" Rachel repeated, unable to keep the sense of betrayal from rising. Sunny had ended their call saying they needed to have drinks soon. Rachel had suggested Monday or Thursday of the following week, but Sunny wanted to email her dates later. She said she still needed to figure some things out. So this was why Sunny had dropped off, because she was too busy fucking Rachel's little brother? In the lengthening silence, Rachel felt dizzy, unfit for the world. "What about Nick?" she said. "You know she has a husband—you met him."

"Please, don't get on your high horse," Jesse said. "You've done your share of shady things."

Rachel tensed. "What about the fact that Sunny is one of my closest friends?"

Jesse went still as he tried to read his sister's face. "You don't seem that close." It came out as neither statement nor question.

Tears sprang to the corners of Rachel's eyes, and she tipped her head up, as if she could push them back inside. "No, maybe we're not," she said slowly. "She never mentioned this to me. Too bad you aren't rich. Otherwise you just might be her type for the long haul."

Jesse stared at his sister with a mixture of incredulity and pity. Rachel was too angry to feel sorry for what she'd said. How could Sunny do this to her? Did she even like Rachel, or had she just been using her to get to Jesse from the start?

"I should have kept my mouth shut." Jesse scooped up his bike helmet and headed toward the door. "I wasn't trying to upset you. This has nothing to do with you."

"I get that," she said coldly.

Rachel didn't wash her face that night. She didn't change into her pajamas either. She just ripped off her jeans and crawled under the covers in her ratty cashmere sweater and underpants. At 2:23 she was up again, the cogs of her mind whirring. Alone in bed, she lay rigid and awake, thinking about Sunny and her brother. What did they talk about? Did she tell him her secrets? Rachel wondered, but couldn't begin to imagine, what it was like to be alone with Sunny in the dark.

# 27

When Sunny rolled over in her bed at five in the morning on a Thursday and kissed Nick good-bye, she didn't know she was about to leave him. Not immediately anyway. What she understood in the predawn darkness, as she lay under the covers listening to her husband zip up his suitcase and slip out the door, was that it was unequivocally over. This wasn't to do with Jesse, not really. He was just a kid. Sunny's marriage was no longer alive, and nothing was going to revive it. All she could do was untangle her life from Nick's and try to figure out what was supposed to happen next.

Sunny's plan had been to spend the day working, which meant a morning painting session before shopping for bread and premade salads that she and Jesse would hardly touch. But the second time she woke up, in an empty bed at ten past seven, just when Nick's flight was boarding, her eyes were sticky and slightly itchy. She'd had pinkeye enough times to recognize the symptoms. Sunny's ophthalmologist refused to call in a prescription without seeing her. The earliest appointment wasn't until one thirty, which ruined the day workwise. Figuring she could at least get in some exercise, Sunny put on her track pants and running shoes and set out to walk the forty-odd blocks to the Murray Hill medical complex. As she headed up Park Avenue South, she didn't see a single building without at least one plaque bearing a doctor's name. They were unquestionably fabulous, in so many fonts and shapes. Sunny started thinking about a potential series of sketches. She preferred to mull this over rather than think about how she should really be meeting with another kind of medical professional, one who could help tame her feelings.

The sadness pressing down on her was both familiar and unfamiliar, a hue she was accustomed to in watercolor, never in oil. Maybe she was pregnant. Her period was a couple of days late, but then again it often was. Sunny came to a sudden halt in front of a person suspended a foot above the sidewalk, balancing on the base of a lamppost. If it weren't for the girl's Tretorns, just like the ones Sunny had worn in grammar school, Sunny would have walked right by her. Instead she watched the girl tape up a sheet of paper.

MURRAY HILL STUDIO AVAILABLE FOR SUBLET NOW.

NO FURNITURE. SUPER-LOW PRICE. TOO GOOD TO PASS UP.

"Is it . . . is it your place?" Sunny sputtered haltingly.

The girl nodded. "I'm moving to the Upper West."

Hearing this made Sunny feel old. When she had first arrived in New York, people still took the time to say "Upper West Side."

"It's a perfectly nice apartment," the girl said. "My boyfriend just got off the waiting list for Columbia Business School. He's moving here from San Francisco. It's all happening fast." The girl had striking kohl-rimmed eyes and looked clean. Sunny imagined her apartment would be, too.

"Are dogs allowed?"

The girl grinned. "Do you know any Murray Hill girls who don't have dogs?"

Sunny didn't know a single person who lived in Murray Hill but gave a laugh. The girl hopped onto the sidewalk. "I'm Chloe," she said, extending her arm.

"Hey," Sunny said. It took her a moment to remember to give her own name. "Sorry, I wasn't expecting this." Chloe was giving her a funny look, as if she were considering whether Sunny were fit for the position. "The other thing I had just fell through," Sunny told her, and Chloe nodded understandingly. "Can I see it?"

Sunny showed up the following afternoon, and the Keetsa mattress truck arrived by evening. Chloe had cleared out all her belongings save for a couple of utensils and a potted fern that Sunny couldn't stop herself from watering. She had never been in an apartment with so little character for more than a few minutes. She had no desire to dress it up, no interest in injecting the apartment with reminders of her fucked-up self.

Sunny was ripping the plastic cover off the mattress when her phone twitched across the hardwood floor like an injured insect. She was expecting it to be Jesse, who had insisted he didn't care if he contracted pinkeye.

Everything cool? Nick wrote.

*I left you and moved into an empty studio apartment in Murray Hill today*, she didn't type back. Instead she replied as the other Sunny, not the one who'd bundled a week's worth of clothing, her computer, and some art supplies into four laundry bags and ridden with Stanley in the back of a taxi to the corner of East Thirty-fifth Street and Second Avenue.

Cool City! Sunny immediately regretted the exclamation mark. She was a promiscuous punctuator, but given the circumstances the symbol struck a chord of immaturity bordering on cruelty. She began a new text.

I saw a teenage version of you on the street. Tried to take a picture, but his mom was staring me down. Best to let Nick enjoy one last weekend inhabiting the reality he'd worked so hard to build for Sunny and himself. She'd paid for her rent and her new mattress in cash.

On her first night, Sunny lay down with her computer and watched a couple of episodes of a Netflix series about the murder of an alcoholic veterinarian in the Cotswolds. The double mattress was hard and tight, as was the sleep it afforded her.

Stanley was eager to get moving early in the morning, as he had every right to be, so Sunny took him on a walk in the park by the United Nations building. On the way back, she picked up an egg sandwich to eat in front of the computer. She had no intention of going outside and found another series with which to anesthetize herself. She finished the final episode a little after eight in the evening. She was famished. Outside, all the bars were packed. So were the restaurants, many of which appeared to have cleared the majority of the chairs and tables and transformed into bars. She walked a bit, looking for a place that wasn't a meat market. It was Saturday night, after all. She came across a shop called Kozmo's Treasure Trove. Somebody had arranged vintage elves in a Halloween scene in the window. Sunny couldn't not go inside, where she found a gingham flannel sheet set and a three-pack of pom-pom ankle socks worth much more than the asking price of six dollars.

When Sunny came back out, a gaggle of college-age girls teetered past in platform stilettos, their arms wrapped around one another. Sunny felt an ache of loneliness and located her earbuds so she could put on the latest episode of *Pod People.* She'd already listened to Geraldine's show a couple of times while working in the studio. She'd liked what she'd heard. It was hard not to feel a little envious.

Now Sylvie was interviewing Esme Ford, a young comedian who'd just returned from a long weekend at a resort in the Dominican Republic. "I went with this guy I've been seeing. It was nice, don't get me wrong, but traveling with somebody can be . . . intense. I've worked in cubicles that are bigger than the room we shared, and every time you need to poop, you have to decide if you want to trek all the way down to the lobby or just *go* for it."

Geraldine let off a shuddering laugh and shared the story about her miserable Jamaican vacation with Peter—she was using his name now. Sunny remembered the story well. She'd still been living in Toronto, in her old apartment, when Peter had taken Geraldine to Round Hill, the resort his family descended on for two weeks every Christmas. Peter and Geraldine had gone without them, in February or March, after a year or so of dating.

"I was so sure something was wrong with me," Geraldine was saying on mic. "There I was, in my thousand-dollar-a-night villa, with all the shades pulled down, watching my boyfriend sleep through the afternoon. I wanted to throw myself in the ocean."

Esme guffawed. "There's nothing like a vacation to make you feel like you're a total failure. You plan everything perfectly, smile all the way down there on the plane, and then you get imprisoned in paradise with somebody you realize you want to kill."

As the two continued talking, Sunny was transported back in time. She recalled sitting with Geraldine in Rosebud Café on Dundas Street right after the vacation. They'd sipped herbal tea with José González playing on the speakers while Geraldine confided in her about Peter's behavior. He'd snuck off a couple of times after Geraldine had fallen asleep and partied on the beach with a group of English music producers. Geraldine had only found out about this at the end, when she'd run into one of the English guys' girlfriend at the hotel gym. The woman had rolled her eyes at Geraldine and muttered something about "your bloke really knowing how to live on the edge" while pounding away on the elliptical. Afterward, when they were in the locker room, the woman had inquired about Geraldine's "sleep disorder" that supposedly made her incapable of staying up past nine, and Geraldine had coaxed out of her that Peter had become friendly with the woman's nineteen-year-old half sister. "Can you imagine how humiliated I felt?" Geraldine asked Sunny. He tried to make me sound like a narcoleptic freak just so he could get serviced on the beach by a bimbo named Petronella."

At the time Sunny had felt certain that Geraldine was coming to her for some sort of absolution. And so she had given it, telling Geraldine that Peter was complicated, and worth it, so long as that's what she wanted. "It goes with being with a powerful man. Look at what Hillary Clinton has to go through," Sunny had told her. "I'm sure Seamus has his secrets, too."

Geraldine had stared at her uncomprehendingly. Sunny's boyfriend of the moment, Seamus O'Connell, was a big-bellied Irish actor-in-residence at Soulpepper Theatre. "But Seamus is completely smitten with you."

"I wouldn't be surprised if he had a thing going on with Lallie," Sunny said, naming the first actress to come to mind. "Look, Peter loves you. You should see the way he touches your hair when you're at parties. And the way other people watch. Everyone wants what you have."

Geraldine's shoulders had eased at that bit. "Really?"

Sunny had given Geraldine what she thought she wanted to hear: permission to do nothing. It was easier than exacerbating her friend's doubts, and it got her out of the café faster. There was no point in contributing her own footnotes about Peter, who often managed to place his hand on her arm or the small of her back when they were going over layouts. Sunny didn't particularly mind when he did this. Geraldine was smart; surely she knew what she was signing on for when she'd started dating Peter Ricker. He had a vintage two-seater, for Christ's sake. Sunny had her own problems to deal with, like plotting her move to New York. Her job here was to listen.

As it still was. If Geraldine wanted to return to Peter, so long as she was happy, or happy enough, they might actually build an interesting life together. Stranger things had happened. And who was Sunny to interfere? Sunny's thoughts dimmed down, and she turned her attention to the conversation Sylvie and the comedian were having. They'd moved on to the pleasures of reading Amazon reviews. "God bless the people who take the time to write three paragraphs about a nail clip—" Sylvie started to say.

Sunny tugged the wires out of her ears and kept strolling through the neighborhood, which felt exotically American to her, the way for-profit walk-in medical clinics and hair-dry bars did. A Japanese-influenced beer garden called Orange Tango had a Dog-Friendly sign. Sunny found herself seated at a table in the back of the garden, near a margarita machine that cast a chartreuse glow. She ordered the salmon special, a grapefruit juice, and a bowl of water for Stanley, who was splayed out on the brick floor by her feet.

The crowd was noisy, but flatly so. No matter whose lips Sunny focused on, she was unable to make out the words being said or access the emotion behind them. The only exception was a girl who was walking around the grounds with a tray of tiny white paper cups. She wore a T-shirt printed with a pug eating an ice-cream cone and had an expression of upbeat violation. Sunny caught herself staring and quickly averted her eyes when the girl turned her way. She looked down at her phone and studied the texts that had rolled in over the last couple of days. She still hadn't told Jesse anything, hadn't even reached out to say hi since she'd canceled their Thursday-night plan, on supposed account of her pinkeye. He'd written twice today, and she'd been missing him. She wanted to find him and curl into him, but her morals wouldn't stand for it. Not before she told Nick she'd left him.

Sunny felt a familiar discomfort in her lower back and grimaced. She had been getting her period long enough to know exactly what was happening. So much for her fantasy of running away from everybody with a baby to keep her company. She felt tears prick her eyes. At least this was better for Jesse. She liked him in a way that sometimes felt maternal. With a steadying inhale, she typed a response to Jesse: You around for a call?

In 10, Jesse wrote back instantly.

Sunny's dinner materialized. The salmon was a shade of pink too close to flamingo to be something that belonged in her body. She ate half of it anyway and slipped a few bites under the table to Stanley.

Sunny felt a spasm in her heart when the phone vibrated. "Can you hear me?" she said.

"Where are you?" Jesse asked. "Where have you been?"

She guessed he could sense that something had shifted, and she gripped the phone tighter.

"I left Nick." The only sound that came back was the echo of the beer garden. "Don't worry, I didn't do it for you." Her words came out sharper than she'd meant them to.

"I know." He sounded tentative. "Are you okay?"

"I don't know." She ringed the edge of her glass with her right index finger. Her wedding band was still on her other hand.

"Can I see you?" Jesse asked, and Sunny glanced around the beer garden. The noise of the crowd was becoming louder and duller. She felt a bottoming-out.

"Not till I talk to Nick," she replied. "He gets back tomorrow night."

"Wait—so you did or didn't leave him?"

"I needed some space first. I'm still . . . taking it. Preparing myself for the shitshow." Trying to envision what the next few days would be like, her mind went blank and she felt overwhelmingly sleepy. When she got stressed as a child, she would retreat to bed. "How are you doing?" she asked.

"Does that really matter?" She could hear him sigh. "Let me know how it goes. Or, you know, if you need anything. It doesn't have to be scandalous. I can also be a friend."

"You *are* my friend. You might be my best friend."

"Same," Jesse said, and Sunny bit down a smile. When she hung up, the pug girl walked over to her.

"This is Do-Yo. It's small-batch frozen yogurt, created for dogs." The girl extended the tray. "Take as much as you want. And please use our hashtag."

Sunny reached out to accept the offering, if only to be left alone. A moment later her phone buzzed on her lap. It was a blank text from Nick, which used to be their code for all the love they couldn't articulate. Now it was just convenient for the times when they were too lazy to think of anything cute to say. Sunny looked around for her server. She was still waiting when she saw that the Do-Yo had melted and taken on the consistency of marshmallow fluff. She dipped her pinkie finger in the paper cup and brought the substance to her mouth. It tasted like sweet nothingness. A couple helped themselves to a nearby bench and began kissing. A sense of claustrophobia closed in as she watched the guy's Adam's apple move like an automated valve. She tossed sixty dollars on the table and yanked at Stanley's leash.

# 28

So what can I tell you?" Rebecca Sattenstein flashed Geraldine an uncomfortable grin and bridged her hands on the thick white tablecloth. They were at the Water Grill, a corporate-geared restaurant near Ffife's office known for its good taste and tasteless salads.

"You can tell me where you could most use some more support," Geraldine said.

Rebecca did not immediately respond. Stacks of rings glittered over her fingers and obscured her marital status. Geraldine knew from Elinda that Rebecca and her husband, Charlie, a stay-at-home dad who fancied himself a music producer, had separated not long ago. Their youngest child was in high school, and Charlie spent most of the time at their weekend home in Rhinebeck.

This was Geraldine's third stop on her "listening tour." She had yet to meet an editor in chief who didn't have an internal clock that dinged four minutes into their meeting, signaling the end of the chitchat portion. To Rebecca's credit she'd waited until they'd placed their lunch orders (crispy Thai chicken salad for Geraldine, tuna burger sans bun, side of sautéed spinach for Rebecca) to get down to business.

"I'm excited to hear about your plans," Geraldine said. "I've read *Smart* since before you took over. You've made it so much sharper."

Rebecca was, if not a legend, close to it. She'd started out as a hard-hitting journalist and made waves a decade ago with *Awake*, her literary insomnia memoir. Rebecca was the kind of woman who used to send Geraldine into paroxysms of inarticulateness. Now Geraldine simply felt embarrassed about what Elinda had put her up to and what Elinda had said about Rebecca, which was that she'd fire her save that she was the breadwinner and it would just about kill Rebecca and her children. This job was awkward from every angle. If only Geraldine and Sylvie's show, now on a weekly recording schedule, were enough to justify her visa. Yet Geraldine could do no wrong by Elinda, who was convinced that Geraldine had the fresh perspective to save Ffife. "You've seen things while you were lost at sea, and that's going to help us discover new lands," Elinda had told her.

"My plans," Rebecca said, and cleared her throat. "We should have met in the office. I could have walked you through the planning room and shown you the boards for the next issue."

"I don't think I need to see the issue at this stage," Geraldine said.

Rebecca looked up. "This is going to be a *stages* thing?"

Geraldine smiled meekly. Elinda had appointed her creative director of audio, yet Geraldine didn't consider herself a creative, and she definitely wasn't directorial. Had she possessed these qualities, she might have been able to come up with a corporate role for which she was better suited, or at least one that didn't require her being here, doing her best to appear tolerant while Rebecca stared her down. It didn't help that Geraldine was overdone, with her hair blown out and her nails painted a rich emerald green for Peter's fund-raiser, whose theme was Enchanted Forest. A car was picking her up after lunch and taking her directly to La Guardia.

"I'm more interested in the larger direction," Geraldine said. "Elinda thought a positive first step would be my meeting key team members and hearing about your greatest challenges and thoughts about the coming year before we firm up the audio strategy."

"Why do we need one? My readers are in their forties and early fifties. They are readers. We already did a podcast, and nobody cared."

Geraldine nodded. "I heard a few episodes. We can do something great."

A feral look came to Rebecca's face. "I believe what you mean is *you* can do something great, and *I'm* supposed to act as if I'm enthusiastic about this shift away from the printed word?" Rebecca twisted her napkin. "Imagine if you'd been in charge of a magazine for six years and then your boss told you to clear your Thursday afternoon so a charming girl from Toronto could come in and rearrange your goddamn life."

The rest of the lunch was no less strained, and Geraldine had never been so happy to hear somebody turn down coffee or tea. At last she was able to lean into the cool backseat of her car as it lumbered through heavy midtown traffic. She checked her email and calendar, now tended to by someone called Katie. Her agenda for tomorrow afternoon looked more packed than she remembered, with two hour-long "touch bases," as Elinda liked to label meetings, and a five thirty drink with somebody she'd never heard of named Sam Lloyd. Geraldine definitely would have remembered saying yes to that. She needed to talk to Katie.

Geraldine's flight landed a little after five, which gave her enough time to take a cab to the Y. Her membership was still valid through February, and she needed a place to freshen up. She hadn't told anybody in Toronto that she was coming to town, not even her mother, who was making noises about visiting Geraldine in New York. She hadn't said anything to Peter either. She was coming up to see him, but she wasn't coming *for* him, and there was a difference.

In the locker room's hair-drying station, she studied herself in the mirror. She'd slightly filled out since she used to come to the gym regularly, her cheeks less hollow, the lattice of bones on her chest contained deeper within her body. In her long jade gown and glittery lip gloss, Geraldine felt less beautiful than Disney Princess–like, a suspicion that was confirmed when a little girl in a sopping-wet bathing suit and goggles stopped to stare. The girl's mother called her over and wrapped her up in a towel. Geraldine felt a softening within and could almost remember the feeling of hugging herself in her favorite dolphin towel while her mother knelt down and rubbed lotion onto her body.

At the gala Geraldine steadied her nerves with food. Trays groaned under the weight of enormous risotto balls and dumplings filled with hot onion soup that Geraldine witnessed squirt all over more than one guest's shirt. Champagne proved a more wieldy source of calories, and she sipped on her second glass of bubbly while leaning against a column, one of many that had been draped in brown burlap and adorned with real branches. Peter was all too easy to locate, chatting and gesticulating grandly across the crowd. When he finally noticed Geraldine, his face lit up, but she could tell he wasn't completely surprised.

He paused for a moment, as if deciding whether to run to her, then motioned for her to join his group. Fair enough, Geraldine thought. She'd told him that if she ended up coming—and it was a big if—he had to behave platonically. She took her time, saying hello to the few familiar faces and trying to ignore the tightening in her chest as she made her approach. A couple of people asked what she was doing there, and she blushed. There was no real answer. She had gotten into a fight with Sylvie after Sylvie had pried out that she was planning on attending Peter's party. "Hello? Do the words 'Harvey Weinstein' not mean anything to you? How are you possibly going to visit a boss who harassed you?" Sylvie said.

"It wasn't harassment. We were engaged," Geraldine replied quietly. She'd had a crush on Peter long before he started to see her as a romantic prospect.

"It was; you just didn't know it," Sylvie informed her. Geraldine tried to keep Sylvie's words from replaying in her head as Peter wrapped his arm around her shoulder.

"Geraldine, meet Boyd and Sandra Dunfield. We're discussing Sandra's work with Trudeau on marijuana legalization," he told her.

"You have my vote," Geraldine said, and everyone laughed. She tried to laugh with them, but Peter was leaning into her and he'd pressed the pad of his thumb into her skin. She felt a shiver of confusion, as if her muscles didn't remember what it felt like to belong to somebody else.

"Boyd's a sculptor. He's one of the greats," Peter said when Boyd and Sandra had excused themselves to circulate. "I can tell he took a shine to you."

"What? I hardly said a word," Geraldine told him.

"You didn't have to." Peter gave a crooked smile and fingered the strap of Geraldine's dress. He looked across the room. "Christ! Michael Ondaatje came after all. Don't go anywhere."

"K," Geraldine said, and wished she hadn't kept her word, when a man with a beetlelike body stepped up to her.

"I've been asking myself all night, who is that nymph?" he said, staring directly at her neckline.

It took her a second to place the face. "Tom?" she said. "Geraldine Despont. We met in New York. . . . We talked about podcasting."

Tom Newlin went slightly pink and stood straighter. Geraldine recalled how smug he'd been at their meetings, taking phone calls and making her wait.

"How are you?" he said. "I'm sorry we couldn't bring you aboard. I loved your ideas. It's just so hard to make anything actually happen. You know how it is."

"I understand." Geraldine peered into the distance and saw Peter dancing with the ideas editor of the *Globe and Mail.* Peter was crouched down and making happy zigzags with his bottom.

"So you've given New York the middle finger and repatriated, too?" Tom asked.

Geraldine shook her head. "I'm here for the night. I found a job down there."

Tom looked slightly incredulous. "I hope it's far from the hell of media."

"I'm in the inferno," Geraldine said. "I'm working on all the podcasts at Ffife Media and cohosting one of my own." Tom's excess fat resided higher on his torso than the bellies of most men. This gave him the aspect of a disgruntled chicken, especially now that he was flustered.

"Good for you," he said. "And you can thank me for doing nothing for you. Seems I did you a favor." He waited for Geraldine to agree, but she remained silent. "How long are you in town for?" he asked. "You should come into the office and meet with the team."

Geraldine bit back a smile. Men really were vultures, homing in when they were no longer needed. She opened her purse and fished out her card. "I'm going back in the morning," she said. "Let me know if you come back down to the city, and we can meet. I'll show you the studios we're building."

When she made her escape, Geraldine kept busy studying the National Parks art on the walls and watching Peter chat up donors from afar. He sustained Geraldine with occasional glances that warmed her belly, and he sidled up to her a little before nine.

"I can see you're wilting," he told her.

"Not at all," she lied. "Take your time."

"I need to stay, but why don't you get out of here? I'll find you later."

"You want me to go?" Geraldine felt a stab of hurt and glanced around the party, searching for the woman whose attention had inspired Peter to release her. There was nobody who came close to Peter's taste.

"Do you know how distracting it's been having you here?" he said.

"You invited me," she reminded him. "Like a thousand times."

"And I meant it. I just didn't think about how nervous it would make me." Peter paused. "You have no idea how beautiful you are."

Geraldine felt herself go soft.

"Meet me at home?" he suggested. "George will let you in, and you can lie down. I'll be there soon."

"Okay, but I have to leave super early tomorrow."

Peter smiled. "The hell you do."

"Oh, I definitely do. There's this big meeting."

"Somebody can give you the notes." Peter stroked her wrist, and she flushed with adrenaline. When she looked into his eyes, though, shame trickled in.

The wind hit Geraldine's face as she flagged down a taxi. She gave her old address to the driver, surprising herself with how easily it came to her. They drove through downtown, which felt apocalyptically lifeless, and into the Annex, a more colorful area with old Victorians and leafy streets. Soon enough the car was outside the massive converted warehouse block that had been her home for four years.

Geraldine could see the outline of George's head through the plate glass of the lobby. George had been the night doorman when she'd lived here with Peter. He'd been there to witness Geraldine's first visit to Front Street, twenty-five years old and all wobbly in her heels and jean skirt. Ever the professional, George had broken character only when she'd moved her stuff out, coming around the desk to give her a hug and tell her she was a good girl. George had a daughter named Nitzah, who'd still been in braces at the time. She was probably at university by now. Would George be happy or disappointed to see Geraldine walk through the door again? She wasn't sure which option made her sadder.

Geraldine asked the driver to keep the meter running and dialed her mother's number. "Are you awake?"

"Now I am." Geraldine suspected that Joanne had begun smoking again.

"Can you wait up another half hour?" Geraldine asked. "I've ended up in town, and I need a place to sleep. We could have tea."

"You've *ended up* in Toronto?"

"It was a last-minute decision." Geraldine squeezed her eyes shut. "Peter had a party."

"Oh, Ger." Her mother sighed. Geraldine pictured Joanne sitting up against the headboard, her bedside table a minefield of remote controls and detective novels.

"It wasn't like that," Geraldine told her.

"What were you thinking?"

"Nothing terrible happened."

"I'd say a lot terrible happened. I don't know what possessed you to—"

"I mean tonight. He was perfectly lovely. He was fine anyway."

"Fine." Joanne exhaled. "That's not enough."

"I know." Geraldine drummed her fingers on the phone and watched George turn to face the street. She slid lower into her seat, but she could see he was squinting at the car in befuddled recognition. "Give me two minutes," she told the driver and went in to say hello to George. When she told him she wasn't going upstairs, that she'd just come by to say hi, he broke into a solar smile.

Heading north on the 401, Geraldine opened the window. The sounds of traffic washed over her while she thought about her mother, working out how upset she'd be if Geraldine kept her 8:10 a.m. flight from Pearson International. But she could push it back, couldn't she? The meeting would go on without her. Katie would help her reschedule the day.

# 29

Rachel tugged her Parker House roll in half, pausing to let the steam waft over her palms. It felt wonderful, and she pretended not to notice the strained expression of the waiter who was struggling with the corkscrew. Matt had ordered a bottle of chardonnay, the unfashionable kind that tasted like oak and buttered popcorn and that Rachel loved to bits. The waiter poured an inch of wine into Rachel's glass. She let the cool liquid kiss every crevice inside her mouth.

"It's delicious," she pronounced. When they'd lined up a babysitter and scheduled dinner at Wild Oak, a new restaurant on Vanderbilt Avenue, over a week ago, it had been to celebrate Matt's news. His paper on a brain protein that his group had discovered and named GargaspinB had been accepted for publication by the *New Brain*, pending a peer review, which even Matt admitted it was certain to clear. He had been working on the zebra fish study for more than three years, and Rachel felt a little sorry that his triumph had to be overshadowed by her news. Josie had submitted *Monsters!* to publishers on Friday. On Monday morning an editor at HarperCollins had emailed to make sure world rights were available.

"Who is it?" Rachel had asked her agent in disbelief.

"Jessica Hyphen-Something. It doesn't matter. She's a child—there's no way we're going with her," Josie told her. "And she didn't actually offer. But we *should* send her a box of cake pops when this is over. She just changed your life. One bite is all we need to get heat. Your track record might not be insurmountable after all."

One hundred thousand dollars was the number Rachel had pulled out of thin air and settled on. If she signed for that, they could justify staying in their apartment. So long as she kept producing, drew the book out into a trilogy, they'd be in fine shape. It was Thursday now, and over the past four days Rachel had interacted with Josie more than she had in as many years. One bite gave way to a couple of nibbles. The interest hadn't escalated to a bidding war, but Josie was close to transforming an inquiry about a potential sequel from an established editor at Bloomsbury into a legitimate offer. "I told him you'll write a follow-up in Esperanto if that's what it takes" was the last Rachel had heard from her. "I'll be fucked if we don't have a deal to announce before this weekend."

Matt clinked his glass against Rachel's. "To you, honey. You pulled it off."

"Not so fast," Rachel said. The weekend was only twenty-four hours away now, and they still didn't have anything definite.

"There's legitimate interest, Rach," Matt reminded her. "You're golden."

Rachel felt her cheeks hitch up in a smile. "Thank you for believing in me. And coming up with the Deep Sea of Lost Memories."

"That wasn't actually mine." Matt hesitated. "It was something I remembered from one of the comic books I read as a kid."

"Now you tell me? If I get trolled for plagiarism, it's all on you," Rachel said, leaning back to make room for the first course. She speared her fork into the quail egg that quivered atop a mound of tuna tartare.

Rachel felt a vibration against her thigh. She looked down and saw it was a text from Josie. It was six fifteen, still working hours for most of the world. "Here we go," she said, feeling her stomach lurch as she started to read.

> Bloomsbury finked out. Jessica is offering 35 for world rights. We should close w her in the morning. Pls confirm this sounds ok. xxxx

"She wants to go with Cake Pop." Rachel slid the phone across the table, feeling numb. All the other authors she knew got six-figure deals. Or at least she thought they did. She suddenly realized that her impression of reality was based on hearsay. Maybe thirty-five thousand wasn't so bad.

Matt's eyes narrowed as he took in the message. "She's using a lot of *x*'s," he said. "That's good, right?"

"I think they're consolation *x*'s," Rachel said. "It's not a ton of money for what will amount to more than two years of work. Josie was talking about that Bloomsbury guy like she had his checkbook in her hand."

"It's still an offer." Matt gave a crooked smile. "Didn't you tell me women were always better editors?"

"Did I?" Whatever, at least she *had* an editor. She felt tired from the week of waiting for Josie to get back to her, worn out from entertaining all the worst-case scenarios and downing NyQuil to quiet her anxiety at night. And that was before Toronto was seriously on the table. Matt's former mentor, Phillip Lippman, was not taking no for an answer. He had an arduous book project of his own to worry about and was desperate to pass on some of the more time-consuming duties to a young zebra fish enthusiast. Phillip had convinced the dean to raise the offer by another fifteen thousand dollars. Canadian, but still. Matt was due to go up and meet the team before giving his answer. No timing was specified, but "soon" was a word that seemed to be mentioned a lot. As the Hastings Professor of Neurobiology, Matt would also be co-director of the McWhorter Lab for Addiction Studies. Which was crazy; even though she knew that the late thirties were one's academic prime, Rachel still thought of her husband as a kid who was happiest on a surfboard. The department was based out of a historic house with bay windows, and if he said yes, Matt's office would have its own turret. The salary would be nearly double what he made now. Rachel could be a writer—not a writer-slash-something. And Cleo could have good schooling, for free, and partially in French. It was a no-brainer, that's what anybody would tell her.

Anybody but Geraldine and Sunny. Rachel couldn't stomach the inevitable pitying looks on their faces when she admitted defeat and told them where her family was relocating. Rachel's mind reeled back to the time when, aged twenty-seven, she informed the newsroom that she was ready to return to her native city. She had to leave, before the comforts of Toronto made a permanent expat of her. If Sunny was barely off the plane before she was asked to design an album cover for Yeah Yeah Yeahs, then Rachel, who actually knew the city, had nothing to worry about.

Rachel felt a twist in her gut when she realized how soon she would see the *Province* crew. They were all going to Sunny's Canadian

Thanksgiving dinner, an annual tradition that Geraldine had crowed about the one time she'd scored an invite.

Rachel was tempted to skip the party, but she and Matt had to go, and not only because she'd promised Sunny that she would do her Jewish-mother thing and help prepare. It would be Rachel's one shot at tipping over the domino that would set Geraldine's world right. She'd already let her friend down once before. The day after Peter's gala, when Rachel had located the pictures of Geraldine on the society page of *Toronto* magazine's website, she'd called Sunny.

"I don't think it's a big deal," Sunny said. "They're not together in any of the photos."

Rachel had been momentarily speechless. The way she saw it, Geraldine and Peter's discretion seemed only to underscore their seriousness about each other. If they had nothing to hide, why wouldn't they pose cheek to cheek? "She went up there to see him," Rachel said. "Do you not understand what that means?"

"I'm sorry—I'm actually in the middle of something. Can I call you in a bit?"

It had taken all Rachel's willpower not to ask if that something was her brother. Instead she sighed. "I get that this isn't fun for you. You need to talk to her."

"And what is it exactly you want me to say?"

"Tell her everything that happened between you and Peter."

"It was noth—"

"I don't care what it was or wasn't. Just let her know. We'll hate ourselves forever if we just stand by and watch her fuck her life up."

Rachel felt her jaw click, and she carved off a bite of her husband's dinner. The berry compote that accompanied the duck was perfectly tangy. "Oh, my God, did you taste that? It's crazy good."

"It's very good," Matt said in a measured tone.

"Now is definitely not the time to leave the neighborhood."

"Have you considered that the Toronto neighborhoods might have changed, too?" Matt's dimple was showing the way it did when he was holding back a smile.

"Look, there's a lot to like about Toronto," Rachel conceded. "But there's nothing to love." The disappointment in Matt's eyes was hard to take. "Not for me. If we have to move, can't it be to any other city?"

"You have more friends in Toronto than in any other city."

"Facebook friends," she corrected him. "Who all remember me as the jerk who wrote first-person pieces about leg waxing and trying out for *Canada's Next Top Model*."

"That was a funny article." Matt had read her entire archive, which lived in plastic storage boxes in the Ziffs' basement. He set down his silverware and reached for Rachel's hands. "At least come with me for the meet and greet. We can see how allergic to the city you really are."

"What about Cleo?" Rachel deflected. "She lives for routine and freaks out if we move her nap schedule by an hour. How would she handle a move?"

"Cleo is two," Matt reminded her. "You honestly don't think it would be the best thing that ever happened to her? As opposed to staying in an apartment we're rapidly outgrowing and watching her mother find new reasons to get jealous of everybody she knows?"

Rachel frowned and looked away. The couple at the next table were quietly working on a tower of oysters and clams. They seemed to have agreed to tackle separate levels, and Rachel could tell that they hated each other.

"I'm sorry—" Matt started to say.

"Don't be. I don't want this to be a fight. I'm in your corner."

Matt kept looking at her. "I need more than that. We can't keep living with everything up in the air all the time. Job offers like this come by once in a never."

Rachel searched for a retort. The restaurant was getting loud and hotter.

"Don't you want to stop feeling shitty every time somebody we knows buys an apartment or dares to go on a vacation that their parents don't pay for?" Matt said. "Just think, we could spread out comfortably. We could get a dog, and you'd be able to walk it during the day. That's what you want, isn't it, to write from home and spend more time with Cleo?"

"In New York," Rachel said. "That was always a very important part of the vision."

"Why? When's the last time you went to a museum?"

"You know I'm not a museum person," Rachel said quietly.

"The opera? A concert? Central Park?"

"I went to that book launch at McNally Jackson." It humiliated Rachel that she had no better rebuttal.

"The exquisite alien corpse thing?"

"Matt, please. Do you not think I already hate myself enough as is?"

"Why are you so determined to make yourself miserable?" Matt looked perplexed, and a little heartbroken. "When will you ever grasp how wonderful you are and stop making everything so hard on yourself?"

"Stop." Rachel brought her hand to her throat and swallowed hard. "You're going to make me cry."

# 30

Rachel showed up at Sunny's door a little after lunchtime. Her arms were groaning with bags of food, and she had a sleeping toddler strapped to her back. "You sure don't mess around," Sunny said, relieving her visitor of her load while Rachel arranged her daughter's limp body on top of a cluster of pillows on the den floor. Cleo's lips were pursed like a flower about to open. Sunny felt a tug of the bittersweet and headed into the kitchen.

The autumn sunlight flooded through the windows and cast a warm glow on the wood. "So what can I do?" Rachel asked, slapping her hands together.

Sunny looked around and tried to come up with a game plan. "Should we start with the turkey?" she asked. "I thought I might spatchcock it this time."

"Groovy," Rachel said. "How honest is your oven?"

"It's good. Just don't use the convection setting."

The nice thing about having Rachel on hand, besides her cooking skills, was that her presence prohibited Sunny from snooping around, as she'd been doing all morning. The clues to Nick's solitary life were now restricted to Sunny's peripheral vision. With Rachel in the room, she could not dwell on the bottles of Dom Perignon at the bottom of the recycling bin and the garden furniture that had been rearranged to accommodate what Sunny assumed had been a small party. She had to peel six pounds of butternut squash and try not to cut her finger off, all the while pretending that she still lived here.

"Who's coming again?" Rachel asked.

Sunny went through the guest list, fifteen or so lucky expats. She saved Geraldine's name for last.

"Notice how I'm not saying anything?" Rachel said. She was bent over a turkey carcass, her hand burrowed under the skin.

"That doesn't count as not saying anything," Sunny replied.

"It will feel so much better after you do it," Rachel promised, looking up from the poultry. "I can distract Nick while you talk to her."

Sunny rubbed the back of her neck "Nick can't make it tonight. He had a work emergency." This was the story that Sunny had concocted and Nick had signed off on. They had agreed not to tell people about their separation until it was further along and had begun to feel solidly inevitable, something that didn't require any questioning or counselor recommendations. They wanted to be let alone, so proceeding with Canadian Thanksgiving on West Tenth Street was the logical thing to do. But being here went against all internal logic and was far sadder than Sunny had accounted for. She missed the orderliness of her old life. She missed her conversations with Agnes. Sunny scooped a roasted-red-pepper sesame dip into a pretty ceramic bowl and obscenely licked the spoon clean. "Is it too early to open a bottle of wine?"

Rachel shrugged. "I'm trying to cut back on my weekday drinking."

"On a national holiday?"

"Twist my arm," she said. "Lemme just get the oven going."

Sunny brought two wineglasses and a bottle of rioja to the kitchen nook and waited for Rachel.

"So," Rachel said when she joined Sunny. "I have something kind of crazy to tell you."

"Let me guess," Sunny said. "You fooled around with Nick a million years ago and Geraldine thinks you should fess up?"

"Nick's not my type—no offense. As you know, I have a thing for underpaid academics."

"So what is it?"

Rachel smiled uncomfortably. "Matt just got an offer at the U of T."

*"Toronto?"* Sunny didn't know if she should laugh.

Rachel nodded slowly. "I'm trying to figure out how to say no without blowing up my marriage. We're going to go up in a little bit for a so-called exploratory visit." Rachel's expression turned dubious. "Hopefully it will suck, Matt will understand my stance, and then we'll come home and forget it ever happened."

"And if he loves it?" Sunny asked.

"How could he?"

Sunny could think of a few reasons. The record shops on Spadina. Picnics in Dufferin Grove. The unequaled coziness of tramping through the snow after dark. Besides, everyone who was given a chance to leave New York these days took it. "Don't you ever just want to float away and start over?" she asked.

"The artful dodger, that's not me," Rachel said. "The only thing I'm ducking is migrating north. If Geraldine can figure out how to make it work here . . ."

Sunny tensed. She was becoming more and more certain that Geraldine did not need to know about those twenty-minute sessions, ten whole years ago. How many times? Half a dozen? Not more than that. Too many to be incidental. Too few to mean anything. Peter had been after her, like a hunter on a chase. She'd acquiesced and frankly kind of enjoyed the friskiness of it, and before things had a chance to settle into anything more permanent, she'd been let go, sent on her way. It was pretty clean, all told.

Sunny took a deep inhale. The kitchen smelled of sage and butter and the maple and blueberry pies that she'd made earlier in the day. The nice thing about people thinking you had no emotions was that when you did have them, nobody tended to search your face for signs.

"Besides," Rachel said, "how could I leave now that I've finally made it onto your list? Do you know how many years I've been hearing about Canadian Thanksgiving?"

"I think this is going to be the last one," Sunny said softly. "Nick and I are separating. I've been staying in a studio apartment, trying to figure out what comes next."

Rachel appeared to be having difficulty processing. "Is there somebody else?"

"I don't know. I don't know anything." Sunny might have said something about Jesse, but she was starting to cry. It was too much to deal with. "I've been avoiding everybody and everything. I need to sort things out with Nick, but I have to wait till he's not so angry. I've been trying to stay busy finishing this stupid project, as if I can distract myself." She curled her knees into her chest and told Rachel about her show of paintings based on plaques outside doctors' buildings. It was going to be in San Francisco, at the flagship of an online company that was trying to be the Warby Parker of holistic health and beauty. As Sunny spoke of her plans, she could feel her soul drifting out of her body. She was seated on the exact same bench cushion as the one she'd been on when she'd told Nick she was taking a time-out. The wording was juvenile but accurate. "I'm not leaving you. I just need to sort through my thoughts."

She'd been prepared for him to plead for her to reconsider, to offer to give her all the space she needed at home. Instead he'd stared at her stonily. "You hung in for several years, I'll give you that," he'd said. "That's not bad for one of your projects." He'd stood up and lowered his voice. "By the way, real artists don't do projects. And even the most humorless ones know that the kinds of projects you embark on are the stuff of exquisite satire. Everyone sees through you, Sunny, being hired by commercial enterprises to give them the veneer of class." His voice had stooped to a growl. "I mean, I should know, shouldn't I? Isn't that what I did?"

His words had cut off her breath. She'd always thought their relationship pivoted on mutual respect. How had she been so wrong? It wasn't until later that night, as she lay alone in her makeshift bed replaying the conversation, that she wondered if Nick had somebody else, too.

Sunny believed that the secret to a lively dinner party was an equal distribution of old friends and guests who'd never met before, and she'd planned this list accordingly. It was a funny little group—a few people from the *Province* days and a selection of

Sunny's newer friends with a connection to Canada, however tenuous. Pam, the adorable assistant to the director of the Canadian consulate, had been so excited to receive an invite she'd offered to stay and help clean up afterward. Pam and a man she'd introduced as her boyfriend, Derek, arrived first and helped Sunny unwrap cheeses and turn on the stereo. The others slowly trickled in, and by the time Sunny and Rachel had grated just the right amount of Comté into the soup bowls, all the appetizers were gone.

Geraldine was the last to arrive. She was wearing a button-down dress with a faint polka-dot pattern and was holding a bouquet of calla lilies wrapped in brown paper. "I'm so sorry I'm late," she said when Sunny opened the door for her.

"We just sat down. Those are beautiful." Sunny reached for the flowers, but Geraldine twisted away.

"I remember where the vases are," she said. "Go eat." Sunny inhaled the fresh October air and watched Geraldine head into the kitchen. She radiated a flushed, purposeful energy that Sunny still wasn't used to. At the table Geraldine took the one empty seat, next to Vera Dulcie, a Montreal-born screenwriter. Vera could be spiky, but she appeared to be riveted by Geraldine, and soon the two were carrying on as if they were the only people at the table. Everyone else chatted inclusively, and the conversation moved from whether there were Canadian pilgrims to a technology that photographed your gut bacteria in order identify missing compounds. "Mark my words," Matt said, bouncing Cleo on his knee. "In ten years everybody is going to be posting selfies of the insides of their bodies."

"Some of us are eating," Rachel told her husband.

"It's no worse than the selfies most people already blast out," Sunny said.

"To each her own narcissism," Rachel replied.

Sunny couldn't help interpreting Rachel's remark as a personal judgment, but she refused to engage about it. "Has anyone seen my phone?" she asked. She should take a picture of the last supper. She'd want to have it.

"No, I got it," said a familiar voice. "You get in the picture, Sun."

Sunny froze. Nick was standing in the doorway with Jeremy. Her husband—she could still call him that—looked taller than usual in his combat-style boots and navy mackintosh. Jeremy's cheeks were flushed, and he was smiling oddly. The pair had clearly been out drinking. Jeremy headed over to Geraldine, who rose up for a hug befitting long-lost siblings. Sunny had already explained Nick's absence to the group and felt her neck go hot as her mind tripped around for an excuse for his sudden appearance.

"Niko Suave," Matt said cluelessly. "I thought you couldn't make it."

"Wouldn't dream of missing Sunny's party. The lengths people go to for an invite." Nick looked around the table, inhaled deeply through his nose. "Is that tarragon? Smells delicious." Sunny wondered how many of her guests detected the curl of sarcasm in his voice.

Matt brought a chair from the kitchen and placed it between Rachel and himself. Derek offered Jeremy his seat. "Pam and I will share." Sunny felt light-headed, a little woozy. She'd decided to proceed with tradition to prove to herself that she hadn't entirely lost purchase on the world she'd gone to pains to create. The party was having the reverse effect. This had been a terrible idea. Now she was sitting directly across from the husband who loathed her and the woman who had the same enormous, soulful eyes as the guy who'd inspired her to leave said husband. She gripped the edges of her seat and tried to force an expression of serenity.

"So what have you been up to, Sunny?" Jeremy was staring at her in a strange way. Nick must have told him everything. At least he didn't know about Jesse. Nobody did, as far as she was aware.

"I have a show in San Francisco coming up," Sunny said airily.

"I saw some of the pieces," Rachel said, and Sunny loved her for it. "Very cool stuff. And you have that project with my brother."

"That's right," Sunny said, trying to sound dull. The sex was still mind-altering. The problem was the moments surrounding it. On their most recent date, they'd gone to a Steve Carell movie, and when they walked out of the theater, Jesse had asked her why she didn't like to laugh out loud.

Sunny looked down the table. "Geraldine! Vera!" she shouted. "What are you two conspiring about?"

Vera jerked her head upright. "My fault—I've been interrogating Geraldine about her life odyssey. Sorry to monopolize her."

"I understand why you'd be fascinated with Geraldine," Sunny said. "She's one of my oldest and dearest friends," she added, as if kind words could cushion the blow that she was meant to hand to Geraldine after dessert. Maybe, Sunny suddenly thought with a flash of hopefulness, Nick's arrival would ruin things to such a degree that she and Rachel would have to postpone their plan.

It was as if Nick could tell that Sunny wished he would kick up a scene. He made amiable, if loud, conversation with his fellow diners. It emerged that Derek wasn't Pam's boyfriend so much as a guy she'd met at a party two weeks ago, and so that made it all the more intense between them. By pie course they were making out, and in a complete reversal of Pam's promise they were the first guests to disappear. A few others followed quickly, including Matt and Cleo, who'd been rubbing her eyes in that way children did when they were about to melt down. Nick and Jeremy went into the garden to get even drunker. It fell to Rachel, Geraldine, and Sunny to clear the table.

Rachel claimed the sink. "Why don't you two just sit down in the den and catch up?" she said as she adjusted the water temperature. "I can get a lot more done if you guys move out of the way."

The other two looked slightly stunned and made motions relevant to appearing useful, picking up dishes and setting them down closer to the sink.

"We can all go sit down?" Rachel said, eyeing Sunny. "Or not, if you really don't want to," she added, in a tone that was not entirely sympathetic.

"I've got it under control," Sunny said.

Geraldine came to a stool on the other side of the kitchen island and smiled unsurely as she took her seat. "You have what under control?"

Sunny backed against the refrigerator and laced her fingers together, avoiding eye contact. "Rachel wants me to tell you something that I'm not sure you need to hear, but I'm not going to hear the end of it if I don't." Sunny pressed her lips together. "I did something very stupid a very long time ago."

"What's that?" asked Geraldine.

"I messed around with Peter."

"I see," Geraldine said, and Sunny nodded slowly, as if her head were weighted down with a thousand stones. "When?"

Sunny drew in air through her teeth. "When I was still at *Province*."

"So when Peter and I were a couple, you and Peter were also a couple." Geraldine took a seat at the kitchen's round table.

"No, no, we weren't a couple—not at all! He was just acting reckless, and I guess I thought I could calm him down."

"By sleeping with him?" Geraldine sounded befuddled.

Sunny glared at Rachel, who was just standing there. "He was persuasive, you know that," she told Geraldine.

"He was also her boss," Rachel chimed in.

"I was your boss, too," Geraldine reminded Sunny. "And your friend."

"You were my best friend," Sunny allowed.

Geraldine let off a bark of laughter. "Sorry, this is just . . . Wow . . . When you two were having your little phone calls and dinners, I wasn't crazy to think I wanted to kill you both."

"Only a few times," Sunny said.

"Times." Geraldine bowed her head. "Plural."

"Just a couple," Sunny said. "A few. The last time was right before I moved to New York. I was barely twenty-seven."

"I know how old you were. I threw a party for your birthday." Geraldine shook her head, dumbfounded. "And why are you telling me this now?"

"It seemed like something you should know," Rachel butted in. "I didn't tell you before because I thought it might kill you. But when you started seeing Peter again, it just seemed like you should—"

Geraldine turned to Rachel. "Wait, *you* knew about this?"

"Nobody told me, per se. I just put the pieces together," Rachel said.

"And you stood by. Even when Peter and I got engaged?"

"I was happy for you two." The pitch of Rachel's voice went up. "It wasn't like it all happened on the same day. Years passed before you got engaged."

"Yes," Geraldine croaked. "Years of my fucking life."

"Hey, don't be mad at me," Rachel said. "I'm not the one who . . . And let's be honest, it's not like you *didn't* know."

"Excuse me?" Geraldine said.

"Why did you put Sunny on Ed's list?" Rachel said. "I saw you and Ed on your walks around Harbourfront, right before the layoffs. You advised him on who to cut, right?"

Geraldine's face went splotchy in parts, like an heirloom tomato. "I didn't have the final say."

"You had some say," Rachel said. "A say. You made sure Sunny went on the pink-slip list, and we all know it wasn't for anything to do with her work."

"*You're* the one who had me fired, Geraldine?" Sunny couldn't help feeling a bit impressed. "I didn't know you had it in you."

"It wasn't my choice," Geraldine said. "We had to lower the head count."

"But you gave Ed advice. And then Ed ejected Sunny," Rachel said. "I always suspected that's what went down."

"Yup." Geraldine gave a frustrated laugh. "After all these years, you're still a little girl detective, Rachel. Well done. I'll have to find a star sticker for you in my bag."

Sunny laughed. "Sorry! I know this isn't remotely funny. But she's right, Rachel—you have an epic Harriet the Spy complex."

"Not so fast," Geraldine said to Sunny. "Peter was obsessed with you, and I hated both of you for it. But that's not why you were let go. We had to weigh all sorts of factors. You were the one person who could afford to start over." She gestured around the apartment. "You kept telling me—you kept telling everyone—how much you wanted to move to New York, and about all the interest in your work."

"When Ed told me he was letting me go, I came straight to your office," Sunny said, the memory growing brighter and clearer. "And you pretended to be shocked. But you knew. Is that why you had those cookies ready for me?"

"I didn't know anything for sure," Geraldine insisted, and turned to Rachel. "Are you happy? You did your job. She told me. You can put your notebook away."

"We just don't want Peter to hurt you again," Rachel said.

Geraldine paused to gather her thoughts. "Peter and I are not seeing each other. I met somebody else who's really . . . good." Geraldine's eyes darted between Sunny and Geraldine. "This is the part where you're supposed to tell me that you're happy for me."

"Of course I am," Sunny said, filling with shame. "I didn't want to say anything in the first place."

Geraldine's eyes were glazing over. "You don't want to do *anything* that will affect other people's feelings."

"What's that supposed to mean?" Sunny said.

"It means we're just props for you." Geraldine came off her stool. "You don't actually like people, which is inconvenient, since you need to keep some of us on hand to make you look better."

"Okay," Rachel said in a breathy exhalation. "Maybe we should all take a break."

"Will you stop telling us what to do?" Geraldine said. "You mess other people up just as badly. The only difference is, you pretend to be warm and uncalculating. But you're totally calculating, creeping about and taking mental notes and trying to shock people with your so-called observations. Sadly, you're just too consumed with yourself to actually see anything for what it is."

"What the fuck?" Rachel cried.

Geraldine fixed her gaze on Rachel. "You're mad at the world for not giving you the recognition you crave, and you're mad at me for working hard and starting to get some myself. You've been mad at Sunny for being the center of the universe since the beginning of time, and I don't even know what you'll do when you learn she's fucking your little brother."

Sunny felt herself drain of color. A crashing sound trilled through the air, and she realized she'd dropped a nut bowl. Rachel leaped to sweep up the shards. Geraldine didn't offer to help.

"I already knew about that," Rachel said from below. "He's slept with half my friends. It doesn't matter."

Sunny's body relaxed when she saw that Nick and Jeremy were still outside, bent in toward each other. They hadn't heard anything.

Geraldine was watching Rachel in a way that made Sunny nervous. "Do you remember how you used to write about me in your columns?" Geraldine asked at last. "I always think about how after we'd gone out together one night, you handed in a story about how socially awkward people were actually cool. You described your friend 'D' as 'a shy and earnest sort,'" Geraldine paused. "I remember the wording after all these years. Do you know what it feels like to see yourself reduced to an '*earnest sort*' in print? I was so crushed."

"I honestly don't remember the piece," Rachel said. "I'm sorry if it hurt you."

"Not if." Geraldine clenched her jaw.

"It's horrible to read about yourself," Sunny said. "I absolutely refuse to do it."

"The only thing anyone could possibly feel when they read the stuff that's been written about Sunny MacLeod is the urge to . . . forget it." Geraldine waved her arms in the air. "You two are something. You don't know what to do with me when I'm not the pitiful spectacle. You both wanted to break Peter and me apart tonight, to hurt me under the guise of helping me. As if you've ever known how to be helpful!"

"That's not fair," Sunny said. "I was always there for you when you needed me."

"You were available to witness me try to make sense of the senseless, to watch me come undone," Geraldine said. "While you were seducing my fiancé."

"He was your boyfriend," Rachel interjected.

Geraldine raised her hand to silence Rachel. "Sunny," she said. "What I don't get is what was in it for you?"

"Nothing, he meant absol—"

"I'm not talking about Peter," Geraldine told her. "You and me, why did you bother? Did you need my jilted ass around for all these years in order to feel better about yourself? Did you just want me to take over your lease? You certainly didn't need me because you liked me."

Sunny felt an ache in her chest. "You're misreading this," she said. "You're wonderful—strong and smart. There's so much about you I admire."

"Admire." Geraldine gave Sunny a shaming look. "Is there anyone you actually feel anything for? Besides Jesse—or are you over him already, too?"

Again Sunny's heart quickened, and she checked through the garden window. Nick and Jeremy appeared to be busy smoking a joint. She turned back to see Rachel watching her intently, her eyes growing even heavier. Now Sunny felt the fool. The garden erupted into thunderous laughter, and the empty branches looked as if they were scratching the night air. "The Jesse thing is not something I planned on."

"Just like you didn't plan on sleeping with Peter." Geraldine clapped her hands. "I absolutely love how effortless you are about everything. It doesn't matter—why try when it all still works out for you?"

Sunny tasted a bitterness in the back of her throat. She was going to be forty in just over two years. She was supposed to be building her life, not setting it on fire. "Why would I have planned any of this?" she muttered. Geraldine and Rachel just stood there, still and cruel. "What is wrong with us?" Sunny cried into her palms. "Are we ever going to get to a point where we can just *be*? Where we're not a group of women bearing grudges and sizing ourselves up against one another?"

"It's a women thing?" Geraldine said. "*That's* what you've got? This is all the patriarchy's fault?" She rolled her eyes. "I sincerely hope this evening provided you both with the empowerment you were looking for."

"I should go," Rachel said.

"Same." Geraldine pursed her lips.

Sunny wanted out, too. On top of everything, Nick was still on the premises, so she had another fight ahead of her. Her shoulders curled as she shimmied into her navy quilted coat and grabbed the spare leash from the hook in the hallway. "Stanley needs a walk," she said, her voice a quiet panic.

# 31

Geraldine moved into the top floor of a narrow brick house in Vinegar Hill, two and a half blocks from the Brooklyn Navy Yard. The building was painted a slate blue, and it was covered in vines that clung to it like moss. She lived above her landlords, a pair of elderly sisters who appeared to barely tolerate each other and who ordered nearly all their meals from Seamless. Tiny and noisy as her new apartment was, it was hers alone, and she loved it with a frightening intensity.

On Geraldine's second Friday as a Brooklyn resident, she and Art were seated on her new couch, one of the few pieces of furniture in her new apartment that had required no assembly. Art's stated purpose that chilly November afternoon had been to help her settle in. They'd gone to a garden shop on Atlantic Avenue, where they'd purchased a pair of potted fig trees. They'd packed them into the back of a cab and lugged them up the stoop and two flights of stairs.

The trees now bookended the rear window and were surrounded by boxes of IKEA furniture. Art and Geraldine completed two out of seven items and decided that building the rest was a task better suited for Sylvie and Marina, who actually enjoyed handiwork.

While Geraldine zoomed around the Internet in preparation for the meeting she had to go to later that night, Art studied the bundle of old *Province* issues that Barrett had mailed down to her. "'So now with the basic facts out of the way, we can all agree that swingers' clubs exist,'" Art recited from an old Rachel Ziff column. "'But how does one go about scoring an invitation?'"

"Please, enough," Geraldine said. She didn't want Rachel's spirit haunting her apartment.

Art ignored her and went on, "'The first person I think to ask is Laetitia, a College Street bartender who has that sex-goddess je ne sais quoi.'"

"Okay, stop." Geraldine moved to snatch the magazine out of his grasp. "I'm not in the mood for Rachel."

Art made a puppy-dog face. "Sorry." He knew all about the Canadian Thanksgiving fiasco. "I will say another twenty-five-year-old's prose caught my eye. The mini review of *Kill Bill* is fantastic. Excellent nostril description."

"Thanks." Geraldine could feel her cheeks warming. All she could remember from that movie was Uma's yellow jumpsuit.

Art got up and went into the kitchen. Geraldine could hear the refrigerator door open, then a hiss as a bottle cap came loose. "Want one?" he called out.

"No, I'm meeting Elinda soon," she reminded him, cocking her head back and anticipating the evening. They were having dinner with a pair of virtual-reality kingpins. A growing part of her job was accompanying her boss on outings with potential partners. Elinda usually asked Geraldine to meet her at the bar of whatever overpriced establishment they were patronizing half an hour before the official start time, and Geraldine would munch on nuts and listen to Elinda's train of thought. Mostly personnel problems, a bit on her husband. He'd gotten into vaping. "Art?" Geraldine called into the kitchen. "Maybe I'll have one."

Art was smiling when he came back into view, a beer in each hand. "*Kill Bill* is very timely."

"Who now?" Geraldine took the bottle and waited for another name to add to the list of disgraced men. They were dropping like litter, a new one every day. She was enjoying it quite a bit.

"No, nothing like that. I just rewatched it."

"Refresh my memory?"

"Uma plays a former assassin who wakes up from a coma and discovers she's lost her unborn child and fiancé. She vows to kill everybody who contributed to the undoing of her life."

Geraldine lifted her chin. "So you're saying I've come undone?"

"I'm saying you're killing it."

As Art resumed his spot on the couch, he lifted Geraldine's feet and placed them on top of his lap, pressing the heels of his hands into her arches. Her head filled with confusion, and she felt the rest of her body relax. Art had been back from Los Angeles for a little over a week, and things between them had settled into a pleasantly platonic rhythm. Art had mentioned on a recent episode of his show that he was seeing somebody, and he and Geraldine now interacted like exes who were still incredibly close friends.

Art was telling her about a chance encounter with one of Uma Thurman's brothers, and Geraldine studied his face as he talked. He was one of the few men on earth who was more handsome than he knew. Even she hadn't realized it at first. It was a good thing they weren't involved, Geraldine reminded herself. She was in no shape for that sort of thing. A month had passed since that car crash of a night at Sunny's. She'd exhausted replaying the conversation in her head and had moved on to deeper reaches of her memory vault, vivid visions from years and years ago that made her ache with embarrassment. It wasn't Peter she was upset with. She'd sent him an apology for ghosting after his party.

Sunny and Geraldine were the ones who'd hurt her the most. She'd tried to work some of this out at her and Sylvie's last recorded interview, with Stephen Bledersoe, a UPenn professor who had a hit behavioral science podcast. His current obsession was future happiness and how humans were likely to incorrectly predict how good their choices would ultimately make them feel. "I love this idea," she'd said. "It brings me great comfort to hear that we're all wired to make decisions we'll regret." She proceeded to give Stephen a revised account of the fiasco. "One of my best friends betrayed me with my boyfriend, and the other watched the whole thing go down without saying anything."

"Not that I'm trained to say this, but the guy sounds like a bit of a sociopath," Stephen said. "People with personality disorders are too tricky to neatly fit into future-happiness theories."

"He's not the issue," Geraldine said.

"Dude, it's the women that did a number on her," Sylvie clarified. "They're supes toxic. Time to move on, Gerry."

Geraldine gave a wistful shake of the head. Sylvie didn't understand. It would be another ten years at least until Sylvie realized that the mediocre, imperfect people she'd happened to align herself with would end up being more significant to her than she could possibly fathom. Who knew, maybe Geraldine would be that person for Sylvie. "They thought they were doing the right thing by rustling up the past," Geraldine said wistfully. "I know they were trying to keep me from falling down."

"Into the hole *they* dug!" Sylvie cried.

Geraldine sighed now and looked up at Art. He was tapping his fingers on her calves and appeared to be sinking into thought. "Can I ask you something?" she said. "Who's the lucky lady?" Geraldine had hoped it would come out sounding funny. But Art just stared at her, looking startled. "You said you're seeing someone. In your interview with the Fitzpatrick brothers."

"I said I was *sort of* seeing someone." Art's cheeks reddened. "I'm not sure what she'd call it."

He stopped working on her feet, and the atmosphere changed. Geraldine held her bottle tighter, as if she could make the eels stop swimming around her fingertips.

"Have you asked her what she'd call it?" she said.

Art looked up at the ceiling. "She's been going through some personal issues."

"All the more reason to be there for her." Geraldine inched close enough to hold Art's hand.

Art watched their fingers intertwine, then leaned down to kiss her. He smelled like cloves, and his lips were soft. He reared back before she was ready to stop.

"Was that okay?" His eyes were pools of hope. Geraldine couldn't remember the last time anybody had looked at her that way. She moved in for another kiss.

Her mind went empty with pleasure, and then the worries came marching in, like little ants. Though she didn't know for certain, Geraldine was fairly sure the women Art had dated before were in their twenties. It was possible he'd never touched somebody who wore cotton briefs and didn't shave all her pubic hair. She shimmied onto her knees and pulled her dress over her head. Better to get it over with, she figured. Art looked terrified, then fumbled with his shirt buttons. His skin wasn't nearly as pale as she'd feared. Placing her palms on his chest, Geraldine could feel the heat rising from him. She kissed his shoulders. "I like your skin," she told him.

Art gulped. "I like your . . ." Art squeezed his eyes tight. "I just like you. A lot."

Geraldine was smiling so hard she could feel the tension in her temples. She'd forgotten that it could be like this, forgotten how happiness could hit you like a truck. She buried her face in the crook of his neck and reached down to unfasten his belt.

"Should we turn off the lights?" she whispered. Art appeared to be massively overwhelmed, his body rigid as a matchstick.

"God no," Art said, and came back to life.

# 32

Rachel saw Sunny first. She was exiting the elevator, her bright eyes casting about the gallery. Rachel felt something catch in her throat and cocked her head, pantomiming serious consideration of the installation in front of her, a lifelike woman sitting on a bench, her opaque pantyhose bunching around her ankles. The sculpture was made of wax and appeared to be perspiring under the hot gallery lights.

Sunny was dressed in dark gray overalls, and her hair was pulled up in a not-quite ponytail, revealing her pointy ears. She reminded Rachel of a baby bat. Rachel realized her hands were shaking, and she had to remind herself that Sunny didn't have the right to be mad at her. Sunny had sounded surprisingly tender when she'd reached out. She'd heard the news and needed to see Rachel before she left town. For once Rachel was the one who could hardly find a time that would work, what with all the cardboard boxes to be scavenged and final play dates to be arranged and accounts to be canceled. She had a doctor's appointment on the Upper East Side, so Sunny suggested the Met Breuer.

"Hi, you," Sunny said, and Rachel felt her heart hitch. Sunny's voice was a running brook, her every utterance a benediction. "So great, isn't it?" Sunny gestured at the sculpture. Rachel stared and came up with a Muppety noise. Looking at art with other people made her nervous. She never knew what to think, what to say. She followed Sunny around a corner. The wintry light filtering in from behind a window shade amplified the museum's cold atmosphere.

Rachel had only the dimmest memory of coming here with her parents when it was still the Whitney. This was her first visit since the big conversion a few years ago, and it felt exactly the same to her, quiet and tomblike. She swelled with premature nostalgia for the city she'd allowed to be wasted on her.

Sunny and Rachel moved around the museum, darting among the slab-walled galleries as if they'd really come to see art and not each other. Sunny gravitated toward pieces seemingly at random and stared at them, moving her head this way and that. Rachel tried her best not to get swept up in reading the wall placards, a habit she hadn't been able to break since middle school, and was not disappointed when they came into a minuscule room on the ground floor and Sunny sighed and clapped her hands, signaling the conclusion of their gallery crawl.

"Want to go outside?" Sunny asked. "For a walk?"

"Sure," Rachel said. "We can look for a post office, if that's okay? I have to pick up some forms."

It was uncomfortably cold out, and the only people on the street were women pushing strollers and shop workers smoking cigarettes. They walked north on Madison Avenue and chatted about the trauma of moving. "I made the mistake of trying to do a little bit every day, which has just expanded into a packing session that's taken nearly a month," Rachel said.

"You don't need much stuff," Sunny told her. "I learn that again every time I move."

"But I like stuff." Rachel gave a shrug. This was getting strange, not talking about Sunny's Thanksgiving dinner. "Have you . . . heard from her?"

"Geraldine?" Sunny gave a slight smile and looked away. "I don't even know what I'd want to say to her. I'm still processing. It was a terrible night."

"Don't say I never have brilliant ideas," Rachel said. "I'm sure you guys will sort it out. She loves you."

"And what about you and me?" Sunny asked, and Rachel suddenly felt warm. "Are you as mad at me as I suspect?"

"About Jesse?" Rachel asked. "I'm getting used to it."

"There's nothing for you to get used to. He and I talked, and—"

"I don't need to hear the details," Rachel said. Truth was, Jesse had already come over to eat tacos and debrief his sister on his romantic travails. She wasn't surprised. The long haul didn't make sense for either of them. "Jesse's not what I'm mad about," she said. "You think I'm some meddling dork. That's why you were never nice to me."

"That's not true," Sunny said. "You always scared me. You're so judgmental. And you've always been especially brutal with me."

"Maybe you're not used to people being tough on you," Rachel replied.

"You've made your point. I know what you think of me."

"No. I find you fascinating," Rachel said after a moment.

"That's not what you'd say about somebody you like." Sunny gazed up at the sky, composing her thoughts. "Do you even *wonder* about me? Does it occur to you how sad I am most of the time?"

The fragility on Sunny's face was almost too much to bear. "About what?" Rachel said softly.

"It's not important." Sunny shook her head, and Rachel didn't press it. She didn't trust herself to locate the empathy Sunny needed.

Rachel filled with wistfulness for the person she used to be, before worrying about being irrevocably left behind had become a full-time occupation. What were her pluck and curiosity worth if she was always keeping score? "We should have left each other alone," Rachel said. "There's probably a reason we've always stayed apart from each other."

Sunny nodded with understanding.

"Sunny?" Rachel went quiet. "I'm sorry for whatever you're going through."

They were at a street corner, and the light had turned green so they could cross. Rachel reached for her arm, but Sunny had become limp and was turning away, sinking into herself.

# 33

Of the fifty or so passengers riding the ferry to Governors Island, only two dared speak above a whisper. There was a man talking nonstop in German on his phone, his guttural stream breaking every so often for a recognizable phrase such as "star power" or "VIP boat." A woman closer to Sunny was regaling her seatmate with the intricacies of the New York City public-high-school application process. "It's Stuy or die," she said in a manic tone.

Fog clung to the windows, intensifying Sunny's sense of entrapment. Why did so many art fairs have to take place on islands? She stared down at her hands. She still hadn't taken off her ring. She and Nick were going to see a lawyer for the first time the following week. He was going to slaughter her. He owed her nothing. Her parents would try to help, but she wasn't going to let them. She would need health insurance, so that meant an office job, her first since her early days in New York. Anxiety colonized her mind, and she'd had to stop using organic deodorant. She looked up at Jesse, who stealthily rubbed his thumb against her knee. She was grateful to have him in the seat next to her, his body like a protective boulder.

The ferry finally pulled into port, and Sunny rushed off, pretending not to hear when a woman said that she liked her boots. Sunny had dressed monastically, in a shapeless navy dress, and thrown on a pair of vintage duck boots at the last minute. A fleet of festival assistants stood in a line, offering branded tote bags and signature cocktails that were a medicinal pink. They contained what looked like poisonous berries. Sunny located the single tray of sparkling waters.

"Ready?" Jesse asked.

"Yup." She made the effort to smile. She'd been to more of these fairs than she could count and really didn't see why she needed to attend one more. Her preview evening tickets had come courtesy of Forma Editions, a Beijing-based art-book company that had paid through the nose for the rights to reprint in a coffee-table book two of her paintings of used-up lipstick. If it were up to Sunny, she'd be home watching murder mysteries on the British streaming service she'd just signed up for. Yet Dominique, her new therapist, argued that it was important that she show face, bound as the fair was to be filled with people from her and Nick's world. Dominique was a chicly graying Jewish woman who worked out of a building on the Upper West Side that smelled reassuringly like stew. "Your inclination is to retreat. It's important to keep up long-standing habits. Bring a friend if it makes you feel safer. Just not Jesse."

But their session had been on Tuesday afternoon, mere hours before Nick mentioned that he'd been "hanging out" with a mother from Agnes's school. Sunny didn't know what hurt her more—that he'd seemed so giddy when he told her or that the mother was a lawyer at Human Rights Watch. Just in case she didn't understand where she stood in Nick's estimation. Even the emails that came through the info@sunnymacleod.com account, requests for magazine illustrations and indie-film posters, all pointed in the same direction: The world found her insubstantial, the human equivalent of a vintage rain boot.

She'd made a portrait of Geraldine and sent it as a housewarming gift. She hadn't heard back yet, wasn't sure she ever would. There was no undoing hurt, never any guarantee of forgiveness. For the first time in her life, Sunny was trying to be good—not good *at* something but good. She'd started reading the newspaper and practicing her own form of walking meditation, circling Gramercy Park slowly and silently as if through water.

Jesse and Sunny began working their way along the pavilion's east wing, occasionally stopping to say hello to people Sunny knew. She was careful to keep moving before anybody asked about Jesse. She had no way of explaining him, even to herself. He was her temporary anchor? A thirty-three-year-old who had no health insurance and who regularly Airbnb'd his spare bedroom to Brazilian tourists? They clicked with each other, but he wasn't the answer. They both knew that. Sunny needed to make up for lost time, not lose more time. There was nothing clearer. Jesse was well behaved, only pressing his nose into the back of her neck once, in a darkened video room.

"Is that Sunny MacLeod?" came a raspy voice. She swiveled and saw the outlines of two girls peering from behind a temporary wall. She returned to the art she'd been examining, a collection of drawings that reminded her of the pages of her childhood sticker books. A moment later Sunny heard the same voice say, "She's so overrated."

Sunny glanced at Jesse before slipping out of the booth and

rushing to the end of the hangar. Jesse caught up with her in the corridor by the bathroom and grabbed her by the shoulders.

"Sun, they're jealous."

"No, I shouldn't have come," she told him. "It's too much."

"Let's find your booth, and then we can leave and get dinner," he said.

Sunny gazed into the main space and went queasy just looking at all the teeth and eyes glinting under the blue lights. The idea of locating her work and playing the part of Sunny was too much. "I'll email them, say I got sick," she told him. "I just need to be alone. Okay?"

He kissed her softly and hugged her tight. Part of her didn't want to be anywhere but enfolded within him, yet she needed to escape. She shouldn't have pushed herself to separate from him so quickly, because when she did, she was face-to-face with Nick's ex-wife. Zoya's eyes were wide, unable to contain the shock of seeing Sunny making out with a stranger in front of a public restroom. Sunny had no choice but to give a sheepish wave. "Zoya, hi!"

Zoya's head remained tilted at a forty-five-degree angle. "I wasn't sure if that was you."

"This is Jes—" Sunny started to say, but Zoya waved her hands in the air. "I didn't see anything! Just your lipstick pieces," she added awkwardly, and scurried off.

Sunny felt weak, tried to remember the last time she'd eaten. "I thought I was doing the right thing leaving Nick," she said to Jesse as Zoya disappeared from view. "I feel sick with myself. How did I mess my life up so completely?"

Jesse shook his head reassuringly. "You weren't happy."

"Do I look happy now?" She bit down on the inside of her cheek.

Jesse reached for her chin, but she wouldn't let him. "I'm so sorry I dragged you into my mess," she said. "I'll call you soon. Promise."

Sunny could feel him watching her as she cut through the crowd. Outside, the air was smooth and slightly warm for late November. An attendant at the ferry terminal informed her she'd just missed the 6:40; the next one wasn't coming for another fifteen minutes. She waited on the edge of the bench and stared at the water, trying to still her horrible thoughts.

# 34

"You're going to love this: Canadian girls are the new French girls." Geraldine watched Sunny blink behind her new tortoiseshell glasses. "Our web czar, Declan, said that any video with the words 'Canadian Style' or 'Canadian Beauty' is bound to perform bonkers."

"Don't people have more important things to read about?"

"Like Russia and sex offenders and deportations?" Geraldine said. "Exactly why everyone wants to numb their brains."

The pair were seated at a tiny marble table near the front of the café, and gusts of wind blew in every time the door swung open. Geraldine had kept on her scarf and hat, and Sunny was wearing Levi's and a black Patagonia parka. Geraldine had never seen her in anything so practical.

"So you have your own web czar?" Sunny smiled with what looked like bemusement. Geraldine could feel the café's spindly chair pressing into the backs of her thighs. No wonder she'd been avoiding actually getting together with Sunny ever since Sunny had reached out and asked to see her for a "holiday drink," as if that were a thing. Geraldine had said yes, then rescheduled it, then asked to change it to a coffee. The place where Geraldine's assistant, Katie, had suggested they meet up, Elio's, didn't even serve coffee, just matcha, a revolting phenomenon that Geraldine had managed to avoid until now.

Geraldine didn't show up to brag about having somebody work for her, or being able to surf the Internet acrobatically. She wanted to let Sunny see that she was okay—good, even. And she needed to do it now, while everything was still fresh—not just Thanksgiving but that hideous and eternal chapter of Geraldine's life when she felt dead if she didn't have a trip to New York coming up. She could still summon the fluttery feeling of trudging up Rachel's stairs with her suitcase and waiting to be buzzed in so she could fawn over Rachel's swelling belly or crying baby, all the while harboring the hope, like some lovesick teenager, that she might get to really be with Sunny before her flight back home.

"I have something for you," Sunny said, reaching under the table. Geraldine tensed; she hadn't brought a Christmas present for Sunny. Was there anything in her bag she could repurpose? She'd just received an essential-oils kit in lovely gold packaging. Had she thrown it into her tote or left it in the office? Her mind went blank when she saw the notebook Sunny had placed on the table. The Book of Indignities.

"I found it when I was packing up my studio," Sunny said. "I'm sorry I took so long."

Geraldine ran her palms over the marbleized cover. "I thought I'd never see it again."

Sunny gave a sideways smile. "What are you going to do with it?"

"I don't know . . . have some witchy ceremonial burning?" Geraldine thumbed through the pages, stopping at a spread in the back. Sunny had drawn a picture of herself lying on the grass with headphones on. In the thought bubble above, Geraldine was speaking into a microphone. She glanced up at Sunny. She was embarrassed and saw that Sunny's cheeks had flushed. "Maybe I'll keep it," Geraldine said. "Where are you living?"

"I'm staying in Murray Hill, but that ends in the New Year, so I'm more or less a nomad."

"That sounds glamorous," Geraldine said, and felt lousy when Sunny didn't reply. She just sat still, as if she were fighting a tremendous headache. "About Thanksgiving," Geraldine said abruptly. "I said things I wish I could take back."

Sunny pulled at the edge of her sleeve. "I deserve it all. I only wish you'd found out about everything sooner. Before it had a chance to fester."

"Wishes for the fishes. My grandfather used to say that." Geraldine got a smile out of Sunny. "I only have one question. You and Peter, you weren't in love, were you?"

Sunny gave a vigorous shake of the head. "God no. It was all so stupid. I realize this is not an excuse, but I didn't think of the pain I was causing at the time. It seemed separate. I should have told you everything. Things could have been so different. . . ."

"No, I knew he was a dog. It's all in there." Geraldine pointed at the journal. "You'd think I was determined to make myself miserable."

Sunny didn't say anything, but she was listening intently.

"And I'm a little sorry, too," Geraldine said.

"For the layoff? I found my way."

"No, for all the pressure I put on you. I lodged myself in your life like some seed that gets stuck in your teeth. You tolerated me, and sometimes you even let me in."

Geraldine watched Sunny constrict. She'd seen her do it many times before, at moments of excessive display. Sunny didn't cross her arms or bend into herself. That would have been too obvious. She brought her nose to her shoulder and looked at Geraldine out of the side of one eye, like a swan.

"Geraldine, that's too much. I always valued you as a friend, and I never thought of you like—"

"There were times when I thought I'd die in your apartment in Toronto, with Barrett finding me rotting in my bed and some movie you'd told me about playing on the iPad. You know I watched every film you ever mentioned?" Geraldine took perverse pleasure in seeing Sunny flinch. "Books, too—I have a Sunny library."

Sunny wouldn't hear it. "You're the one who got me reading Eve Babitz before anyone else was talking about her," she reminded Geraldine.

Geraldine remembered how Sunny had included a vintage paperback of *Slow Days, Fast Company* in one of her old *Cassette* columns and how when she'd first glimpsed the psychedelic cover bracketed by a Polo Lounge toothpick and an autographed Peter Falk eight-by-ten, it had felt as though Sunny were winking at her from the magazine page. She could almost laugh at it now. Sunny closed her eyes, and Geraldine watched her carefully. All these years later, she still marveled at how beautiful Sunny was, a composition in cream and inky black. "And what about the rest? I want to know how you're doing with the separation."

"Separation." Sunny tapped her fingertips on the table. "Such a weird word. Like something that belongs in a cake recipe."

"Are you thinking about unseparating?"

"No." Sunny smiled. "The last time Nick and I spoke, he was too busy shopping for a lawyer to have time to buy his daughter a Christmas present."

Geraldine gazed up at the girl working the cash register. She was cleaning a miniature Christmas tree that had been fashioned out of gummy worms. "Are you making art?" She wasn't just trying to make Sunny feel better. She would always be jealous of Sunny's ability to work through her storms.

"I'm playing with some ideas. They're different from before."

Geraldine stirred her drink and took a sip. It tasted worse than terrible, like boiled pencil shavings.

"Cheers," Sunny said, draining her cup. "This is my big indulgence of the day. I'm off everything—coffee, alcohol, men." Geraldine gave her a dubious look. "Jesse and I aren't seeing each other anymore." Sunny fidgeted with the gold cuff around her little wrist. "Well, we're not touching each other."

"Want to hear something?" Geraldine said. "I used to have a massive crush on Jesse. Now that Rachel's fled town, I wonder if I'll ever see him again."

Sunny started giggling. "Sorry, the idea of Rachel surrounded yet again by Canadians cracks me up."

Geraldine nodded in agreement. "It *is* funny. I hope it works out for her. Rachel's not a bad person."

*Just super annoying*, Sunny's expression seemed to say before it changed to something more dignified. "And that guy you said you were seeing?"

Geraldine felt a pleasurable lift in her stomach and told Sunny it was still on. "He's been in L.A. for work. I'm planning on going to visit him over the holiday."

"I really like it out there—fake tits and all," Sunny said. "I haven't been in a little while. I should go, sunbake my woes away."

Geraldine could sense that Sunny was descending into her own thoughts. This couldn't go on much longer. This was all Geraldine was ever going to get from Sunny, who had never offered her heart to her. She had intimated as much, but she'd never done it. Whereas Geraldine had offered Sunny everything she had, every time she saw her. Even when they'd been hundreds of miles apart, Geraldine had placed all of her hopes and heartaches at Sunny's feet.

"I've been listening to your show," Sunny said. "It's really good."

"That's sweet of you."

"No, I'm not being sweet. And neither are you. You sure can throw shade. Sometimes it's a little hard for me to listen. I was surprised to hear the way you talk about your time coming to New York. I had no idea you were so lonely."

"In the very beginning," Geraldine said tentatively.

"But you had friends here," Sunny sounded uncertain. "You had me."

Geraldine wasn't sure how to respond. "I had your events to glom on to, but tagging along gets embarrassing."

"We saw each other one-on-one. We had teas, remember?"

Sunny's obliviousness was starting to wear on Geraldine. "Sunny, we had *a* tea. And then there was the time I brought a tray of iced teas to your doorstep and we sat on your stoop for half an hour. You didn't even invite me in." Geraldine couldn't believe she'd expressed this, and held the composition book tight against her chest.

"I wish you had said something—to *me*. Before taking your indignities public on your show."

Geraldine sat up straighter and looked down at her book; she hadn't thought of the connection before. Was she some masochistic collector of pain? She inhaled hard. "Even if you're trying to be nice, it can be painful to be around you." Sunny was looking at her with an expression of violation. "When I come to your events and you barely talk to me, I feel like I'm on some distant, invisible planet."

"I never meant to make you feel less than you are." Sunny closed her eyes. "I miss you, and I miss the time we used to fritter away whole days together."

"God, that was so long ago," Geraldine said.

"We used to tell each other our secrets. Now I learn about what you're up to by listening to your podcast. There was something you said on the show that I liked, the way you described your past life—what was it, about a shipwreck?"

"That I was swimming between sinking islands," Geraldine said.

"That's it. I wouldn't ever wish that on you, but it's beautiful. And now you're on land. Which is also beautiful."

"Sometimes I think the world has gone mad."

"Or maybe you've found your way in it." Sunny granted her old friend a melancholy smile. "Better you than anybody else."

# 35

Let me get this straight," Matt said. "Your new editor comes to town, asks you out to a fancy lunch, and then at the last minute tells you to come to her hotel room instead."

"Hotel lobby, not room, but otherwise, yeah, you got it," Rachel said, and cocked an eyebrow at him. They were walking down Wellington Street, around the corner from their new, temporary, and kind of wonderful condo in downtown Toronto. There was a gym at least twice the size of the one Rachel belonged to in Brooklyn and a squad of supers ready to come running anytime a lightbulb went out. Matt and Rachel were supposed to find real housing by the spring. The provost had yet to give them a hard date.

"You'll be careful with her?" Rachel cupped her hand around the back of their daughter's head. Matt was walking his bicycle, with Cleo strapped in the plastic baby seat like a tiny princess atop a rickshaw steered by a drunken supplicant. Matt was coming off an all-nighter, and his steps were a little jagged. He and his new research partner, Marcus, needed to submit a research proposal before winter break, which gave them two more days. At least Cleo's parka was heavily padded, Rachel told herself. She was trying not to freak out. She had to be somewhere else, soon.

"This hotel thing sounds like a come-on," Matt said.

"I don't have the bandwidth right now for your ribbing."

"I thought that's why you agreed to come up here, to get more bandwidth."

Rachel kept moving down Wellington Street. All around her a blur of business attire and briefcases fed into the revolving doors of shiny office buildings. When people said Toronto was so clean, Rachel suspected what they meant was that everything was so spanking new. The city's grand wonder, the CN Tower, had been constructed in the same decade Rachel was born. But there were Old World charms, too, streets of brick homes and magnificent trees.

Rachel glanced back and saw that Matt was steadying the bike as the crowd pulsated around him. He was having a harder time navigating the foot traffic than she was. She slowed down.

"I know I've just sat through six straight hours of sexual-harassment training," he said when he caught up to her, "but doesn't asking you to meet in her room at eight in the morning strike you as a little—"

"How many times do I have to tell you? Lobby restaurant. But eight a.m. is rude, I'll give you that." Her new editor, Jessica Mayo-Brodsky, was in town to visit the set of *The Theory of Danger*, a film adaptation of one of the books she'd edited.

Matt didn't say anything. Rachel felt a surge of excitement when she thought she recognized a woman rushing past him. For a split second, she thought it was Elsie, the receptionist with the spiky attitude from *Province.* Rachel had become a ghost hunter, always on the lookout for slivers from her past. She'd had a few legitimate sightings. The other day she'd spotted Peter Ricker standing outside Canadian Tire, passionately arguing on his cell phone with what must've been a repairman about botched grouting. "Bone white! Not white—bone white!" Cleo had even pointed and asked her mother what was the matter. "It's just a grown man throwing a tantrum," she'd replied, tempted to take a video with her cell phone and send it to Geraldine. But there was no point. Geraldine had walked out of that Thanksgiving dinner and become one with the ghosts. She'd sent Rachel an email saying she needed time and would reach out when she was ready to talk. There was nothing Rachel could do now but wait.

When they came upon the corner of Simcoe Street, Rachel saw the navy hotel awning and her stomach gave a hungry flip. "Why am I so nervous?"

"You've got nothing to worry about," Matt said. "Remember, you're the talent. And you're incredibly cute." He rubbed her back and kissed her.

Rachel sighed a little doubtfully and turned to Cleo, who grabbed a handful of her mother's furry hat. "I love you, Schmoopie," Rachel said, planting a kiss on her daughter's nose. Cleo blinked in what Rachel was certain was total solidarity.

A Christmas tree stationed near the fireplace filled the lobby of Hotel Simcoe with a sharp aroma of pine. There was no question that the wispy girl waiting on the couch was Jessica, but Rachel pretended to look around, as if she hadn't Googled her new editor to death and didn't know she had a mop of strawberry-blond hair and transparent beige glasses that reminded Rachel of the old Italian ladies who had nightly cocktails in deck chairs on the sidewalk when she was growing up. In Jessica's case they were meant to be ironic, Rachel could only assume.

"Rachel?" Jessica Mayo-Brodsky stood up. She was wearing a green eyelet skirt and red block-heeled Mary Janes. A vegan-looking bag with a typewriter pattern sat on the couch. "Can I hug you? I feel like I already know you so well from your writing."

"It's so great to meet you!" Rachel murmured into Jessica's sweater as they embraced.

"Is it okay if we just sit here?" Jessica asked. "The restaurant is pretty grim."

Rachel lowered herself onto the couch while Jessica kept talking.

"I'm so sorry I had to switch things on you. One of the actresses got mono, and they had to rearrange the entire schedule. I'm not a breakfast person, but I'll have a coffee. Want anything to eat? There's a bagel bar by the elevator."

"No, no, coffee is perfect." Rachel didn't want to waste any of their limited time and prayed her stomach didn't growl. She'd eat something after.

"I'll get the drinks," Jessica said. "It's so funny that I have two Canadian authors," she added, returning with two mugs.

Rachel nodded smilingly. Now was not the time to explain that she was from Kensington, Brooklyn. Instead they chatted about the logistics of Jessica's visit. She liked the hotel's proximity to a pop-up botanical perfume shop.

"We need to discuss your book," she said at last, and Rachel felt her breathing slow. "First let me tell you that it is absolutely on fire," Jessica said. "You write beautifully. But so does my cat." Rachel tried to keep a flat expression on her face. "What kills me is the honesty of your prose. It gets me right here." Jessica pretended to stab her heart. "I'm not just blowing smoke," she said. "I don't do that—you'll see.

I've been editing for a while"—here Rachel bit her cheeks to keep from smiling—"and I'm usually able to keep an emotional distance when I read a manuscript. Yours made me so . . . angry."

Rachel was taken aback. "Angry?" she said. "I was going through some stuff when I wrote the book, I guess?"

"No, it's there in all your work. The other three books have it, too."

"The out-of-print ones?" Rachel spluttered, and immediately regretted it. "They're *angry*?"

"A little." Jessica shrugged. "And sad. Sangry!" She laughed. "Your writing is so *moving*. Your previous editor was crazy not to blow you up."

"I'm not sure it was her choice." Rachel brought her hands back to her lap.

"Oh, she failed, for sure. Your writing reminds me of Mary Gaitskill. She's this—did you see the movie *Secretary*?"

Rachel was speechless. She'd discovered Mary Gaitskill's stories in ninth grade, when she'd been at her most friendless and hopeless. She would spend her lunch periods curled up in a tattered orange butterfly chair in the school library stealthily reading her short stories. That spring Rachel convinced her father to take her to see Mary Gaitskill read at a bar in the East Village. The author had read a story about a girl whose mother is dying and who seduces her best friend's uncle. Joe had turned purple in the face when Mary said the word "ass" and looked right at him.

"I love Mary Gaitskill," Rachel said slowly. "I own multiple copies of *Bad Behavior*."

"Did you read *The Mare*?" Jessica asked. "I sobbed and sobbed."

"Me, too." Rachel swallowed hard, dizzy with new understanding. She wasn't here to win Jessica's approval. It was the other way around. After all those years of clambering for some sort of recognition, here it was, on a hotel couch on Simcoe Street.

Jessica started talking about Mary Gaitskill's forthcoming book, and Rachel half listened. The window was done up in holiday decorations, but she could make out the shapes and colors of movement outside. The scene on the street seemed to sparkle through the tinsel.

She would never be as slippery and exquisite as Sunny, or as savvy and well connected as Geraldine was destined to be. Rachel was reminded of one of Cleo's favorite books, *Banana House.* It was about Muriella, a baby mouse who inexplicably hated cheese but loved bananas. Muriella lived with her family in the walls of a house, and at night she'd scoot through the hole she'd dug and search the kitchen for the fruit bowl. In the morning her siblings would make fun of Muriella because she smelled like bananas. She vowed to stop eating them and switch back to cheddar, and for a few pages she succeeded. And then one night, during a biblical-level thunderstorm, a cat snuck into the house through an open window and Muriella fashioned an escape raft for her whole family out of the peel from a banana she'd stashed in a cupboard. Rachel had read the story to Cleo over two hundred times, but it was only starting to make sense. Everybody needed something to love. Everybody needed something that would save them. Fuck the cheese, Rachel thought. She had her banana.

# 36

"You won't let me in? You've got to be kidding me." Sunny mussed her hair and gave the lounge attendant the shy smile that usually made men trip over themselves. It was two days before Christmas, and she'd endured three-plus hours of airport traffic and check-in and X-ray machines, not once complaining, not even when a woman who'd worn a similar pair nearly made off with Sunny's Keds at security. Now her flight was delayed, on account of freezing rain at Toronto Pearson International Airport, and she'd never needed the lounge so badly. She'd been thinking about the bacon sandwiches since breakfast.

"The account is under Chase," Sunny told the gatekeeper, tightening her fist around the Platinum Rewards card she'd already presented him. "It's Nick. Or Nicholas?" She forced a gentle expression. "We've been members for a decade. If not longer."

The attendant consulted his iPad, and Sunny watched his eyebrows raise in a way that indicated good news was coming. "It's here," he said at last. "But you're not listed in the account."

"What? He kicked me off?"

"I'd advise you to call Mr. Chase and ask him to contact the—"

"It's fine," Sunny said. A line was forming behind her. She turned around and pulled her old Rimowa suitcase away from the Admirals Club lounge, overcome with the strange urge to laugh at Nick's brilliant Christmas present. He'd found a new way to fill her stocking with coal. Nobody could accuse Nick of not being clever.

Every table in the Sbarro–McDonald's–Panda Express complex was taken, and there were encampments on the floor. The pubs were filled, too. Sunny finally found a seat at a faux-upscale wine bar near gate 22. She ordered herself a cheese sampler and a glass of sparkling water with lime. "Actually, wait a moment," she said, scanning the menu on the wall, and put in a request for the most expensive red on the menu, pinot noir. If there were ever a time, Sunny told herself, and opened the Candy Crush app on her phone.

A glass and a half in, she could feel the bridge of her nose blazing. She was delightfully tipsy. She ate the last of her brie and watched a piece of striped licorice explode on her screen. Sunny's game was interrupted when her mother texted for her ETA. Dad will pick you up. This warmed Sunny and slightly hurt her pride. Not once since she'd moved to New York had anyone come to the airport for her. Most of the MacLeods were already up at the family cottage. Sunny glanced at the departures monitor.

Still pending, hopefully not too late, she replied.

As she typed, a discussion taking place behind her came into focus. The women had southern accents, and one of them was vowing to be more mindful in the New Year. "I'm going to start drinking tea and collecting my thoughts each morning."

The other said she was done with "putting the pressure on Jackson."

"That's not a resolution," Tea informed her.

Sunny located their reflections in the mirror behind the bar. They both wore red lipstick and were dressed in busily patterned active-wear. If Sunny had to guess, she'd say they were around her age. "There's a sperm bank in California that has a catalog that tells you what movie stars the donors look like," said the one who was going to take it easier on Jackson. "It's right there on the Internet."

"Now you're talking," Tea said. "You're going to have Brad Pitt's fucking baby."

Sunny gave a dry cough and recovered only to feel herself smiling hard. Too hard—the bartender glanced over at her in a way that embarrassed her. Signaling for the check with one hand, she picked up her phone with the other and pretended to be in the middle of an amusing exchange when in fact she could not think of a single person whose banter could make her feel less lonely. She suspected she would make a lousy mother. She was terrible at dealing with people, with their whims and needs. Why should a baby be any different? What if she simply wasn't cut out to connect? Sunny could now feel the skin around her mouth start to tremble, like a vole sniffing around for food.

Several hours later, when the city lights were no longer visible and the man in the next seat was safely absorbed in his action movie, Sunny hooked into the plane's Wi-Fi. She found the site the women were talking about and scrolled through the donor inventory, a clearinghouse of hair color, eye color, medical history, educational background, special talents, and interests. Potential mothers were asked to submit an essay about themselves and the attributes they were looking for. God, she had no idea.

Sunny turned over her phone and closed her eyes. Words from her favorite Elizabeth Bishop poem were ticker-taping through her mind. *Lose something every day. Accept the fluster / of lost door keys, the hour badly spent.* Sunny could feel her eyes watering up. Airplanes always had this effect on her, though not so soon after takeoff.

She felt a tickle in the back of her throat and raised her palms to cover her cheeks and eyelids. Saving face, literally. Her mouth filled with the taste of salt. Next year was going to be a better one. It had to be.

From: GDespont@rogers.com

To: GDespont@rogers.com

Bcc: ContactList2

Subject: Change of Scenery

Happy New Year, folks! As some of you may know, I've been in New York for the past little while. My work papers came through, so I've officially moved here. I'll explain, but first pull up your contacts list (don't you miss Rolodexes?) and write this down:

Geraldine Despont
86 Ship Street, Apt. 3
Brooklyn, NY 11201

For those of you who are wondering what I'm up to, I'm a bona fide podhead. I've been working on a podcast that's nominally about other podcasts but really about . . . I'm afraid you'll have to listen to it. I also have a "real job," working at a media company in strategy, because Lord knows I'm nothing if not a strategic genius. ☺ I wear pumpy shoes and find myself at a lot of meetings in conference rooms named after dead writers, pretending to be assertive and decisive and—how could I forget—cost-effective. I can now say I've read a book on motivational management and seen Hello, Dolly! with executives from Snapchat. There are worse ways to keep the lights on. New York is fun as hell.

There's not a ton of time for non-work things, but I'm loving what I'm seeing of the city, even in this dark, bloated season. I've been meeting a lot of people who seem cool (we're all so busy it's hard to actually get to know anybody), and I've been seeing somebody, a guy who's also in podcasts and whose idea of heaven is a matinee at Film Forum.

Which is not to say I don't suffer the occasional case of Toronto nostalgia. And by occasional I mean nearly constant. I'm hoping to come up once I figure out how to carve out a week. A long weekend seems like too much of a tease. In the meantime send me a postcard. Text me. Pay me a visit. I miss and think of all of you, more than you know.

Geraldine xx

From: GDespont@rogers.com

To: rachelpapers@gmail.com

Re: Change of Scenery / Very Important Personal Addendum

Rachel,

That pay me a visit thing? I meant it. We're in it too deep to call it off. The truth is that I've loved Harriet the Spy ever since I was a kid. And as the years blur by and I realize what babies you and I were way back in the day, I can say the exact same about you.

Geraldine

# Acknowledgments

Boundless gratitude to Ben Schrank, who urged me to pull the pages out of a drawer; to Claudia Ballard for believing in the pages; and to my editor, Allison Lorentzen, who literally hugged the pages at our first meeting and has never let go.

Norma Barksdale, Lydia Hirt, Sara Leonard, Lindsay Prevette, Andrea Schulz, Kate Stark, Brian Tart, Olivia Taussig, and the rest of the team at Viking are all co-conspirators without rival. Additional thanks to Suzanne Gluck, Jessie Chasan-Taber, Fiona Baird, and Laura Bonner at WME.

I am extraordinarily lucky to have readers in: Chiara Barzini, Pooja Bhatia, Rodrigo Corral, Sarah Fan, Ben Greenman, Claudia Herr, Thessaly LaForce, Eve MacSweeney, Jessica Matlin, Tim Rostron, and Chloe Schama.

Thank you to my family: Linda Schrank, Faith Childs, and Harris Schrank. My parents, Curtis and Sharon Mechling, who raised me on a steady diet of love and laughter. My sister, Anna, and my grandmother, Rhea Jack, extraordinary women both. I am grateful to the city of Toronto, and to all the friends I've loved and lost.

And Henry and Louisa, truest people on earth.